Y0-CAP-652

There was one thing Jessie had to ask . . .

"Why are you wearing a tuxedo?"

Kale glanced down as if he couldn't recall what he was wearing. "Oh, this?"

"You have to admit your attire doesn't quite fit the image of a man out to apprehend a criminal."

Kale had thought he couldn't feel more awkward and uncomfortable. He'd let his quarry get away. He'd tried to arm-wrestle a car and had been tossed on his tush for his trouble. And it had all happened in clear view of this most attractive woman.

He couldn't tell her that he'd worn the tux in the rather arrogant anticipation of catching the thieves and still making an appearance at tonight's faculty reception. Sure, his pride was injured, but it wasn't dead. He shrugged and offered what had to be the dumbest excuse in the world....

ABOUT THE AUTHOR

Karen Toller Whittenburg claims her love of reading inspired her writing career. She enjoys all kinds of fiction, but romance holds a special place in her heart and in her life. She loves to share her romantic daydreams with her readers, and hopes that they enjoy the adventure as much as she does. Karen lives in Oklahoma and divides her time between writing and running a household, both full-time and fulfilling careers.

Books by Karen Toller Whittenburg

HARLEQUIN AMERICAN ROMANCE

197–SUMMER CHARADE
249–A MATCHED SET
294–PEPPERMINT KISSES
356–HAPPY MEDIUM

HARLEQUIN TEMPTATION

303–ONLY YESTERDAY

Don't miss any of our special offers. Write to us at the following address for information on our newest releases.

Harlequin Reader Service
901 Fuhrmann Blvd., P.O. Box 1397, Buffalo, NY 14240
Canadian address: P.O. Box 603,
Fort Erie, Ont. L2A 5X3

KAREN TOLLER WHITTENBURG

DAY DREAMER

Harlequin Books

TORONTO • NEW YORK • LONDON
AMSTERDAM • PARIS • SYDNEY • HAMBURG
STOCKHOLM • ATHENS • TOKYO • MILAN

For Don

Published January 1991

ISBN 0-373-16375-4

DAY DREAMER

Copyright © 1991 by Karen Toller Whittenburg. All rights reserved.
Except for use in any review, the reproduction or utilization
of this work in whole or in part in any form by any electronic,
mechanical or other means, now known or hereafter invented,
including xerography, photocopying and recording,
or in any information storage or retrieval system, is forbidden without
the permission of the publisher, Harlequin Enterprises Limited,
225 Duncan Mill Road, Don Mills, Ontario, Canada M3B 3K9.

All the characters in this book have no existence outside the
imagination of the author and have no relation whatsoever to
anyone bearing the same name or names. They are not even
distantly inspired by any individual known or unknown to the
author, and all incidents are pure invention.

® are Trademarks registered in the United States Patent and
Trademark Office and in other countries.

Printed in U.S.A.

Chapter One

American Gigolo, Jessie thought as the man in the tuxedo walked past her table. She sipped her Irish Coffee and watched him make his way to the last booth on the right. His broad shoulders filled the black dinner jacket to perfection and the satin stripe on the trousers ran, unwrinkled, the length of his long, powerful legs. King-size bed, Jessie decided. No frills or throw pillows. No-nonsense in the bedroom, either.

He dropped his topcoat onto the vinyl seat and slid in beside it. With minimal effort, he adjusted the black sleeves and white cuffs at his wrist and, after a rapid perusal of the pub's clientele, picked up the menu.

Jessie studied him openly, noting with interest the downward slant of his dark brows, the way his sable-brown hair feathered in natural waves away from his rugged face, his unconventional attractiveness. And he didn't even seem aware of the way he stood out in this crowd. She narrowed her gaze and pictured him lying on the black-gray-and-claret stripes of the American Gigolo sheets. The image was wrong, somehow, and she mentally flipped through the linen patterns she'd designed during the past six months, trying to find the right one.

Caribbean had too much turquoise. Siesta was too bold. Cloud Dancer looked altogether too feminine and Jessie just couldn't imagine the black tuxedo draped across the pastel florets of Fancy Free.

Forget the clothes, Gretchen would say if she were here. Visualize him naked and seductive on the sheets. Think like an advertising exec. Jessie sighed in mild frustration and turned her attention back to the coffee. Her sister was much better than she was with these pretend games of "Between the Sheets." While Gretchen romped right past inhibitions to match the perfect linen pattern to the perfect male, Jessie got waylaid by details. The truth was, Jessie just didn't have Gretchen's knack for stripping off a man's—pretensions. And she wasn't much interested in acquiring it, either.

Jessie tapped the table leg with the toe of her shoe and looked around the crowded interior of Dakota Jack's Juke Joint. College students lined the wide oak bar and couples gyrated to a Top 40 song blaring from unseen speakers. The pub was one of several frequented mostly by the University of Arkansas populace and Gretchen had said it was the place to mingle with the U of A jocks. But Jessie wasn't a mingler, she wasn't a fan of Razorback sports, and she was a long five years removed from being a college coed. In fact, if Gretchen hadn't arranged this meeting with some hayseed Romeo, Jessie would not have been in Dakota Jack's rowdy pub. She wouldn't even have stopped in Fayetteville and she'd have been at Grandad's house at this very moment, drinking his homemade cider and enjoying the first night of her first vacation in four years.

The waitress breezed past Jessie's table and stopped beside American Gigolo. Jessie couldn't make out the breathy words of the waitress, but the man ordered coffee, black coffee, in a deep voice that convinced Jessie he was not where he wanted to be.

She wondered what he was doing in Dakota Jack's. He was at least ten years older than the young men and women gathered around the bar, maybe as much as twenty years older than some. He was also, without exception, the only man in the room wearing a shirt with more than three buttons and Jessie was fairly certain he wasn't a regular customer. No one spoke to him and he frowned over the menu with obvious distaste. Was he meeting someone, as she was?

And where was Pancho, anyway? It was past eight. And why did Gretchen always forget things? Why did she always ask Jessie to do just "one little favor"? Why did Jessie always say yes? After twenty-odd years, though, she should have been used to it. Although Gretchen's IQ was a cool one hundred and forty-seven, she fell far short of average in simple common sense. Jessie was sure she was the only member of her family who knew when it was time to come in out of the rain. It was probably a genetic quirk that out of five people; mother, father, sister, brother, and herself, she had received the single accountability gene.

So here she was in a college pub, pinch-hitting for her sister and playing a mental game of strip poker with a man in a tuxedo. And losing the game, at that. So much for common sense, Jessie thought. By this time, Gretchen would have had him reduced to biceps, triceps and a pair of sinewy pectorals. She'd have undressed him...in her mind, of course...and stamped him either Approved or Rejected. Jessie tried to whip her imagination into gear, but she only got as far as his bow tie—which was made of a black, nubby type of fabric; a silk blend, probably—before she realized he was returning her stare with one of cool indifference. Jessie sighed. She never had been very good with fantasies.

She lifted her cup in a gesture of surrender and decided that with eyes that blue, he really belonged with the Swashbuckler linens. Too bad she'd decided to discontinue that pattern.

"Jessica Day?"

The voice was male, the accent a far and foreign cry from an Arkansas twang. Jessie glanced over her shoulder to see a young man of slight build and long black hair. If he'd been a few years older, his manner might have made her nervous, but he couldn't have been more than eighteen. "I'm Jessica," she said. "Are you Pancho?"

He nodded as he slid into the chair opposite her and leaned across the table. "Your sister sent me," he said. The word came out, "seester," and Jessie barely restrained a heavy sigh. What had her "seester" gotten her into now? "She told me to look for a woman with golden hair and a stiff back." He grinned. "I spotted you right away."

Jessie shifted in her chair. She would get Gretchen for this. "Do you have a package for me?"

"First, tell me the password."

"What password?"

"She didn't tell you the password?" His eyebrows went up, the words hissed from his lips, and he hunkered down as if he were going to slither over the table and tell her a military secret. If he'd been a spy, Jessie thought, someone would already have shot him.

She leaned back, swept a hand through her blond curls and wondered where Gretchen had met this long-haired James Bond. Peripherally, she noticed the man in the tuxedo getting to his feet, but she kept her attention on the youth in front of her. "Gretchen asked me to be here, at Dakota Jack's, at eight o'clock to pick up a package. I don't know anything about a stupid password. Now, if you want to play games, go put a quarter in the pinball machine and let me go on about my business."

His grin flashed a glimpse of a gold tooth far back in his mouth as he reached into an inside pocket of his coat. "Mees Day said you would be cranky. Don't worry, there is no password. I have the package for Gretchen, but first I must ask you to do me the favor—"

"Take that hand out slow and easy." A shadow fell across the table as the command dropped low and ominous into the air.

Pancho's grin went slack, his face blanched beneath his dark complexion, but he did as he was told. His hand came away from his coat slowly, so slowly. Jessie looked up at the man in the tuxedo, stunned. His very blue eyes shifted to meet her glance and a tremor of anxious excitement washed through her. The eye contact lasted a second, no longer, but in that instant, Pancho made his move.

In a flash, the wiry young man was on the floor, scooting between the threatening man and the table, using both hands and feet in a ridiculous spider crawl for the exit. The man in the tuxedo lunged after him, catching a shoe and holding on for dear life as the crowd in Dakota Jack's, drawn like curious children to the scene of the scuffle, surged forward to see what was happening. One hulking athlete stepped right in the middle of the struggle, knocking the man in the tuxedo to the floor and giving Pancho a reprieve. He hit a table and sent it crashing in his wild scramble for freedom. Then he was gone, the door closing behind him with a slow whoosh.

For a moment, there was an almost pure silence. Then, as everyone realized the show was over, the crowd returned en masse to the bar, someone picked up the overturned table, and the athlete offered a helping hand to the American Gigolo. The gesture was brushed aside as the man in the tuxedo levered himself off the floor. Jessie watched as he furiously hand-dusted the front of his trouser legs. He caught her gaze and returned it with utter frustration and no small degree of anger.

Now, what had she done to warrant such a look, Jessie wondered? Until a few moments ago, she hadn't known Pancho from a knot in the wall.

He approached her table, still brushing pub dust from his sleeves. "You didn't get it, did you?" he said, his voice holding all the concern of a wounded bull. "And I don't suppose there's a chance in hell you have any way to contact him again, either, is there?"

"Contact who?" she repeated, puzzled by his anger and his question.

"Pancho." The man's mouth tightened in a heavy frown. "I've been looking for that little punk all day and I want an explanation."

Jessie could only stare at him.

"Look, lady," he said between clenched teeth. "I've got you dead to rights. I saw you with Pancho. He was getting ready to hand over the information. Now, I'm going to sit down here and you're going to tell me what in hell you were planning to do with it."

"I don't think so." Jessie glanced past him, searching for the waitress and the bill for her coffee...and a way of escape. She wasn't scared, exactly, but she saw no good reason to encourage this man. "I'm leaving."

He continued to stand beside her chair, frowning, waiting, as if he thought she would tell him what he wanted to know. Finally, Jessie fumbled through her purse, tossed a five-dollar bill on the table and rose, pulling her coat along with her. "Excuse me," she said crisply, but he showed no inclination to let her pass. "Excuse me," she repeated with more bravado than she felt.

"No, I won't excuse you." He sent his very blue gaze streaking toward the ceiling and, with a deeply frustrated sigh, brought it back to her. "I'm really tired of this runaround. I want the truth and I want it now."

"Very well," Jessie said, slowly and distinctly. "The truth is, I don't know what you're talking about."

"Oh, for Pete's sake! Stop pretending you don't know about the stolen research."

"Stolen research?" Jessie couldn't seem to do anything except parrot his ridiculous accusation. "Whose research was stolen?"

"Mine. As if you didn't know." His jaw was set in a line firm enough to write on.

It was becoming painfully obvious that he was in no mood to listen to reason and Jessie was in no mood to deal with a stranger's misplaced anger. "I didn't know." She made the words as final as possible and tried to stare him down.

"I would—" his voice dropped to a steely baritone "—prefer not to make a scene, here."

"A little late to think of that now, mister."

"Doctor," he corrected without the least bit of courtesy. "Dr. Kale Warner. I'm a professor at the university."

"Then you ought to know better than to accost women in public places." She made a move to step past him, but he reached out to detain her. His fingers didn't make contact with her arm because she pulled out of range, but she met his gaze head-on. For an instance, a warm swirl of sensations rippled through her body, spiraling in a slow spin of awareness, but she didn't let the pleasure linger. This man was threatening her. Jessie couldn't take the chance that he was just overwrought. She reached past him and grabbed hold of a passing waitress. "Please call the manager," she said clearly. "This man is harassing me."

The college-age waitress looked at the man with eyes that widened in surprise, then recognition. "Dr. Warner? Is anything wrong? Should I call Jack?"

"That won't be necessary," Dr. Warner said, and the waitress nodded and turned away.

Jessie frowned up at him, thinking his eyes were really too blue to belong to a masher. However, facts were facts. With the slightest tilt of her lips, she ducked down and around him and hurried toward the door. "Wait a minute," he called and she increased her pace.

She reached the door, jerked it open and felt a cool blast of air on her face and arms just before he snagged her by the elbow. "Wait a minute, I said."

Jessie shook off his touch. "Look, Dr. Warner, or whoever you are, I don't know what's wrong with you, but I'm warning you to leave me alone." She glanced around the restaurant and saw that they were beginning to attract attention. Keeping an eye on him, she tugged at her coat and managed to get one arm into the sleeve before he stepped closer. She stiffened with new suspicion, but he only grasped her coat collar and guided her arm into the other sleeve. With a stroke of his hand, he adjusted the fit across her shoulders and then moved away from her.

"There," he said. "Now, would you please just sit down and talk to me."

A smile made a brief pass across her lips before she answered. "No, Dr. Warner, I won't."

Chapter Two

It took a full ten seconds before Kale registered her answer and another five before he followed her out the door. "Wait," he called for the second time that evening. But this time he tried to cool his rising irritation and put a note of conciliation in the words. Catching a thief was proving to be much more difficult than he'd expected.

"Wait a minute." He scanned the row of parked cars and saw her unlocking the door of a foreign-made coupé. It was red, he noted, which only made him madder. "Damn it," he muttered under his breath as he forced a pleasant expression and hurried toward her.

She saw him coming and panicked, jerking open the car door and scrambling inside. Kale rounded the front fender and made a grab for the door frame, narrowly missing getting his fingers caught when she slammed the door and locked him out. On top of total frustration, he was beginning to feel a tad embarrassed. The woman was acting as if he were trying to abduct her or something. He tapped on the window. "Hey, I just want to talk to you a minute. Is there anything wrong with that?"

The look she turned to him through the window was classic and Kale decided he hadn't handled the situation with enough diplomacy. But hell, how was he supposed to be diplomatic when thieves were making off with two years' worth of his research? The engine roared to life and then sputtered to a stop. He could see her chagrin as she ground the ignition, trying to get the engine going again and he realized he had only seconds to figure out how to stop her.

"It's important that I talk—" The engine kicked in before he could finish the sentence and he heard her release the emergency brake. Desperate situations call for desperate measures, he told himself as he jumped and clung spread-eagled across the hood of her car. Thank God, the hood ornament was flat not vertical. He grappled for a firm hold along the rim of the windshield. Miraculously the car didn't move. He lifted his head and looked through the windshield at the driver. It wasn't exactly the way he'd pictured it, but at last he was face-to-face with the woman who was his only link to the stolen research. She had to listen to him now.

What are you doing? Her lips formed the words he couldn't quite hear. She had an interesting mouth, he thought. All curved and soft-looking. The interior of the car was cast in shadows, but he could see her face clearly as she leaned forward, her eyes wide and unblinking. They were brown, he noticed. A pretty ash brown. And angry.

"*What are you doing?*" He heard her this time, even over the idling of the engine beneath him. "Get off my car!"

"I have to talk to you," he said.

"You're nuts." She rolled the window down a scant inch. "I'm going to back out of this parking space. You'd better get off before you get hurt."

Kale felt like an idiot, but he'd come too far to just let her drive away now. He clung to his position. "Please, give me five minutes to explain. Just five minutes." He could see her hesitate and he searched his brain for something that would reassure her. "Trust me," he said. "I'm a college professor."

Her hesitation vanished, replaced by a new determination. "It's no wonder our educational system is in critical condition," she muttered as she rolled up the window and shifted into reverse.

Kale didn't know what he'd said to upset her, but he knew he'd better hold on. Surely she wouldn't—

The car began a steady roll backward and Kale held fast, determined not to slide off. She'd stop, he thought. Of course, she'd stop. She would stop, wouldn't she?

Another car pulled off the highway and into the parking lot with a squeal of tires. Kale closed his eyes and told himself that in thirty-seven years of living, this was the stupidest thing he'd ever done. He felt the car jerk as the brake went down hard and fast and then, without further ado, he sailed over the left front fender and landed roughly on the graveled pavement.

Jessie slammed the gear shift into Park position, pulled the emergency brake and jumped out of the car. If she'd killed that idiot, she'd never forgive herself. What had she been trying to do? She knew never—ever—to put a car in gear when a man was lying on the hood. Rounding the front of the car, she paused in the glare of the headlights and scanned the darkness for her victim.

He sat in plain view, knees pulled to his chest, hands clasped loosely at his shins. He didn't look as if he were badly injured. He didn't even look very disheveled for a man who'd just fallen off a moving car. Jessie hurried forward. "Are you all right?"

He gave her a baleful look. "Are you talking to me?" Jessie became aware of the painful thud of her heartbeat against her ribs and realized how frightened she'd been. "I'll call an ambulance. Wait here."

"I don't need an ambulance." He brought his hands away from his knees and inspected the palms for damage. "I could use a hand up, though, if you wouldn't mind."

Jessie wasn't sure she should touch him, but with the man sitting there with his hand outstretched, what else could she do? Extending her arm, she grasped his hand and pulled as hard as she could. He came easily, if a little stiffly, to his feet and Jessie wondered why such an attractive man had had to behave with such complete stupidity.

"I'd better call an ambulance." Jessie said, trying to pull her hand away from his. He clung. "You might have a . . . a concussion or something."

"I don't have a concussion or something," he said curtly. "My pride's a little sore, that's all. And my good suit is a little the worse for the wear, but there's no need to panic."

"Maybe I should get the manager of the pub. Jack, that's it. I'll get Jack."

"No." Kale Warner emphasized his objection by tightening his grip on her fingers and brushing at his clothes with his free hand. "Jack will only laugh, which will not be edifying for my pride. And he certainly isn't going to show any concern for my clothes. So, there's no point in getting him out here."

"But you could be hurt."

"I'm okay." The word came out tight and clear with just the slightest tinge of embarrassment.

He looked okay, Jessie decided, running her gaze upward from his scuffed shoes to his tousled dark hair. He actually looked more than okay, but this was hardly the time to notice that. "Well, if you're sure." Her voice brimmed with uncertainty. What was her liability in this awkward situation, she wondered. "I could follow you in my car, if you want to drive to the emergency room. . . ."

"Forget the first aid. If you want to make sure I'm uninjured, then follow me back inside Dakota Jack's. It's warm in there. There's plenty of medicinal beverages and I'd feel a hell of a lot better if you'd give me just a few minutes of your time. I know I haven't handled this very well, but I really must talk to you. It's important."

Jessie weighed her disinclination to talk to this man against the possibility of being sued at a later date for assault with a moving vehicle. Fear of the lawsuit won out and she capitulated with a sigh. "You have to let go of my hand."

He accepted her terms graciously and motioned for her to precede him into the juke joint.

Wrestling doubts all the way, Jessie walked to the last booth on the right. Someone had better have one heck of an explanation for all this, Jessie thought as she brushed his topcoat and wool scarf to one side of the bench and sat beside them.

"Care for anything to drink?" the professor asked. Jessie shook her head and he summarily dismissed the waitress before setting his clasped hands on the table and leaning forward. "How long have you known Pancho?"

Jessie drummed her fingertips on the tabletop once, then once more. This man had all the subtlety of a locomotive. "Five minutes, maybe less. How long have you known him?"

"I don't know him. Well, I mean, he works in the lab but he's fairly new and he works nights and I—" Dr. Warner stopped talking. "Why am I telling you this? You know all about Pancho."

"Wrong. I'm only a bystander in this melodrama."

He frowned, obviously unwilling to believe that. "All right, then, we'll play this your way. Suffice it to say, I never even noticed the kid before...until some important information was stolen from the lab a couple of days ago."

"And you think Pancho stole it?"

"Of course he did. And as his contact person, you're as guilty as he is."

Jessie wished she'd hit the brake harder and knocked some sense into this man. "You don't teach in the School of Diplomacy, do you?"

"The University doesn't have a school of—" He grimaced. "You were kidding, weren't you? Sorry, I'm a little slow to see the humor in this. The loss of this research..." His voice trailed to a somber bass rumble. "I must get it back."

That much, at least, Jessie had already figured out. "Why do you think I can help you?"

Impatience flashed in his eyes. "You were with Pancho," he said as if that explained everything.

"Purely circumstantial evidence, I assure you."

"Ah, but you were here at Dakota Jack's at eight o'clock and—" he paused for effect "—you're blond."

"Well, that's certainly damning proof." Jessie tucked a hand in her coat pocket, making sure her car keys were accessible. "Frankly, Dr. Warner, I think you're grasping at straws."

"You're right, I am. But you're my only lead." He cupped his hands and stared at them for a long moment. "When I discovered the research was gone, well, I panicked and followed the only person who had the opportunity to take it."

"Pancho. You're sure no one else could have taken it?"

"Yes. Pancho started working in the lab at the beginning of the semester, only a couple of months ago. It's logical to assume he's a plant and was put there to get the information."

"Logical," Jessie repeated, not at all convinced. "And how did you know he'd be at Dakota Jack's tonight at eight with a blonde?"

"I was told—by a reliable source—that he meets you here every Friday night."

"Not me. This is my first time in Dakota Jack's."

"You're denying that you came here to meet Pancho?"

Trapped, Jessie decided that sooner or later she would have to drag Gretchen's name into the conversation, although she hated to give out any information that might get her sister into trouble. "No, I'm not denying that, but I know nothing about your research. What kind of research is it, anyway?"

Kale considered her question and her for a moment. She had to be lying. Even though her eyes stared back at him with convincing innocence. Even though her hand lay calmly on the table. Even though her expression reflected unruffled serenity. Some elemental awareness stirred deep inside him, an attraction evoked by the soft prettiness of her eyes, the stubborn set of her chin. He swallowed an impulse to throw away his suspicions, smile and say, "What the hell...how about dinner?"

This must be his night for stupid ideas. He pursed his lips and debated how much he could tell her without revealing all the cards in his hand. "It's genetic research," he said. "The information that was stolen has to do with a study I'm conducting on...developing certain genetic traits in, uh, lab animals."

That was vague enough, Jessie thought. "Who would steal genetic research?"

"Lots of people. But that's beside the point. Who did it is not as important to me as recovering the information."

"Why is that? I mean, you do have copies of the information, don't you? So it's not as if you've lost the research."

A pained look crossed his face and Jessie experienced a sinking feeling. She knew, suddenly, what he was going to say.

"Well, actually, I only recently put my notes on the computer and—so I still have my notes, of course. But it's all organized on the diskette that was taken and...it's important that I get it back.''

Jessie shook her head. "You didn't make a copy?"

Kale frowned. Did she think he hadn't kicked himself already a dozen times for not doing so? "I intended to copy the disk, but some things happened and it didn't get done.''

He forgot to take care of details. Jessie didn't need it spelled out for her. For twenty-seven and a half years, she'd listened to her family offer the same lame excuse. And she'd spent almost that length of time trying to straighten out the resulting chaos. Dr. Kale Warner needed help. No doubt about that. But Jessie was not getting involved.

"I see," she said. She'd tell him just enough to extricate herself from his suspicions and leave him to pursue some other poor blonde. She hoped to heaven that other blonde didn't turn out to be her sister. "Look, Dr. Warner, I'll tell you all I know about Pancho. My sister called me on Wednesday afternoon from the Little Rock Airport. She asked me to meet Pancho here this evening and..." Jessie made a quick decision not to mention the package she was supposed to pick up and mail to Gretchen. That would only confuse the professor and put him off on a wrong scent. That package had nothing to do with genetic research. "...tell him she'd had to go out of town unexpectedly. I believe the boy is, well, infatuated with my sister, and she's trying to let him down easy. She's blond and probably has met Pancho here before. I know she often counsels undergraduates and even socializes with them once in a while. But just because someone saw them together a couple of times is no reason for you to assume he was going to pass stolen information to her.''

"She called you Wednesday? That's the day the diskette disappeared. Well, that night, actually.''

"Then, obviously, she had nothing to do with it. She was gone before it disappeared.''

He pursed his lips in a moment of pensive thought. "Where is she now?"

"On the West Coast somewhere. I'm really not sure where." It was the truth and for once Jessie was glad she didn't know Gretchen's exact destination. She was also glad she didn't have to tell this man the dramatic reason for the trip.

"So you're just filling in for her? Meeting Pancho so his heart wouldn't be broken?" Skepticism registered clearly in his blue eyes. "That's not even a convincing lie."

Jessie stiffened. "Gretchen is working on her doctorate in sociology and I can assure you she had nothing to do with the theft of your research."

Kale realized he would make no inroads with that tack, so he backed off the question. He'd just begun to get this woman to talk. He didn't want her to stop now. "Sorry." He hesitated. "Do you think your sister might be able to talk Pancho into returning the computer disk? Is there some way we can get in touch with her?"

"I don't know what kind of influence she has with the boy and besides, unless she calls me, I don't have any way to reach her." And I wouldn't even if I did, she added silently. "Are you positive Pancho is the guilty party?"

"You saw the way he tore out of here when I questioned him."

Jessie decided there was no point in mentioning that in similar circumstances, she had "torn out of there," too. Dr. Warner had proven he could be effectively threatening. "Yes, well, I'm sorry, I can be of no assistance to you and I do hope you find your missing research." She bit her tongue to keep from telling him he should be more careful with his precious research. "Good luck, Doctor, and—" she rose from the table, clutching her car keys "—goodbye."

He was on his feet, his coat in hand, before she'd taken two steps. "I'll walk out with you."

Protesting would be useless, Jessie thought, so she allowed him to open the door for her and walked with what she hoped wasn't a frantic step to her car. He stood quietly as she slid into the bucket seat and made an unnecessary adjustment to the rearview mirror.

"Will you let me know if you hear from your sister?" he asked. "It might be of some help if I could talk to her."

Jessie agreed with a nod and hoped he wouldn't tell her how to contact him. Not to worry, she told herself a minute later. Phone numbers were forgettable details to people like Dr. Warner. "I hope your...pride isn't still sore tomorrow." Jessie offered a smile with the wish, but he didn't seem to be paying attention. She started to close the door, then stopped. There was one thing she had to ask.

"Why are you wearing a tuxedo?"

He glanced down as if he couldn't recall what he was wearing. "Oh, this?"

"You have to admit your attire doesn't quite fit the image of a man out to apprehend a criminal."

Kale had thought he couldn't feel more awkward and uncomfortable. He'd let Pancho get away. He'd tried to arm-wrestle a car and had been tossed on his tush for his trouble. And it had all happened in clear view of this most attractive woman. He couldn't tell her that he'd worn the tux in the rather arrogant anticipation of catching the thieves and still making an appearance at tonight's faculty reception. His pride was injured, sure, but it wasn't dead. He shrugged and offered what had to be the dumbest excuse in the world. "This was the only black outfit in my closet. I didn't want to seem—conspicuous."

He seemed to realize the incongruity of the statement and offered a persuasive little shrug as conciliation. Jessie smiled because, despite the loud groans of her common sense, his gesture struck a responsive chord inside her. It was more likely, she thought, that he'd forgotten to get his laundry from the cleaners and the tux was the only clean suit in his closet. With an understanding nod, she closed the car door, put the car in gear and lifted her hand in a farewell wave. He tapped on the window and she rolled it down. "I forgot to ask your name," he said.

He hadn't even thought to ask her name before now. Really, that was just too much. She started to drive away without telling him. She actually took her foot off the brake. But then he smiled. A slow, shy, expectant kind of smile and her indignation drained away. "Jessica," she said. "Jessica Day."

He nodded, as if her name pleased him somehow, and stepped back from the car. With a warm glow that Jessie couldn't explain, and tried hard to ignore, she backed out of the parking space.

Kale forced himself to stand still, even though he wanted to sprint for his car to lessen the chance of losing her in the Friday night college traffic. But she'd have to drive a couple of miles before turning off the road and he'd be able to catch her before that. He waited until she pulled onto the street, noted the direction she took and then walked quickly to his sedan.

As he unlocked the door, he touched the wool scarf he'd worn into the pub. He hesitated before tossing it onto the front seat of the car. In moments he was following Jessica Day. When he caught sight of her red sports car in front of him, for the first time that evening, he relaxed a little.

All right, he decided. She'd dropped her scarf. He'd picked it up, tried to signal her, but she'd already driven away. He'd had to follow her to return it. Kale frowned at the plan. She probably wouldn't believe him. On the other hand, she might believe he'd thought the scarf belonged to her. He had nothing to lose by offering the excuse and besides, he had to know where she was going. It was just that simple. Maybe, he told himself, he'd just gotten off to a slow start at this espionage business.

His heartbeat quickened with sudden anticipation. Whether she believed him or not, Jessie would be surprised to see him. And that was exactly what he wanted.

THE HEADLIGHTS SWEPT the porch, rounded the corner of the house and focused on the detached one-car garage. Jessie parked in the driveway and grabbed a duffel bag from behind the seat. She always packed overnight gear in an easily accessible bag, separate from her other luggage, for just such occasions as this. With her family, emergencies happened more often than not, so Jessie had learned to be prepared.

She locked the car and walked up the steps to the wide porch that spanned the front of the old, wood frame house Gretchen called home. Jessie walked directly to the far window, found the niche where her sister kept the extra house key, and pulled it out.

A car slowed on its way down the street and Jessie glanced over her shoulder, curious at first, then concerned as the car turned into the driveway and caught her in the glare of its headlights. In a moment the engine died, the lights went off and Jessie reached for the snap of her purse. Within moments, she touched the cool metal of the mace can.

"Hello? Jessica? Jessica Day?"

It was Dr. Kale Warner's voice and Dr. Kale Warner's body that emerged from the car almost in unison. Jessie first felt relief, followed quickly by a return of concern. Her instincts told her this man wasn't a threat, but she certainly couldn't prove that by his earlier actions. She pulled the can of mace from her purse and slipped it into her coat pocket . . . still out of sight, but handy. "Dr. Warner?" she responded hesitantly.

"Good." He slammed his car door. "I was afraid I might have followed the wrong person."

"You followed me?" Jessie moved to the top of the porch steps. She wanted to be able to spray him square in the eyes, if it turned out to be necessary. "Why?"

"Why?" He advanced on the porch. "Um, you forgot this." He held up a dark object and it took Jessie a minute to realize what it was.

"That's your scarf," she said.

"My scarf? Are you sure?" He lifted the wool scarf toward the porch light and looked closely at it. "I thought it was yours."

Jessie suppressed a frown. Either Dr. Warner belonged in the Hall of Fame for Absentminded Professors or he was one clever fellow. Since he'd followed her with such a weenie of an excuse, he obviously hadn't believed her denial and still thought she knew something about his lost research. But he already had all the information he was going to get from her, regardless of how many scarves he "returned."

"I believe you're right." He shrugged with far more confidence than embarrassment. "This is my scarf. How silly of me to think it belonged to you."

Jessie wasn't going to argue that. If nothing else, his ridiculous subterfuge had put her at ease. He might be eccentric, but Kale Warner was no menace to her health and well-being. And she did admit to a reluctant admiration for his persistence. "It was thoughtful of you to make the unnecessary effort, Dr. Warner."

"Oh, please, don't mention it." He looped the scarf around his neck and smiled . . . a charming, easy, quiet kind of smile. "And since you're not one of my students, you can drop the formality."

Jessie intentionally looked puzzled.

"You can call me by my given name," he explained.

He deserves this, Jessie thought as she raised her eyebrows in question. "Your given name? I'm sorry, if you told me, I've forgotten."

"Kale." His voice stiffened a degree. "And I don't think you forgot."

"And I don't think you believed that was my scarf."

He picked up one end of the fringed wool and regarded it before offering a wry shrug. "It could have belonged to you."

Not in a million years, Jessie thought as she took a step back toward the door. "Look, why don't you just tell me why you followed me here."

"I followed you because..." He pursed his lips as if considering what to say next. "I, well, I wanted to make sure you didn't meet Pancho someplace."

Jessie wondered why the admission didn't annoy her. By rights, it should have. Was it because he was so attractive or because he was so awkward in the role of detective? "As you can see, there's no one here but you and me. And frankly, Dr.—Kale, I'm tired of this 'I spy' nonsense. I am not meeting Pancho tonight or any other time. Now, it's late and I want to go in."

"Do you need some help?" He came up the three steps to join her on the porch.

"I've been going in by myself for years, now. Thanks, anyway." Jessie slipped her hand into her coat pocket and grasped the mace can.

"Is this your sister's house?"

Jessie shot him an irritated glance. Would she have better luck getting him to leave if she went into the house and shut the door in his face? "Yes, this is where my sister lives. Now, if you don't mind—"

"Well, here." He stepped forward as she positioned the door key. "Let me open the door for you. You have that bag to carry and all."

"It's not heavy...." But he was already stepping past her to open the door and reaching inside to switch on the light.

"Here you go..." The last word drew into a 'oh' of surprise and the next thing Jessie knew he was gripping her elbow and propelling her toward the steps. "I'm sorry, Jessie, but you'd better wait out here. Someone has ransacked your sister's house. I'll go in and call the police."

Chapter Three

Jessie shook free of Kale's grasp and walked to the door. The front room was a mess. Clothes draped the furniture. Books and magazines covered the floor, the tables, the couch, and chairs. Papers were strewn from one end of the room to the other. Three shoes, a pair and a single, lay upside down on the coffee table. Clothes hangers hung from the window casing; wiry silhouettes against the rose-colored, priscilla curtains. The place was a mess.

But then, so was her sister. Jessie looked back at Kale. "It's always like this."

"You mean someone's broken in before?"

"No. I mean, this is the way Gretchen lives. In chaos. Every day of her life."

Kale's blue eyes met Jessie's brown ones and she saw disbelief register there. "No," he said, taking a step into the room.

"Yes." She followed, taking her hands from her pockets and crossing her arms at her waist. "I swear no one has been in here except my sister. Well, maybe some of her friends and a few of her students. When she's home she entertains a lot. No one seems to mind the clutter."

"If this is clutter, I never quite understood the meaning of the word before." Kale was careful not to step on anything except the floor...no small task. "Are you sure it's...uh, that you want to stay here tonight?"

"There's no reason not to. It looks ransacked, but it's not filthy. My sister has her faults, but she's no threat to the public health."

"Clean or not, can you find a bare space to sleep in?"

"Don't worry. I shared a room with her for sixteen years. I'm used to this." Jessie paused to look at the room. "And every day, I say a prayer of thanks that I no longer have to live with her."

"I take it this isn't your idea of how to live?" Kale asked and won the small reward of one of Jessie's smiles.

"Let's just say that, even at its worst, no one has ever thought my apartment had been ransacked." She put down her bag and placed her small hands on her trim hips.

Kale noted the grace in her movements and reminded himself that it was the good-looking women a man had to be careful of. Jessie's poised femininity *could* disguise a criminal mind. He didn't really think so. Her eyes were a little too clear, a bit too large, for that. But still... He began to glance around, casually looking for the stolen diskette. It was like looking for a needle in a haystack, but he had to start somewhere. "What do you do, Jessica?"

"Oh, I just try not to disturb her system too much. Believe it or not, Gretchen can find things in here."

He doubted that, but saw no reason to argue. "No, I meant, what do you do for a living? Are you a graduate student, too?"

She looked surprised that he'd asked. Or maybe she was surprised to realize he had been listening when she'd told him about her sister. "No. I've been out of school quite a while and have a business in Tulsa."

"A business." He was impressed, but not surprised. She looked like a businesswoman. It was something about the way she met his eyes. Evenly. Directly. He was more accustomed to students who regarded him with deference and a healthy respect . . . if not for him personally, at least for the grade he could give. And the female colleagues with whom he came into contact . . . well, he'd never paid much attention to how they looked or how they looked at him. He was only interested in what they knew. But Jessica didn't fit either of those categories. And the way she was looking at him now, created an odd, expectant sensation inside him. Was she waiting for him to say something? He retraced his thoughts and came back to being impressed. "What kind of business?"

"Are you really interested?" Her tone was impatient and he straightened his shoulders in self-defense.

"Well, yes, I'm interested." He realized suddenly it was true. Jessica Day was his only link to his missing diskette, but he would have been interested in knowing more about her anyway. "I want to know what kind of business you're in."

"Bedrooms and baths." She'd put her hands back in her pockets. "I design bed linens, wallpaper, shower curtains, towels. If it goes in the bedroom or bath, Day Dreams provides it . . . either through special order or at our retail store."

"Day Dreams," he repeated. "Well, if I ever need a bedroom, I'll know where to find one. Decorate a bedroom, I mean. If I need to decorate a bedroom."

Jessica's lips lifted in a smooth curve. "Yes, I knew what you meant. And speaking of bedrooms, it's time we called it an evening. I'm tired and you must be, too. It can't be easy chasing after a youngster like Pancho."

He felt old all of a sudden. The kid was younger, sure, but that didn't make him an octogenarian. "I never felt better," he lied. "I keep in shape."

Her gaze ran over him, assessing the truth of that, and he held his breath, hoping that he hadn't developed a hangover-the-belt belly since the last time he'd looked. It bothered him that she might find some physical flaw, bothered him even more that he cared about her opinion. But the worst part was that he couldn't tell if she found him wanting.

"Even Olympic athletes have to rest, so..." She took a step toward the door, but Kale pretended not to notice her broad hint. If she was determined for him to leave, he was just as determined to stay...at least until he saw whether or not he could wheedle any more information from her. He'd just have to be subtle about it.

Kale stepped over a cardboard box and examined a picture on the wall. It was a snapshot of Jessica and her sister—the resemblance was too strong to be anyone else—hamming for the camera. They'd scrawled their names across the bottom of the photograph... Jessie and Gretch. Jessie. He liked that. It suited her, made her seem more approachable than Jessica. "When was that taken?"

"A couple of years ago. Now, really, Dr. Warner—Kale. I'd appreciate it if—"

"I can't leave, Jessie." He tried out the nickname as he turned to her. "I...uh, thought of something else I need to ask you."

Her sigh was audible. "What?"

"Do you prefer Jessica or Jessie?"

"Honestly, isn't there someplace you need to be? Isn't your wife keeping dinner for you or something?"

"No wife. No dinner, either. Are you hungry?"

"No," she said crisply. "I'm tired. I worked today...all day. I drove all the way from Tulsa, not planning to spend the night in Fayetteville, but because of you, I don't have a choice. It's too late now to drive to my Grandad's, so I'm going to stay here until tomorrow, but I don't need your company and if you don't leave in the next five minutes, I'm going to call the police." She sent a rueful glance around the room. "If I can find the phone."

He felt uncomfortably cloddish and forgot his resolve to proceed with subtlety. "I'm sorry, Jessie. I know I've behaved poorly this evening, but I'm desperate to get information about the stolen research and you're the only—"

"—link you have. Yes, I remember. But I've already told you I don't know anything about it. I don't know Pancho. And I don't know you. So, you see, I can't help."

Why was it so hard to get her to tell him, he wondered. She looked so innocent, but she had to know something. It couldn't be pure coincidence that she'd met Pancho tonight. "You must know something."

Jessie tucked a few strands of hair behind her ear. "I don't even have the faintest idea of who would want to steal your research, Dr. Warner."

"Oh, I could name two or three corporate farms engaged in similar research and one or two researchers who'd give their mother's molars to have access to my genetic studies. It's my bet that one of them hired Pancho to steal it and got you—" Kale held up a hand to halt her protest "—or someone like you, to be the go-between. I can't prove it, but I think it's likely. In research, the line between profit and the good of mankind occasionally blurs and the idea pops up that the end always justifies the means."

"And do you subscribe to that theory?"

He laughed because the idea was so ridiculous. "Of course not. I'm one of the most upstanding citizens you'd ever want to meet."

"Well, upstanding citizen, you're about to be arrested for trespassing."

"Trespassing?" He realized, reluctantly, that she did have a point. She hadn't invited him to come inside. "Oh, I see. Do you think you could tell me—" He noticed the warning lift of her brows. "No. Okay, then. I'll go on and let you get to bed."

"Thank you." Her lips curved slightly and he was struck by the appearance of a slight indentation in her chin. It wasn't a dimple, but it was intriguing. Most intriguing.

"You'll let me know if you hear from your sister or Pancho?"

She nodded as she urged him toward the door. "If the phone rings, you'll be the first to be notified."

He stopped just outside the door and faced her. "I know this may be a game to you, Jessie, but it's very serious to me. I'd appreciate being told anything you think might help."

She lifted sober and curious eyes to meet his plea for assistance. "I'll let you know."

He brought up a finger, intending to touch that tempting cleft on her chin. Luckily he stopped the impulse before it could reach its objective and his hand went back to his side. His heartbeat had quickened, he realized. And was that his breathing that sounded so quick, so uneven? All because of a little dimple in a pert little chin?

"Good night," Jessie said.

"Yes," he answered, still standing there, staring at her chin. "Good night."

When she stepped back and closed the door, Kale snapped to his senses. What on earth was he thinking? Jessie was involved in the disappearance of his research. At least, he had to go on that assumption until evidence of one kind or another pointed to another possibility. He'd certainly gotten no information out of her. And he certainly had no business getting diverted by a dimple that wasn't quite a dimple.

As he walked to his car, his thoughts churned with new irritation. Somehow, someway, Pancho was going to get that computer diskette to Jessie. Kale had a hunch about the two of them. They'd looked very conspiratorial sitting in Dakota Jack's and Kale had no intention of letting the matter rest.

He started his car, turned on the lights and drove away from Gretchen's house. After rounding the corner, he made another right turn, then another, and another and ended up on the same street where he'd begun. He shut off the engine and the lights and coasted to a stop across the street from Gretchen's house. He'd keep an eye on it tonight. If Pancho tried to see Jessie . . . well, he, Kale, would be right on the scene. He saw Jessie's silhouette move past the window and he frowned into the darkness.

Bedrooms and baths, he thought. What kind of business was that?

But as he settled in for a long night, he did wish he had a pillow.

Chapter Four

What a night!

Jessie leaned against the door and released a whooshing sigh of relief. At last, he'd left. What a persistent, one-track mind Kale Warner had. He was attractive, too. But that was neither here nor there. The man had accused her of aiding and abetting a thief, jumped on her car, followed her and then tried to convince her Gretchen's house had been ransacked...probably just so he could come inside and look for his missing computer disk. After a glance at the messy room, Jessie deleted the last charge. Kale might be misguided in his suspicions, but he wasn't blind, and finding anything in here would be closer to a miracle than a scientific discovery.

An image of his too-blue eyes floated to mind. Tall, dark, well built, he could have posed for any number of photos advertising Day Dream linens. She could see it now...a room—a man's room—with bed covers tousled, barely covering the long length of his bare legs, the sensual angle of...

Jessie stopped the day dream before it got out of hand. She'd do well to forget Dr. Warner and his angles...all of them. The man needed looking after in the worst way. Any one who'd forget to copy important research was either too busy or too distracted. And then, to wear a tuxedo to track down a suspected thief…well, he needed help, that was for sure.

Jessie didn't want another needy person in her life. She hoped someday to find a man who could take care of his own details. Someone she could depend on. Someone to share life's responsibilities. She didn't want to have to find lost articles or be the one who always made the dinner reservations. Her Mr. Right would be self-sufficient, but he'd be as much in love with her as she would be with him. She meant to be number one in his heart. No secondary affections for her.

She glanced at her watch. It was an hour later at her parents' Maryland home and she debated calling. But, on the outside chance that Gretchen had phoned them with a message, Jessie decided to hunt down the telephone. It lay in the corner, piled under a telephone directory and five assorted throw pillows. Jessie shifted them aside and dialed home.

"Hi, Dad." She cleared a space on the floor and sat, Indian style, on one of the discarded pillows. "Working late?"

"What? Oh, yes, yes. Working. Always working." He chuckled. "Who is this?"

"It's Jessie, Dad."

"Oh, Jess. Hi, honey. How are you? Is something wrong?"

"No. Everything's fine. I'm on my way to Grandad's for my vacation."

"Vacation? I thought school just started."

Jessie let her lips curve in wry affection. For as long as she could remember, her father had seemed out of touch. He was a linguist and was usually lost in the study of one language or another. Jessie never knew when or if she had his full attention. "I'm out of school, Dad. I graduated four years ago."

"Oh, that's right. It's Gretchen who's still at college, isn't it?"

"Yes, Dad, and that's why I'm calling. She took off Wednesday to help clean up after that oil spill. You know, the one somewhere off the coast of Washington state?"

"There's been an oil spill? I hadn't heard that. I've been working on some translations. A fascinating dialect of an obscure South American tribe. It's just uncanny... what?" His voice went soft with distance, then strengthened as he came back on the line. "Jess? Here, your mother wants to talk to you. Maybe she knows about Gretchen's oil spill."

Jessie sighed, knowing the call had been an outside shot at best. Millie and Robert Day hardly ever knew where their children were. "Hi, Mom," she said when her mother came on the line. "I thought Gretchen might have called you. I sort of need to talk to her."

"Well, she isn't here. Where are you, dear? I thought you were going to Grandad Joe's."

"I'm on my way. Gretchen wanted me to stop at her house and get something for her, but I ran into a problem and—"

"I wouldn't worry about it, Jess. You know your sister. She'll turn up sooner or later. And by the way, I spoke to your brother yesterday... or was it last week? Well, anyway, he said to say hi when I talked to you. He's going to be home for Christmas and guess what?"

"He's going to bring his new puppy with him." Jessie had heard this story already. "The one he bought because it reminded him of Snooker in 'The Revenge of The Time-traveling Ninja Warlords.'"

"You're thinking of the wrong comic book. Snooker was in 'The Warlord Returns.'"

"You're right, Mom." Jessie didn't know why she liked to call her parents. Reaching out to touch someone at her home was a risky business. "Eric has written so many comic books, I can't keep track of all of them. Tell him I said hi and I'll see him at Christmas. And if you should hear from

Gretchen, tell her—'' Jessie stopped. It was pointless, she knew, to leave a message. ''Never mind. Bye, Mom. Tell Dad bye.''

''I will. Now you enjoy your trip. Oh, wait...your father wants to know if you remember where he put his extra pair of glasses. He's misplaced one pair and can't seem to find the others.''

''Tell him to try the top shelf of the bookcase.'' It was a guess, but Jessie figured she'd be close, if not right on target. She waited as her mother relayed the message. ''Oh, and Jessie,'' her mother said, ''while I'm talking to you, would you mind writing down the name of that ice cream you like so much. I want to have some the next time you're home.''

''I'll send it to you, Mom.''

''Good. Well, you have a nice vacation. And don't worry. Your father's keeping busy with some new dialect he's found and I'm in the middle of a new book, which I'm calling *The Final Diet*. Perfect title for a science fiction novel, don't you think? So you just go on and have a good time. Don't spend a minute worrying about us.''

No, Jessie thought as she hung up the receiver. She'd spend a lot of minutes worrying. But not now. She'd done all she could. She'd tried to get the package from Pancho and she'd tried to contact Gretchen. There was nothing else to do but to continue her plans. Grandad's farm sounded like heaven at the moment...and tomorrow she'd be there. Away from the demands of her business, away from her obligations to her family, and away from that crazy Kale Warner.

Jessie tossed the throw pillows back on top of the phone, turned on Gretchen's answering machine, and hoped her sister hadn't tried to call in her whereabouts during the past two days. It was just like Gretchen to say she'd leave a message and then forget to turn on the machine. With a shake of her head, Jessie picked her way into the bedroom and cleared the bed.

She'd just gotten comfortably sleepy when the telephone rang. Gretchen didn't have an extension, so Jessie sat up and pushed back the covers. She grappled for the flashlight she'd placed beside the bed, knocked it to the floor and had to reach under the bed to retrieve it. Finally she picked her way past the bedroom clutter and found the light switch. The answering machine clicked on just as she got to the living room and she decided to monitor the call. It was probably that crazy Dr. Warner again.

With a sigh, Jessie sank onto the pillow, placed her head on her arms and waited for the message.

"This is Pancho. Pancho Diaz." His accent was heavier now than it had been in the restaurant and Jessie wondered what country he was from. *"Please, Miss Day, if you are Gretchen Day's seester and you hear this message, I request the honor of your appearance at the Daybreak Donut Shop on University Street. It is important."* There was a pause and then a hurried, *"Please, eight tomorrow morning."* There was a beep signalling the cutoff of the conversation and Jessie realized, belatedly, that she should have picked up the phone and told Pancho she was not going to meet him.

It would be silly to go. She'd tried to take care of Gretchen's request, but enough was enough. Gretchen could just do without whatever was in the package Pancho had. She hoped he didn't have Kale's stolen diskette.

Jessie sighed. It looked as though she had no option other than to meet Pancho tomorrow, if only to satisfy herself that Pancho—and consequently, Gretchen—had had nothing to do with stealing that research. She wasn't sure what she'd do if Pancho did hand her a computer diskette. Call Kale, she supposed. Or maybe turn the whole thing over to the university's security police. That was all highly unlikely, though. If the truth were known, Kale Warner had probably just lost the thing and wanted someone to blame for his own negligence.

The memory of him sliding off the hood of her car brought a soft frown to her lips. Whatever had possessed him, she wondered. Did he often pull stunts like that? Somehow, she didn't think so.

Well, upstanding citizen or not, she didn't owe him any explanations. Jessie punched her pillow into a softer shape. Tomorrow she'd meet Pancho and try one last time to straighten out whatever Gretchen had left undone. Then she'd get on the road to Pottsville and the restful peace of the farm.

At least, Grandad Joe had good sense. Jessie thought she must have inherited it from him. He wouldn't expect her to do anything more than enjoy herself and keep him company. Quite a vacation after smoothing the details of too many other people's lives.

Jessie pulled the covers over her shoulders. Now, if she could only stop thinking about how Kale Warner would look all tangled up in the Swashbuckler sheets.

THE PURRING NOISE increased to a zippy hum and Kale awakened just in time to see a red sports car shift from reverse to forward gear and zoom past him. Damnation, he thought as he blinked the sleep from his eyes. Jessica Day was escaping.

It took mere seconds to start his car, make an awkward U-turn and get on her trail. His station wagon was a little on the staid side, but it had power where it counted…under the hood. Unfortunately Kale felt that his own under-the-hood power was not hitting on all cylinders this morning. Sleeping upright in the car had left him with a stiff neck and no earthly idea of what, if anything, had gone on in Gretchen's house during the night. Pancho and Jessie could have tap-danced up and down the street for all Kale knew.

The closer he got to Jessie's car, the more irritated he became. And the fact that Jessie seemed completely unaware that he'd spent the night within a hundred yards of her front door irritated him even further. Of course, it was entirely possible she did know and was at this very moment, leading him on a merry chase. Maybe he was only kidding himself. How difficult could it be to spot a full-size station wagon with a man in a crumpled tuxedo asleep at the wheel?

The red car made a left turn on Garland and breezed down the hill and through the stoplight. The light went from green to amber to red and Kale had to stop. Luckily Jessie turned into the shopping center at the foot of the hill and Kale figured he could catch up to her there. There was little activity in the shopping center at this hour of the day. It was too early for the art supply store to be open and . . .

The doughnut shop, he thought. Where else? So much for early morning sleuthing. He'd followed Jessie's sweet tooth to the Daybreak Donut Shop.

Kale tapped his fingers restlessly on the steering wheel. So what did he do now? Park outside and wait until she left? What would that accomplish? Damned, if he knew. Allowing himself a half yawn, he drove through the intersection and turned into the large parking lot. Yes, there was her car parked in front of the art store and he could see Jessie pulling open the door of the sweet shop. He thought about following her inside, if only for a cup of coffee, but decided to drive past the shop first and see whether or not she planned to consume her greasy breakfast there or take it with her.

Doughnuts, he thought with disgust. Didn't she know that wasn't a decent breakfast? He would have bet she counted calories, as slim and lithe a body as she had. He remembered her body quite well, considering he'd had a limited time for observation. But, well, some things made an impression right off and he—

Kale slammed on the brakes as he looked through the plate-glass windows of Daybreak Donuts. Jessie was there, all right, and she was sitting at a table—in plain view. And at the same table, also in plain view, was good old Pancho.

So she hadn't seen his car, Kale thought, or else she didn't care that he'd followed her. He drove on, pondering his next move. He could go in there and confront them. The idea was appealing, but was quickly followed by the memory of how little he'd gained from confronting the two of them the night before.

He could wait. If Pancho was handing over the computer disk, Kale would simply accost Jessie on her way out and she'd have to turn it over to him. Simple. Meanwhile, though, he had to find somewhere to park so he could see the door of the shop. How long could it take? he wondered. Surely a breakfast of so little nutritional value could be eaten in fifteen minutes or so. His stomach churned with the thought, or hunger; he couldn't be sure which. He *did* wish he had a cup of hot coffee.

"I REALLY DON'T CARE for any," Jessie said when Pancho set the thermal cup and jelly roll in front of her. "I'm not a big doughnut fan." Pancho's expression took on a wounded look and Jessie wordlessly took a tiny bite of the roll. "Do you have breakfast here often?"

Pancho bit off a section of a bear claw and nodded as he chewed. "Every day," he said. "I have the sweet tooth. Your seester, too."

Jessie wasn't sure if he meant that Gretchen also had a sweet tooth or if he had a sweet tooth for Gretchen. It was probably better not to know. "Do you ever meet my sister here?" Jessie asked. "For breakfast?"

"No, no. We meet at Dakota Jack's on Friday nights. That is our only time together."

Smart move on Gretchen's part. Jessie cupped her hands around the cup as she glanced around the small shop. It was a typical, college-town store, catering to students and offering a full-range of fried and iced doughnuts every day of the week. The greasy smell had killed Jessie's appetite as soon as she'd walked through the door.

"So, Pancho." Jessie took a small sip of the coffee and ignored the gooey jelly roll. "How did you meet Gretchen in the first place?"

His dark eyes took on a dreamy, romantic glow. "It was what you would call kiss-me."

"Kismet?"

Pancho shrugged his indifference to technicalities. "I saw Mees Day and my heart stood still. It was beeutifull."

"Are you one of her students?" Jessie took another drink. "Are you a sociology major?"

His grin was youthful, swift and proud. "I am studying agriculture so I can improve my family's farm in Ecuador and make us very reech. I take sociology, too. And that is how I met your seester."

His dark eyes and wistful expression reminded Jessie of the kitten Gretchen had once brought home—the three-legged kitten that Jessie had reluctantly acquired ownership of when Gretchen had had to devote her time to another project. Jessie had fed and cared for that cat through all of its nine lives and it still had first and always adored Gretchen. Unless she was much mistaken, Pancho was another three-legged cat. Jessie decided it was time to get on to the reason for this early-morning rendezvous. "Did you bring the package?"

"The package, yes." Pancho finished his last bite of doughnut in one gulp and furtively licked his fingers. "I have it here." He patted the paper sack on the floor beside his chair. "Mees Day asked me to collect these things and give them to you. She said you would know where to send them. It is important."

"Yes," Jessie agreed with a pointed look at the sack. "I'll mail them as soon as possible." As soon as Gretchen thought to let her know where in the world she was. "Why don't you give the sack to me now, Pancho?"

For a moment, he looked uncomfortable and Jessie wondered if perhaps Kale Warner had some grounds for his suspicions of Pancho. But Pancho was just a kid and he didn't seem overly blessed with good old common sense. It was hard to believe Pancho could have stolen Dr. Warner's computer disk and gotten away with it.

"You'll mail it to Mees Day?" Pancho reached for the sack and held it securely in his lap. "It is important she knows to trust me."

"I promise." Jessie didn't want to tell him that Gretchen pretty much trusted everyone, regardless of how well she knew them...or didn't know them. It was one of her most endearing personality flaws. "I'll let her know you did just as she asked, Pancho."

He smiled at that and handed the sack across the table. It was bulky and Jessie unrolled the top to glance inside.

Pancho shrugged. "I put everything in a box...for mailing purposes."

"I see." Jessie pulled out the shirt-size box and placed it on the table. "What did Gretchen ask you to get?" In reality, Jessie knew she was only looking for a computer diskette. One that belonged to Kale Warner. She didn't see how it could be there, but she had to satisfy herself that it wasn't, just the same. It was her way of protecting Gretchen and Gretchen's student.

"Don't." Pancho tried to keep her from opening the box, but Jessie was quick and determined.

"I have to know what's in this, Pancho, before I can mail it."

He seemed to accept that and leaned back in his chair, but he did look embarrassed. Jessie flipped back the lid and looked inside. There was a notebook, which upon examination, contained pages of notes in Gretchen's handwriting. The notebook rested on a dark blue sweater, which was folded neatly on the bottom of the box, and next to the notebook was a plastic container. Jessie sighed and reached for it, knowing it held computer disks. Pancho should have known better than to be so obvious, she thought.

"What are these?" Jessie asked, holding up the plastic container. "Did Gretchen ask you to send these?"

Pancho nodded quickly and fiercely. "Yes. They were in her office. Just like that. All three."

Jessie opened the box and took out the disks. There were three, as Pancho had said. Three disks, all bearing stick-tight labels on which Gretchen's handwriting was unmistakable. Jessie checked all edges of the labels, but could find no evidence of tampering. The chances that Pancho could have substituted a disk and changed the label without a trace were remote. With some feeling of relief, Jessie put the disks back in the box with the sweater and notebook. "All right, Pancho. I'll get this mailed to my sister today. And I'll let her know how much help you were."

Pancho nodded. "I put in the sweater," he said. "It is mine, but I didn't want to think of Mees Day in the cold weather without a sweater."

He was obviously proud of his gift and Jessie didn't have the heart to tell him Gretchen had worse problems than being without a sweater. "I know she'll appreciate that," Jessie said. She stood, sack in one hand, thermal coffee cup in the other. "Best of luck to you, Pancho. I know you'll make a wonderful farmer."

"Reech farmer," he said.

"Rich farmer," she repeated as she turned to go.

"Mees Day?"

Jessie turned back to the small table. "Yes, Pancho?"

Pancho scuffed his feet on the linoleum and met her eyes reluctantly. "I have the favor to ask you."

"Favor?" Jessie vaguely remembered he'd started to make the same request last night. "You want me to do a favor for you?"

He nodded. "I have a geeft for your seester, but I could not give it to her before she left."

Jessie saw it coming. "You want me to mail it, too?"

"No, no." Pancho looked surprised at the suggestion. "Just keep it until she returns."

"She'll be back in a couple of weeks, Pancho. Then, you can give it to her yourself."

"But I cannot keep a pet in the dorm. It is not allowed."

A pet. Visions of the three-legged kitten came to mind. "Pancho," Jessie began. "I can't—"

"Just a couple of weeks." His dark eyes pleaded with her for understanding. "I rescued it, just for Mees Day. She will be so proud."

Jessie didn't doubt that for a minute. "Pancho, I'm leaving Fayetteville this morning. I can't take care of an animal."

"But I have already put it in Mees Day's garage. Please, you must do me the one favor. It is important."

Apparently Pancho's life was full of one important thing after another. With a sigh, Jessie capitulated, promising herself that cute, cuddly or whatever, the pet would blend into the scenery at Grandad Joe's farm and if Gretchen wanted it later, she could go and get it. "All right, Pancho," Jessie said. "I'll take it with me. It's in the garage?"

"Thank you, yes. This will make your seester most happy."

Jessie nodded and started for the door again. Halfway there, she paused and looked back. "Does it have three legs?" she asked.

"Three legs?" Pancho looked concerned and puzzled.

"Never mind." Jessie walked to the door and outside. The air was crisp and cool, as it often is in mid-October. For the first time since her arrival, Jessie thought there might be hope for her vacation yet. She did love Arkansas autumns and the thought of the farm ablaze with color was soothing. She—and Gretchen's pet—should arrive by early afternoon and then . . . two weeks of peace and rest were hers for the taking.

She adjusted the bulky paper sack in the crook of her arm and wondered where she could dump the coffee cup she still held. There didn't seem to be a trash receptacle, so she took another sip of coffee as she started for her car. On Garland Avenue, traffic was beginning to increase with early arrivals for the afternoon football game. By noon, the street would be overflowing with Razorback fans and foes. Jessie couldn't wait to get out of town. Her gaze swept the parking lot as she reached into her pocket for her car keys. Not many people in the shopping center yet, but . . .

Jessie narrowed her eyes at the station wagon parked directly across from where she stood. It was in front of the Chicken Express fast-food take-out window. Who would be getting chicken at this time of the morning, she wondered. And why did that car look so familiar?

Recognition came almost immediately upon the heels of the realization that Chicken Express was not yet open for business. But that didn't seem to matter to Dr. Kale Warner. Jessie clutched her sack and headed across the parking area. She'd tie up this last loose end and then she would begin her vacation.

"Good morning," she said as she circled to the front of the station wagon. "What a coincidence to see you again so soon, Dr. Warner."

If he was embarrassed at having been caught following her, it didn't show. He rolled down the car window the rest of the way and rested his arm on the frame. "Good morning," he said. "I saw you with Pancho, so there's no need too deny that he gave you the information I'm after. Save us both a great deal of trouble, Jessie, and hand it over."

Jessie thought seriously about handing him the coffee cup, upside down, on top of his handsome head. "Why don't you go home and do your laundry? Your good black suit is showing signs of fatigue. And while you're at it, soak your head. You'll be a better man for it." She spun on her heel and headed away from him.

"Wait!"

She heard his door open and close with a frustrated slam, but she kept walking. He caught her in two steps, stepped in front of her in two more and danced a slick two-step when she tried to get past him. "I apologize if I sounded abrupt...."

"Abrupt?" Jessie's voice rose.

Kale made a wide gesture of appeasement with his hands. "Okay, so I was rude. I'm sorry. It's been a long night."

"We all have our problems, Dr. Warner. It isn't my fault you stayed out too late last night."

"No, it isn't your fault, but you're certainly the reason I had a miserable night and a stiff neck this morning."

Jessie blinked against the blue intensity of his gaze. "I beg your pardon, but you were born with a stiff neck."

He frowned. "You didn't see me sitting in front of your house this morning? You drove right past me."

"No, I didn't see you. Why would you—? It never occurred to me you'd do such a stupid thing." It should have occurred to her, she realized as soon as the words left her mouth. He'd been doing stupid things since the first minute she laid eyes on him. "Why did you do that?"

He straightened his shoulders in self-defense. "I don't consider it stupid to try to protect research it took months to develop."

Jessie refrained from pointing out that he should have protected it before it got stolen. The man was clearly determined to believe she had his research. "Look, Dr. Warner—"

"Kale," he corrected with some easing of his brusque manner.

"—I came over to your car just now to let you know that Pancho gave me the package I'm supposed to mail to my sister and your missing research is not in it. So you need to get a new angle on the thief. It wasn't Pancho and it certainly isn't me."

"Impossible." At the swift warning of her frown, Kale changed tactics. "I mean, Pancho has to be in on the theft. I don't now how he did it yet, but he has my research."

There seemed only one way to resolve the issue once and for all. "Come on," Jessie said. "I'll let you see what's in the box and then maybe you'll stop being so stup—stubborn about this." She turned and walked over to a picnic table under the yellow-and-red awning of Chicken Express.

Kale followed and stood beside the table as he reached for the paper sack in her hands.

"Not so fast." Jessie pulled it out of his reach. "Sit down. We're going to do this my way, understand?"

Kale decided two could play this game. He sat. He smiled his most disarming smile. He clasped his hands as if he could wait forever. "Did you have a good breakfast?" he asked.

She glanced up in surprise, her big brown eyes wide and a tad suspicious. "I haven't had breakfast this morning."

"Don't you like doughnuts?"

"Not particularly. Do you?"

"No. I'm more of a whole-grain person." The suspicion in her eyes crystallized and Kale wondered what it would take to bring out that enchanting little dimple in her chin. "I have a weakness for coffee, though."

She glanced from him to her coffee cup. "You want the rest of mine? It's still hot."

He found it somehow appealing to think about touching his lips to a cup her lips had touched. Jeez. It must have been a rougher night than he'd thought. "No, thanks. I can live without it."

"Well, I hope you can live with this." Jessie pulled a shirt box from the paper sack and set it on the table between them. "There are three computer diskettes in here. If you can see how the labels might have been changed or tampered with in any way, I'll be happy to take the disks to a computer so you can check the data on them."

His heartbeat quickened with her mention of diskettes, but quickly faded when he took the plastic sleeve from her hand. "These aren't mine," he stated over a wave of disappointment and inexplicable relief. "The disk I used had a white center. These are black. And you're right about the labels. It's pretty hard to change them without a trace."

"And that's definitely my sister's handwriting," Jessie pointed out, adding proof upon proof. "So you see, you've been barking up the wrong tree all along."

Kale looked up and saw the dimple flash an appearance. No doubt about the charm it added to her already pretty face. And no denying the stir of attraction he felt. But his research was still missing and his last lead was quickly slipping through his fingers. "Do you believe Pancho knows nothing about this?" he asked, for lack of a better question. "Didn't you think he acted just a little suspicious?"

She considered that. "Maybe he did, but that doesn't prove anything."

Kale handed back the plastic box of diskettes. "I guess not. So, what are you going to do now?"

"I'm going to mail this to my sister... if she bothered to call and leave an address. Then I'm on my way to Grandad Joe's for a vacation." Jessie closed the shirt box and slipped it back inside the sack. "What are you going to do now that your suspects are cleared?"

"Do a little more investigating, I suppose." He tapped his fingers on the rough wood. "Where's Grandad Joe's? Is that anything like Dakota Jack's?"

Jessie smiled and Kale watched that elusive dimple. "It's more like Old McDonald's. My grandad has a farm on Crow Mountain, just north of Pottsville. And for your information, Pottsville is on the Arkansas map. Potts Tavern used to be a stop on the Wells Fargo line, which is some claim to fame."

Kale liked her easy conversation and wished he had more time to pursue it. Jessie Day had caught his interest, in more ways than one. Unfortunately he had another claim on his time and interest at the moment. If Pancho hadn't given the research disk to Jessie, then he must still have it in his possession. The game wasn't over yet. "Was Pancho still in the doughnut shop when you left?" he asked.

Jessie blinked in surprise. "Uh, yes. Yes, he was."

"Okay." Kale stood and took a step toward his car before coming back to the table. "Thanks, Jessie. You've been a big help. I'll let you know how things work out."

A big help, Jessie thought as she watched Dr. Kale Warner walk to his car and then drive the short distance from Chicken Express to Daybreak Donuts. The man was a mess, she decided. His mind didn't jump tracks, it traveled the same track around and around and around. Why had she even thought she could convince him Pancho had nothing to do with the theft of the research? Why had she even tried? At least, he was off her trail now. She wouldn't have to look over her shoulder . . . or out her window . . . and see him following her. She couldn't believe he'd parked outside the house all night, waiting to see whether or not she met Pancho. For an intelligent man, he didn't seem to exercise much sense.

Jessie wrinkled her nose as she dumped the coffee and cup into the trash can. Dr. Warner was hot on the scent of a new trail and she had better things to do than to think about him. Undoubtedly she would never see him again anyway. So, Pottsville and Grandad Joe's, here I come, she thought and made her way across the parking lot to her car.

It took less than ten minutes to drive back to Gretchen's house and less than five to listen to the two messages on the answering machine.

"Hi, Jess. Hope you found everything. I'm in Seattle. Well, not really Seattle. It's a place on the coast not far from Seattle. The name of the town escapes me for the moment, but I'll think of it in a minute. Anyway, you should see what we're up against here. Honestly, the things done to the environment in the name of greed make me sick. Poor birds covered in slime. And the seals. Jess, it breaks my heart. You want to come out? We could use more hands. What a job! I can't believe—" Beep! The answering machine cut off the rest of Gretchen's words, then with another beep, she took up where she left off.

—I guess I better give you this address. Send the package to P. O. Box 5943, Seattle, Washington . . . zip . . . oh, forget the zip, it'll get here. At least I hope it will. I'll pay you back later. Pancho did give you the stuff, didn't he? Call me if he didn't, okay? Oh, and tell Mom that she can't use Ecoloam as the name of a planet. There's a company out here with that name. She could change the spelling, I guess, but it might be better to— Beep!

Jess rewound the tape and reset the machine. As she wrapped the package for mailing, she wondered what her sister, and her whole family, would do if she suddenly stopped being the dependable one. What if she rushed off to aid injured animals on the West Coast? What if she took a spur-of-the-moment trip around the world? Would the Day family collapse? Probably not, but Jessie wasn't entirely sure they wouldn't. And even if they didn't collapse, who would take care of the three-legged kittens?

That thought reminded her of the "pet" in the garage. A kitten, she wondered. A puppy? No, a puppy would have howled during the night. A kitten, then. She decided to cover the floorboards of her car with paper just in case the kitten didn't take well to automobile travel. With overnight case packed, and the car protected from possible pet accidents, Jessie walked to the garage.

"Here, kitty, kitty," she called as she pulled open the door. "Where are you, kitty?"

No answering meow echoed in the dusty air. Then Jessie heard a scratchy sound and smelled a vaguely familiar smell.

Chicken.

Pancho's gift to Gretchen was a chicken.

Chapter Five

Heaven couldn't be better than this, Jessie thought as she sat sideways in the wooden swing on Grandad's front porch. The breeze was almost chilly as the full moon crested the tall oaks. She buttoned her sweater and clasped her hands around her jean clad knees. One deep breath didn't satisfy her and she drew in another, loving the clean, earthy scents of the farm. The city was as far from her thoughts tonight as the moon and she didn't intend to give her business or her apartment or any other part of her life in Tulsa a second thought. Not for the next two weeks.

She didn't intend to think about Gretchen or Pancho or the sinfully blue and attractive eyes of Dr. Kale Warner, either. But oddly enough, her memory kept tossing out moments from the past two days . . . Kale flat on the floor in Dakota Jack's; Kale on the hood of her car; Kale standing at the foot of the steps telling her he'd come to return her scarf; Kale driving away from Chicken Express and out of her life.

Jessie hugged her knees tighter and balanced against the sway of the swing. It was silly that she should think of Kale Warner at all. The man had a one-track mind and she had no trouble reading it . . . r-e-s-e-a-r-c-h. First, last, and always, Dr. Warner was going to love his work.

Gretchen was a lot like that, too. In fact, every member of the Day family, except Jessie and Grandad Joe, had much in common with the good Dr. Warner. Which was all the more reason not to give him another thought.

Oh, but the moon was gorgeous. Full and white and huge in the canopy of dark sky. Pinpoints of stars pricked their way through the fabric of night, unblemished by the vapor lights of highway and street lamps. This was a night for romance and lovers and Jessie felt the first blush of a wish that she had someone with whom to share it. Not Grandad Joe, of course, who'd retired for bed shortly after eight-thirty. Not Anthony, the man who lived in the apartment next to hers and whom she'd dutifully and unenthusiastically dated a few times. Not one of the two or three men who'd passed through her life with relatively small impact, either.

No, she had no one with whom she'd want to sit in the swing and watch the moon. No one to share conversation and private thoughts with. No one to tell about the chicken she'd brought with her from Fayetteville to the farm.

Her lips tilted with a smile. It hadn't been funny at first, but by the time she and the chicken reached the city limits of Russellville, they were fast friends. Jessie had named her Jennifer, after a roommate in college, and she felt the hen liked the name. Of course, it was hard to read approval into a couple of clucks, but...it was a long drive of straight highway and most of the radio stations were laid-back country. Telling chicken jokes had lasted barely ten miles because Jennifer's sense of humor wasn't all it might have been.

Jessie laughed softly at her own nonsense. She'd been without a vacation far too long, obviously, when she could so easily amuse herself in *fowl* company. She bent her head and rested her forehead against her knees. Her "seester" had better be grateful for this favor, that's all she had to say.

In the distance, a car engine hummed and there was the faraway sound of tires on gravel. Jessie raised her head to listen, trying to separate all the distinctly rural noises from the city ones. She couldn't do it. A car sounded like a car and she felt a bit irritated at the interruption in her perfect night. Well, almost perfect night.

With a lazy yawn, she thought about bed; about the scratchy, sun-dried sheets and the big feather mattress and the downy pillows awaiting her inside the house. By the end of her visit, she'd be ready for fabric-softened linens, inner springs, and foam pillows, but for now, nothing could be better.

The car sounds came closer and Jessie glanced toward the road that circled the orchard in time to see headlights sweep the peach trees and swing toward the house. There was a quarter mile of drive to cover. Jessie frowned as the car came closer, then she sighed easily as it took the curve away from Grandad's.

She debated going inside the house and crawling beneath the covers. If the moon wasn't quite so big, if the stars weren't quite so charming...

Putting one foot on the wood slats of the porch, Jess pushed and sent the rocker into gentle motion. She sat there, staring dreamily at the sky and breathing country air, half-asleep for perhaps another ten minutes or so. It wasn't until the headlights cut a swath across the barn that she became aware of the noise of an engine and the return of the automobile.

She wasn't alarmed. Neighbors often stopped if they saw someone outside. Apparently someone else hadn't wanted tonight's moon to go unshared. The car crunched through the dry, fallen leaves of the hickory tree and parked in front of the house. Jessie slipped both feet to the floor and shifted her palms on the curved edge of the swing. "Hello?" she called softly as the door of the station wagon opened.

Wait a minute. *Station wagon?*

"All right," Kale said as he came around the front of the car and walked toward the porch. "What did you do with it?"

Jessie couldn't believe this. She could not believe he had followed her again. "Dr. Warner. Aren't you a long way from the laboratory?"

"I'm a long way from anywhere. Do you know how many farms there are on this dadblasted mountain?"

Jessie bit back a sudden smile. "No, I don't know. Do you?"

"I've been to the Bowdens, the Williams, the Cohans, and the Heathrows tonight looking for you. And that doesn't include the places I stopped and didn't get the name."

"And now you've found me."

"So I have." Kale steadied his breathing with effort. In the shadows of the porch, Jessie's hair caught the moon glow and glistened with a dozen lights. Her face was pale and lovely, her smile a masterpiece of subtlety. Her lips looked soft, kissable, and he wondered if she would taste as cool and sweet as she looked. That was hardly the kind of thing he should be thinking about a thief. But now . . . well, he couldn't quite remember what he'd wanted to say. "May I join you on the porch?"

"Sure." She eased back in the swing and watched his approach. "I almost didn't recognize you without your tuxedo. Aren't you a little under-dressed to come looking for your research?"

He swept his hands in a dismissing gesture. "I didn't figure the farm was formal. You're not exactly dressed for the prom, yourself."

"I thought my part in the great disappearing research caper was over. Apparently, since you're here, you've lost something else."

"You're a cool customer, Jessica Day." Kale leaned against the porch rail and crossed his arms across his sweater-covered chest. "Keeping me talking about the diskette, when you knew all along you had my lab animal."

Jessie blinked. Her tone turned defensive. "Lab animal? How did you manage to lose an animal?"

"I didn't lose it. It was stolen. And I have every reason to believe you have it in your possession."

"If you think I would carry off some nasty little lab rat, you're as crazy as a loon. I do not handle rodents, Dr. Warner, and there isn't enough money in the world to entice me to do it, either."

"You admit it, then. You took money for stealing CTA #43."

Jessie rose, frustration and annoyance in her every move. "I admit nothing because I know nothing about—what is a CTA #43?"

Kale frowned, beginning to doubt the wisdom of having followed her, beginning to suspect he'd made another mistake. "Cholesterol Test Animal #43 is a white, female leghorn. A chicken."

Jessie's lips parted in a small oh of surprise and the anger faded from her expression. "A chicken," she repeated. "You're testing a chicken for cholesterol?"

"Not exactly. CTA #43 is—"

"What in Sam Hill is going on out here?" Grandad Joe opened the front door, pushed back the screen, and stepped out onto the porch, adjusting the strap of his overalls as he came. He was a tall, lanky man with long arms and legs and a thin face that showed no sign of a smile. Kale was bigger, younger, and the better bet in a fight, but he had a feeling he would be no match for Jess's Grandad Joe.

"Good evening, sir." Kale straightened, offered his hand for a handshake. "I'm Dr. Warner. Dr. Kale Warner from the University of Arkansas. I'm here to speak with your granddaughter."

The elder man covered Kale's fingers in a firm and brief grip. "Joe Day," he said politely, but his questioning eyes turned to Jessica. "A bit late for a gentleman to call, don't you think, missy?"

"It's not even ten o'clock yet, Grandad." Jessie moved over to stand beside her grandfather. "And Kale isn't calling on me the . . . the way you're thinking. He's looking for his chicken."

"Chicken?" Grandad Joe narrowed his eyes at Kale. "This is gonna be one of those long stories, ain't it? Let's go inside and Jessie can make us all something warm to drink." He turned and reentered the house. With a slight lift of her shoulders, Jessie followed and so Kale followed, too.

The house was small, but cozy. There was a scent of age and old wood inside and Kale knew without being told that the house echoed with good, solid memories. There was a clock on the shelf and Grandad Joe glanced at it before leading the way through a doorway and into the kitchen. He pulled out a ladder-back chair and seated himself at a round oak table before directing an expectant look to his guest. Kale took the chair opposite and Jessica set a stainless-steel kettle on the stove.

"Now, what're you here about?" Grandad Joe asked Kale. "You a friend of Gretchen's there at the university?"

Kale shifted in his chair. "I have not had the pleasure of meeting your other granddaughter."

"You're here to see Jessie then?"

"He came because he thought I stole his chicken, Grandad Joe." Jessie stood behind her grandfather and smiled across the table at Kale. Her brown eyes showed signs of laughter that were barely hinted at in the slant of her lips. Just enough amusement to make Kale a little uncomfortable, but not enough to bring out the dimple in her chin. "He's the man I told you about," she finished.

After that ambiguous statement, Kale thought he was honor bound to defend himself. "Actually I thought Jessica stole a computer diskette. You see, I knew Pancho... a student who works nights at the lab...took the diskette and was supposed to give it to a blonde at one of the clubs in Fayetteville. So today, when I found out Jessie didn't have the diskette, I followed Pancho again. But there was a football game and ... well, I lost him in the crowd."

There was no look of dawning comprehension on the part of his audience, but Kale plowed on with his explanation, determined to resurrect at least a portion of his pride. "I went back to the lab, thinking maybe I had been mistaken and the diskette with the research data was still there. And that's when I discovered that another chicken had been substituted for CTA #43."

Grandad Joe glanced over his shoulder at Jessie.

Jessie patted his bony shoulder. "CTA #43 is the chicken he lost, Grandad. It stands for Cholesterol Test Animal. Pretty scientific, huh?"

Her attitude annoyed Kale, but he thought he did a good job of hiding it. "I didn't lose the chicken," he said. "It was stolen...along with the diskette. And I'd like to know what Jessie knows about it."

"Jess?" Grandad Joe turned toward her, questioning. Kale did the same.

She made a wry face. "I didn't steal your chicken, Kale, but I might have—accidentally, you understand—driven her getaway car."

"This is serious," Kale stated unequivocally.

"You're right. Maybe I could turn State's Evidence and reduce my sentence. 'Your Honor, this chicken flew in my car window and directed me to Interstate 40. I thought for sure I was a dead duck, if I didn't do exactly as she said.'"

Kale frowned his impatience and Jessie sighed. "This is serious," she said. "I know." She knew that he, for one, was very serious about it. But she couldn't help seeing the humor. After all, it wasn't her fault he was so absent-minded he didn't know until today that his precious CTA number whatever was gone. "Okay, I did bring a chicken to the farm with me today. This morning Pancho told me he had left a gift for Gretchen in the garage and asked me if I'd take care of it until she got back. I thought it would be a kitten or something like that. But when I went to the garage, there was this cage with a chicken in it."

"That's it." Kale jumped up from the table. "That's my chicken. Would you get it for me, please?"

"It's perfectly all right to refer to 'it' as a 'her.'" Jessie squeezed a few drops of fresh lemon into the mugs, feeling irritated that Kale was so pleased at the mention of the hen. "And I'm afraid I can't get her."

Kale sat down...heavily. "Oh, God, you didn't...fry her for supper, did you?"

Jessie spun toward him. "She's in the henhouse, you idiot. I am not the sort of person who would eat a pet!"

"Chickens are chickens, not pets."

"He has a point there, Jess," Grandad Joe said, accepting the hot drink Jessie handed to him. "Chickens don't make real good pets."

"I'll just go find her, myself." Kale started up out of his chair.

"No, sir." Grandad Joe stopped Kale with a look. "You're not going to disturb my layin' hens in the middle of the night. Your chicken's not going anywhere before daybreak. You can look for her then. In the meantime, we've got an extra bed, if you're of a mind to stay."

"I'm not leaving without my chicken," Kale said flatly as he stared at the mug in front of him. "Thank you, I will stay with you tonight."

Dismay had swept through Jessie the minute her grandad had made his suggestion. With Kale's acceptance, it jolted all the way down her spine. "I'll make up the other bed," she said without expression and left the warm kitchen.

It was probably ten minutes before Kale came to stand in the doorway of the back bedroom. He was too tall for the room and although he was in no danger of bumping his head on the ceiling, he looked oversize and awkward in the doorway. He looked good in jeans, Jessie thought. He'd probably look pretty good in sackcloth. But how he looked was not her concern at the moment. How he slept was what she had on her mind. "Did Grandad Joe go back to bed?" she asked.

"He drank his tea and toddled off to the other side of the house."

"This has been a long evening for him. He's usually asleep before nine and he's always awake before four. He's a genuine, up-with-the-sun farmer."

Kale's gaze followed her as she smoothed the sheets and plumped the pillows and Jessie tried to keep her movements casual and even, as if she weren't unsettled by his too-blue eyes. "I'm sorry, I acted like a fool before," he said. "I don't know what it is about you that brings out . . ."

". . . the animal in you?" Jessie couldn't resist teasing him.

"If that were true, I'd be grabbing you and trying to kiss you at every opportunity. Would that be the best way of getting the information I want?"

"Oh, I don't know." Jessie tossed the pillow into his arms. "It couldn't be much worse than what you have tried in the past twenty-four hours."

"Haven't I known you longer than that?"

Jessie let a slight smile touch her lips as she backed toward the door, which led to her bedroom on the other side of the wall. "You don't know me at all."

She slipped into her room and closed the door, leaning against it with a sigh. How could she possibly, possibly, feel any attraction for that man? Why he'd accused her of stealing his chicken and then eating it! She was insulted, irritated, and…her palms were sweaty. Her heartbeat wasn't entirely steady, either, but that could be a combination of…well, a lot of things. Kale Warner didn't, necessarily, have anything to do with the warmth that was even now flooding her cheeks.

Jessie pushed away from the door and prepared for bed. She could hear Kale walking in the next room. The wall was so thin, she could practically hear him breathing. The original house had been built with a living room and kitchen in the center and two narrow bedrooms, one on either side. Over the years, though, as the family increased and the house didn't, this room had been halved and made into two small bedrooms. The wall in between provided more privacy than a sheet, but not by much. She and Gretchen had shared a bed and played whispering games through the wall with their brother. It had been fun then, but the idea that Kale was now on the other side of that wall and probably could hear her breathing was not so exciting.

"Jessica?" Kale's voice was soft, but she could still make out his tone of surprise. "Isn't there any soundproofing in this wall?"

"Not much. The house is pretty old."

"Oh."

The bedsprings squeaked and Jessie felt uncomfortably warm knowing Kale was getting into bed. They might as well be sharing a bed, they'd be sleeping so close together. Jessie backed up her thought processes. There was a wall between them, she told herself. A thin physical wall as well as a thick wall of their differences. There was no reason to make this a personal experience. With that resolve, she slipped into a flannel nightgown and slid under the covers.

"Good grief. I can hear every move you make."

Kale sounded irritated and Jessie flounced onto her side, making the bed squeak as loudly as possible. "You can bunk in the barn, if you'd prefer, Dr. Warner."

There was a moment of quiet. "You're awfully touchy. Is it because you have something to hide?"

He was just like her family. He could go from point *A* to point *Z* without ever straying from point A or passing through the points in between. "I have nothing to hide," she said.

"You hid my CTA #43."

"I put her in the henhouse. What else was I supposed to do with a chicken?"

"You could have turned it over to me."

"I didn't know you wanted her." Jessie punched her pillow and turned over on her stomach. "All I heard was that you were looking for a computer diskette with your research data on it. You never once mentioned a chicken."

"I didn't want to reveal everything about my research until I was sure you weren't working for the thieves."

"You should have stayed in your laboratory and hired a detective. I don't think you're overly talented at sleuthing."

"I don't think I've done too badly." He sounded a bit offended. "I found you, didn't I? And you do have Number Forty-three."

It was hard to argue such profound logic and Jessie found herself shaking her head in the dark. "Don't you ever give them names? Do you always have to call them by numbers?"

"I name pets, not test animals."

"You have pets?"

"A few." His voice got softer and maybe, just a bit nostalgic. "Several, over the years. Right now, I have a couple of dogs and a cat. Actually the cat doesn't belong to me. He's an independent feline who comes in my house when he chooses and leaves anytime he pleases. The dogs love me, though. But they're not too crazy about the cat."

This was a new and interesting aspect of Dr. Warner and Jessie found it intriguing. "What kind of dogs?" she asked.

"What kind would love me, you mean? Or what breed?" He didn't wait for her reply. "One's a Labrador. The other is a cross between a schnauzer and something with a long, fuzzy tail. I've never been able to figure out just what. The Labrador is called Angus and the mutt is Crusoe. The cat doesn't answer to anything."

"I named your chicken Jennifer," Jessie confided for some unknown reason. "I hope you don't mind."

"I mind that the chicken is here and not at the experimental farm where it's supposed to be. How Pancho got this far with his scheme is beyond me. Did you help him?"

"For the last time, Dr. Warner, I met Pancho last night for the sole purpose of getting a package and mailing it to my sister. I don't know Pancho and certainly have no plans to pursue a relationship with him in the future. I got your chicken by default, but I don't believe Pancho stole it. He said he'd rescued it and that Gretchen—that's my sister— would be very proud of him. Now, will you stop accusing me of being a common thief?"

"There's nothing common about you, Jessica. Were you this argumentative as a child?"

"No. At least, I don't think…" She couldn't believe she'd started to answer that. "My childhood is none of your business."

"True." A moment of silence pulsed through the wall. "If you spent your childhood here at the farm, it must have been wonderful."

Her gaze traveled the familiar ceiling to the lace-curtained window, along the painted woodwork to the solid oak dressing table and the silvered mirror. "Some of my fondest memories were made on this farm. I spent a couple of weeks here every summer."

"I thought so. You seem . . . calmer, not as uptight as you were yesterday."

She decided not to point out that if she'd been uptight yesterday, he was largely responsible. "It's hard not to be calm in a place like this."

"My grandparents lived close to Tenkiller Lake and I loved going to visit them. I thought life couldn't be any better when I was there. It's funny how small their house seems now. I used to think the whole world was inside it."

"Yes," Jessie said, understanding more than she really wanted to, liking him better for having special childhood memories. "We'd better get some sleep. Grandad will have us awake early in the morning. He doesn't believe in anyone lying abed after seven."

"Thanks for the warning. Do you have an alarm clock?"

Jessie's lips went wide with a smile. "Tell me, Kale, do you ever work with roosters?"

"It's difficult to breed chickens without one."

"Well, here on the farm, they serve a dual function. You'll be awake before seven, trust me."

"Jessie?"

"Yes?"

"Thank you for making up my bed."

A slow heat wandered into her cheeks. "You're welcome."

No other words came through the wall, but Jessie lay awake listening to the night sounds and the rustle of sheets as the harvest moon scattered champagne-colored shadows across the room. She only hoped Jennifer was enjoying the golden moon and her one and only night in the henhouse with Grandad's rooster.

Chapter Six

The rooster crowed in full voice outside the window and Jessie opened her eyes to pale sunlight and the stimulating aroma of frying bacon. She could hear the rumble of deep voices in another part of the house. With a yawn and a lazy stretch, she flipped aside the covers and shivered as the cool morning air raised a rash of goose bumps on her skin.

Ordinarily she would have put on a robe and house shoes and hurried to the warmth of the kitchen. But Kale's presence in the house prevented such informality. There was just something too intimate about a robe. So Jessie reached for her jeans and flannel shirt. She pulled on a pair of thick socks and the boots she wore when she visited the farm, then blew softly on her cold fingers. Vanity forced her to take a look in the dresser mirror and then she had to brush her hair. Maybe she ought to put a little powder on her nose... She stopped short right there and headed for the door that led to the living room and warmth.

"...the funny thing was, everybody told him he couldn't grow watermelons in that patch of ground."

"That variety of melon is getting a lot of attention now. One of the agronomists at the university is conducting tests on the soil—no thanks, Joe. No eggs for me."

Jessie stepped into the kitchen and caught the men's attention. "Good morning," she said. "What's for breakfast?"

"Eggs, bacon, biscuits and gravy." Grandad Joe took a pan of browned biscuits from the oven. "You rolled out of bed kinda late this morning, didn't ya?"

"Didn't you hear the rooster crowing?" Kale glanced over his shoulder as he stirred the gravy in a skillet. "It certainly woke me right up."

Jessie frowned and slipped into a chair. "This is my vacation. I can sleep as late as I wish."

"Not if you want breakfast." Grandad slid a biscuit from the pan onto the plate in front of her. "Here, try some of Maybelle's blackberry jam. Sit down now, Kale. I'll get a bowl for that gravy."

Kale pulled out the chair next to Jessie and brushed her knee with his as he sat down. "Sorry," he murmured, but he didn't move his leg more than a half inch from hers. "Did you sleep well?"

For some reason, Jessie read more into the question than a literal inquiry on the quality of her sleep. She shifted in her seat and reached for the jam jar. "Yes, I did, thank you. How is Maybelle, Grandad? I haven't seen her in a long time."

"Same old Maybelle."

Kale raised an eyebrow at Grandad's terse answer, but Jessie saw no reason to enlighten him. He was, after all, just an overnight visitor. There was no need for him to know that Widow Maybelle Simms had had her eye on Grandad for quite a spell.

"Jessie?" His voice was deep and tantalizingly close to her ear. She turned and her gaze tangled with the blue of his eyes. Dark hair drooped toward his forehead and she started to reach out to brush it back, but reason reasserted itself.

"Ye-s?" She cleared her throat and tried again. "Yes?"

"Could I try some of Maybelle's blackberry jam?"

Jessie looked at the jar in her hand, the rather large portion of jam on her biscuit, and smiled guiltily. "I really like Maybelle's jam," she said lamely.

"I can tell." Kale took the jar and spooned jam onto his plate. "I'm not used to breakfasts like this. At home, I usually have granola or rice. I seldom cook."

Grandad Joe sat at the table and helped himself to eggs, bacon, and biscuits. "Don't you eat eggs, son? They're gettin' some bad press lately, but you can't tell me they don't stick to a man's ribs and tide him over to lunchtime."

"Sticking to the ribs is the problem with eggs," Kale said conversationally. "Do you know that one egg has more than two hundred and fifty milligrams of cholesterol? Multiply that by the number of eggs consumed daily in this country and it's no wonder Americans are unhealthy."

"You're getting into a touchy area, Kale." Jessie picked up her biscuit and bit into it. "Grandad Joe sells a lot of eggs."

"I'm working on ways to reduce the cholesterol," Kale said.

Jessie licked a drop of jam from the corner of her mouth . . . and swallowed hard when she saw that Kale was watching her. "That's the reason you want Jennifer back, isn't it?"

"Jennifer?" Kale looked confused for a moment. "Oh, you mean the chicken."

"Jessie was always one for giving the work animals names," Grandad said between bites of breakfast. "She and Gretchen treated them all like pets."

"I have to break that habit in some of my students. I tell them the laboratory is no place for misplaced affection." Kale shifted his leg and brushed Jessie's knee again. This time he didn't bother to move away and she had to.

"I don't see why," she said. "What harm can it do to feel some affection for the animals you work with?"

"It ruins objectivity for one thing," Kale said.

"That's nonsense." Jessie wondered when she'd started to sound like Gretchen, wondered why she felt so determined to argue with anything Kale might say. "What time do we leave for church?" she asked her grandad.

"At 9:00 a.m., just like always." Grandad scraped the last bit of egg onto his last bit of biscuit and put the whole thing in his mouth. He chewed, patted his lips, and swallowed before looking across the table. "You're welcome to attend service with us, Kale."

"Thank you, Joe, but I didn't bring a change of clothes with me."

"The Lord don't care what you're wearing. If jeans is all you've got with you, then jeans is what you should wear to church."

Kale nodded. "Well, if you're sure the Lord won't mind, I'll be ready."

Jessie gulped the last swallow of coffee. Why was Kale hanging around on Crow Mountain when he could just get his precious Number Forty-three chicken and head for home? For a man who was obsessed with research, he certainly seemed in no hurry to get on with it. "I'll clean up the kitchen," she offered.

"I'll help." Kale offered her a smile.

"I'll do it." Grandad Joe said decisively. "Now, run along."

Jessie glanced at Kale, who lifted his shoulder in a shrug. Grandad Joe began gathering the dishes. With a sigh, Jessie stood and headed for the bedroom.

Forty-five minutes later, Jessie walked out onto the porch. Kale leaned against the rail. He had on the same blue jeans and shirt as before, but when he turned toward her, she saw that he had put on a tie. A rather thin, bland sort of tie. A tie she might have expected her grandfather to wear.

"Joe loaned me a tie," Kale said. "I, uh, didn't bring one along."

Jessie nodded, knowing he hadn't brought anything along. It was just like him to start off on a wild chicken chase without a change of clothes or anything else. She sighed. "I have an extra toothbrush, if you'd like to have it."

"Do I have blackberries stuck between my teeth?"

Why did she find this man so interesting, Jessie wondered. "Not that I can see. But I figured if you forgot to pack a tie you probably forgot to pack a toothbrush as well."

"Do you always carry a spare?"

"Yes. I'm afraid I don't have any extra underwear, though. Not men's anyway."

Kale straightened and a slow, mesmerizing smile tipped the corners of his mouth. "That's a relief. I was beginning to worry about you, Jessie."

Ha! she thought. Fat chance of him ever worrying about her. "You're welcome to the toothbrush." She walked down the steps and looked up through the branches of the hickory tree.

Kale followed and stood behind her. "You're kind of tense this morning, aren't you? Did I snore and keep you awake?"

His question seemed somehow intimate and a shiver trickled down her back. "Don't be silly," she said. "I hardly knew you were there." She paused. "In the next room."

Kale's eyes swept over her, intensifying that odd little shiver into a thousand ripples of awareness. "You look very pretty all dressed up, Jessie. I'm proud to be going to church with you."

She didn't know what to say to that. It was hardly the kind of compliment to turn a girl's head. Hardly the sort of homage a woman fantasized about. "Here's Grandad," she said as the pickup lurched around the corner and stopped in front of the house.

"After you," Kale opened the door with a flourish and Jessie stepped up into the cab, uncomfortably aware of Kale's gaze on her legs; uncomfortably aware that he found her attractive in her Sunday clothes; uncomfortably aware that she found him attractive in his jeans, wrinkled shirt, and out-of-date tie.

"UP AND OVER." Jessie swung a leg across the rail and climbed down the other side of the fence.

Kale flipped up the latch, opened the gate and walked through. "Doesn't Joe get after you for climbing his fence?"

"No, but he'll be mad at you if you don't make sure the gate latches properly." Jessie brushed back a wayward lock of tawny hair as she led the way to the chicken house. "He hates for the bull to get out."

"I'll just bet he does." Kale fell into step beside her, the swing of his arm bringing his hand within inches of hers. "How many cattle does he keep?"

"I don't now. I never counted them."

Kale shot her a patient glance. "How about the chickens? Ever counted them?"

She shook her head. "Nope. To be honest, I hardly ever get near the chicken house. It makes me sneeze." Jessie lengthened her stride to cover the incline in front of the long, narrow building that housed Grandad Joe's laying hens. "Here we are," she said with a gesture to the door. "Your CTA #43 is somewhere inside, sir."

Kale frowned as he opened the door. "*Somewhere* is the operative word, isn't it, Miss Day?"

Jessie watched as he entered the building, heard him sneeze once, then again...and again...and again. He backed out of the chicken house and slammed the door. He blinked furiously and sneezed some more. "Good Lord, there must be two hundred hens in there." He turned away and sneezed. "How am I supposed to find my chicken in that bunch? Why did you turn it loose in there, anyway? Didn't it occur to you that it would be next to impossible to single out—ah-choo—one chicken?"

"Dust bother you?" she asked sympathetically.

"Dust, feathers, and a lot of other things on this farm." He moved to the wire-screen windows and looked at the chickens—from a distance. "Did you notice if the chicken you brought here had a band on its leg?"

"If there'd been a band I would have noticed. Jennifer looked just like every other leghorn chicken I've ever seen. I can't remember any distinguishing marks at all." Jessie paused, restraining a slow grin. "No scars on her beak or patch over her eye or anything like that."

He started to frown, but a sneeze interrupted. "Do you happen to have a tissue?" he asked. "I came away without one."

She pulled one from her hip pocket and solemnly offered it to him. "Well, what will you do now, Dr. Warner?"

"Put some distance between my nose and the chicken house. What are you going to do?"

Jessie dusted her hands on the seat of her jeans and followed him back toward the gate. "I guess I'll go with you." She felt badly all of a sudden that he hadn't immediately recognized his chicken and she was sorry he couldn't go into the henhouse without sneezing. But it wasn't her fault. Not really. She hadn't known Jennifer was his chicken. And she certainly hadn't known anyone was going to come looking for the chicken once she'd turned it loose in the chicken house. She hadn't even thought Gretchen would be so sentimental as to want a laying hen for a pet. Of course, Kale wasn't being sentimental. He was being—

"If you keep dawdling along, the bull will get out and we'll have to spend the rest of our afternoon chasing him."

She glanced up, saw Kale holding the gate for her and looked over her shoulder for Gringo, Grandad's registered Hereford bull. His old red-and-white head was nowhere around. "Are you trying to scare me?" she asked as she sashayed through the opening and waited for him to close the gate.

"Just trying to hurry you along. We have things to do and places to go."

"We do?" She looked up in surprise and lost any sympathy she'd felt for him when she saw the mysterious gleam of amusement in his eyes. "I think you've mistaken me for someone else. I'm on vacation, remember? I have nothing to do and no place to go."

"You won't help me find my chicken?"

Somehow, she knew she was being set up, but she walked right into it anyway. "Of course, I'll help you do that. But you just said you couldn't handle the dust and feathers and—"

"—and so I have to come up with another way to pick CTA #43 out of the flock."

"How long will that take?"

"Days. Weeks, maybe. It would take a couple of months or more to run tests on every one of Grandad's chickens and find #43 that way. How long is your vacation, anyway?"

"Two wee—now wait a minute. My vacation has nothing to do with this. I can't help you do any testing."

"True, but you can help me pick out a tie." He took her hand as they walked toward the house. His fingers folded around hers like the perfect fit of a made-to-order garment. Jessie didn't have time to protest and, though she wiggled her fingers a little, she didn't pull away. "Why do you...uh...need a tie?" she asked.

"In case I get invited to church again. Grandad Joe said I could stay as long as I wanted and I need more time to figure out how to separate #43 from the other hens. That means I need a few things in the clothing line." He squeezed her hand. "No offense. I like your grandfather, but his taste in ties could use some improvement."

Jessie couldn't seem to find her voice. Kale was staying. She'd thought he would leave, she'd hoped he would, and now... There was no explaining the ripple of excitement that suffused her. It would go away, of course. She was not happy about his intrusion into her vacation. Any moment now, he'd do something dumb and her good sense would reassert itself.

He swung her hand as they reached the porch steps and Jessie, guiltily, pulled it away from his grasp. "I thought you'd return to Fayetteville for a few days, get whatever paraphernalia you need to do this testing and get on with your research. Wouldn't that be easier than hanging around here waiting for an idea?"

He smiled as he pulled open the screen door. "It might be easier, but then, who would keep an eye on you?"

She glanced over her shoulder to make sure he was joking, but Grandad caught her attention from where he stood in the kitchen doorway. "It's about time you two came in for dinner. Wash up and we'll sit down to it."

With a slight shrug and an enigmatic smile, Kale headed for the bathroom. He wasn't serious about keeping an eye on her, Jessie thought. Was he? Surely he didn't still suspect her of consorting with the people who'd actually stolen his chicken. She had brought the chicken to the farm, true, but that was purely circumstantial evidence. It was a mistake, pure and simple. Just like his holding her hand a minute ago. He probably hadn't even realized what he was doing.

"Jess?" Grandad Joe prodded her toward the sink.

She rubbed her hand down the seam of her jeans. "Yes, Grandad. I'll wash up right now."

FOR A COUPLE OF DAYS, Jessie gave Kale the benefit of the doubt. Perhaps he truly was thinking about how to pick out Jennifer from the rest of the chickens. He didn't go near the henhouse and he seemed pretty laid-back for a man with a mission, but that was no guarantee he wasn't thinking.

She accompanied him to Russellville, where he purchased a change of clothes and a toothbrush . . . to replace the one she'd given him. He accompanied her on a walk around the farm. At night, he talked to her through the wall. He asked questions about Day Dreams and designing bed linens. He wanted to know about Gretchen and the other members of Jessie's family. Jessie answered the business-related questions with ease, but she was cautious about the others. For all she knew, Kale might be planning to sue her entire family over the loss of his research. Stranger things had happened . . . the strangest being that she was actually beginning to like him.

Kale Warner was the type of man who brought out protective instincts in a woman. Jessie found herself checking his appearance to make sure his shirttail was tucked in and that his fly was zipped and that his socks matched. So far, no adjustments had been necessary, but Jessie was somehow sure that that was a fluke. Two mornings of careful dressing did not mean this absentminded professor had become a fashion plate. And two mornings of chitchat over the breakfast table did not mean his thoughts weren't racing with formulae and theories.

Two nights of quiet conversation, though, had softened Jessie's attitude. Two nights of gentle sharing through the wall had increased the attraction. Kale was not the kind of man Jessie had in mind as a suitable partner. She wanted someone who would be responsible... and insanely in love with her. Was that too much to ask? Was it selfish not to want to be responsible for the details of another person's life? After all, she'd been taking care of her family for years. Wasn't it her turn?

"Your turn, Jess." Grandad Joe tapped the tabletop and Jessie brought her attention back to the chess game at hand. She deliberated another moment before moving her bishop. Then she allowed herself to peep at Kale, who stood in front of the kitchen sink staring out the window. With his fingers tucked in his hip pockets, his shoulder muscles bunched beneath his shirt with a kind of relaxed tension. The hair on the back of his head lay short and smooth and tantalizingly neat. Jessie rubbed her fingers together in her lap.

"Bad move, missy." Grandad shook his head. "Checkmate. That was too easy." He began clearing the board. "You want to play, Kale? Maybe if you was sittin' here at the table, Jessie could keep her mind on the game. She usually gives me a run for my money, but not tonight."

Kale turned around. "No, thanks. I believe I'll go outside for a while. It's such a beautiful night."

Grandad nodded. "I'm going to bed, so I'll see you at breakfast. Have you had any luck in finding your chicken?"

"No. I can't pick her out by looking and I don't have time to run tests on every one of your laying hens. I keep thinking some simple method of separating my chicken from yours will occur to me, but so far, I'm drawing a blank."

"You'll figure out something." Grandad stood and slid his callused thumbs under the straps of his overalls. He adjusted the strap at the shoulder and walked around the table to drop a kiss on Jessie's cheek. "Good night, Jess."

"Good night, Grandad." She watched him walk from the room before she stood too, and put the pieces of the chess set away. She knew when Kale left the room, although he didn't say anything. She listened for his footsteps and the squeak of the hinges on the screen door as it opened and then closed again. Her throat felt thick with an expectancy as inexplicable as it was real. This was her vacation. She wasn't supposed to be tense . . . or nervous. Impulsively she followed Kale outside.

He stood at the far end of the porch, looking up at the stars, his arms supporting his weight as he leaned against the rail. Jessie slipped up behind him and settled herself in the swing. He glanced over his shoulder, acknowledged her presence with a smile, and went back to his stargazing.

"Beautiful night," she said and wished immediately that she'd left the quiet unbroken.

"I was thinking about Pancho," Kale said. "Why would he come all the way from another country to attend college here and then risk losing his student visa by stealing? Doesn't he realize how self-defeating that is?"

Jessie sighed. Did Kale ever think about anything else? "I don't think Pancho stole anything. I think you're wrong about him."

Kale's gaze swung to her with scarcely disguised skepticism. "That's the reason you and me and CTA #43 are all here on the farm, I suppose? Because I'm wrong about good old Pancho."

"I can't explain how Pancho ended up with your chicken, but I just cannot believe he intentionally stole it."

"You're probably right. He stole it unintentionally, which makes all the difference in the world."

Jessie frowned as she shifted positions to sit sideways in the swing and hug her knees to her chest. "I don't want to argue with you, Kale. I'm sorry I didn't know Jennifer belonged in your lab and that I inconvenienced you by bringing her here. If I knew how to pick her out from the other

chickens, I'd do it this very minute and let you get back to
Fayetteville and your research.''

Kale turned around. "Would you really?" he asked. "Are
you that anxious for me to leave?''

His question caught her off guard. "Well, no. Yes. I
mean, I know you must be anxious to return to work. It
can't be much fun for you here, not knowing how to find
Jennifer and having only one change of clothes and all.''

"And I thought I was enjoying myself.''

What kind of game was this, Jessie wondered. He was
almost, *almost,* flirting with her. "I thought you were waiting for inspiration to strike and give you the means to recover your chicken.''

"Well, I am." He took a purposeful step toward the
swing. "Sort of." He braced a hand on the back of the
swing and placed his other hand on the chain, effectively
holding Jessie hostage. "Is it inconceivable, Jessica, that I
might also be waiting for you?''

"Waiting for me?" Her voice cracked. "Why?''

He leaned close to her. She began to drown in the suspicion that Kale was no longer thinking about his research. He
didn't answer, but he didn't make any moves, either. Not
toward her or away from her. There was an uncomfortable
flutter in her throat, a curious tightening in her stomach,
and a funny dryness in her mouth all of a sudden. Her eyes
lifted to meet his...and the expression she encountered there
unsettled her even further. Her gaze dropped to his mouth
and she swallowed hard. It had occurred to her once or twice
that Kale probably could be quite charming...if it suited
him to be. It had not occurred to her, until this moment,
that she might be susceptible to that charm. But as he slowly
leaned forward, his lips firm and slightly parted, his dark
azure eyes mirroring his determination, Jessie realized she
was in big trouble. When his mouth closed over hers, she
knew she'd underestimated him.

But who would have thought Dr. Warner, dedicated scientist and poultry researcher, would know how to kiss with such expertise?

Expertise wasn't even the right word. It was too technical to describe the soft, enticing movement of his lips against hers. It was too cold to explain the warmth swirling through her body. It was too impersonal, considering the response that rippled from the tips of her fingers all the way to the tips of her toes. She hadn't expected this. She hadn't expected anything like this.

When he drew back, she looked at him with new respect and renewed caution. Her breaths were shallow and quick and she thought it best not to say anything. But he was staring into her eyes with the same intensity with which he'd stared at the stars only moments before. Jessie swallowed. Was he going to kiss her again? Her lips parted, but by some miracle of mind over impulse, she managed to close them...and the open invitation. "I think I'll go inside. I...uh...haven't slept too well the past couple of nights."

He straightened slowly. "I hope that isn't my fault."

"No," she denied. "Of course not. It has nothing to do with you." She'd slept like a baby the past two nights, but she had a feeling that tonight might be different. Was her heartbeat ever going to quit skipping around? "I'll just go on in to bed and let you stay out here and...and think about your chicken."

He nodded as he stepped away from the swing. "I do have a lot of things to think about."

"I'm sure you do." Jessie hardly knew what she was saying and the idea that a kiss...a completely unsolicited kiss at that...could rattle her this way only heightened her confusion. "So I'll leave you to think, then." Aggravated by her betraying chatter, Jessie pushed to her feet and would have gotten clipped by the swing in the backs of her knees if Kale hadn't caught the chain.

"Good night, Jessie."

She turned to the house and safety. "Good night, Kale. I hope the solution to your problem comes to you."

Solution? Kale watched her walk away, watched the soft sway of her hips, watched the no-nonsense set of her shoulders, watched the determined lift of her chin. He didn't know what Jessie had thought about that kiss, but he sure as hell knew it hadn't solved a damn thing. It certainly hadn't accomplished what he'd intended.

He'd been trying for two days to find out what, exactly, Jessie had done with CTA #43. He'd been subtle, respectful, and careful with his questions. She'd been evasive and cautious in her answers. So he'd had the brilliant idea of trying a bit of charm, a little flirtation. So he'd kissed her.

And now look where he was.

Kale couldn't quite put his finger on where that was, but judging by the steady thud of his heartbeat and the uncomfortable heat in his veins, it was not where he'd thought he'd be. And in a few minutes, he'd be lying in a bed not a foot away from where she was lying in bed.

He put a stop to that line of thinking. There was a wall between those beds, he reminded himself. A thin wall, yes. But still a wall.

With a frown, he resumed his position at the end of the porch and lifted his pensive regard to the night sky. If Jessie didn't crack soon and tell him what she'd really done with his chicken, he'd have to do something extreme. He couldn't just shrug his shoulders and forget the importance of his research. His chicken was out there somewhere. Not in the henhouse. Jessie was too smart to have mixed a valuable bird with a flock of ordinary laying hens. But he didn't think she'd passed the chicken on to enemy hands, either. Not yet, anyway.

So, he'd play her game a little longer. When it came right down to it, what choice did he have?

None. At this point, Pancho was a dead end. Jessie was his only lead. But he had to be careful. Her eyes were such a pretty brown, her expressions endlessly appealing, and he couldn't come up with the right formula on how to handle her. The answer was there. She had it. He'd find it. Persistence would win out. If he didn't let himself get carried away by a simple kiss.

Well, maybe it wasn't simple.

He'd enjoyed kissing Jessie.

More than he would have thought possible.

More than he wanted to recall.

He wondered how many more times he could kiss her before scientific research became personal involvement. Or was it already too late?

Chapter Seven

Gretchen's phone call interrupted the evening chess game. Jessie had been trying to demonstrate just how little effect Kale really had on her and that she not only could keep her mind on the game, but that she could win as well. It was slow going. With Kale seated at the table, observing her every move, Jessie was barely holding her own. At least she was until the phone rang.

"Here, Jess," Grandad Joe said after a few minutes of chitchat. "Gretchen needs to talk to you."

Need being the operative word, Jessie thought as she rose from the table.

Kale shot her a questioning, alert-kind-of look. "Your sister?" he asked.

"You want Kale to finish out the game?" Grandad said as he resumed his position on his side of the chess board.

Jessie reached for the phone. "All right. I've got you on the run, Grandad. I guess Kale can pinch-hit until I get off the phone." Kale moved into her place and Jessie put the receiver to her ear. "Gretchen? It's Jessie. Where are you?"

The voice that traveled through the wires was alto-pitched and throaty-smooth, not at all the flighty, soprano notes that would have more closely matched Gretchen's personality. "Hi, Jess. I'm in Washington. The state. We're somewhere—" the sound faded for a moment and Jessie could hear Gretchen asking someone in the background what town they were in "—we're in Seattle."

"Seattle," Jessie repeated. "Is it cold?"

"Rainy. That's why I'm calling."

Jessie knew her sister hadn't called because it was raining in Seattle, but she figured the real reason would be just as obscure. "Do you have an umbrella?" she asked with a wry smile.

"No, but I have the sweater you sent." Again Gretchen's attention turned to someone outside the range of long-distance telephone service. "If they don't have salads, I'll eat somewhere else. How can you even think about eating a hamburger?" The disgust in Gretchen's voice carried clearly to Jessie's ear. "So, what am I supposed to do with it, Jess?"

"What?"

"The sweater. You sent it, didn't you?"

"Oh." Jessie pulled her attention away from the thick strand of dark hair that edged Kale's nape. "The United States Postal Service tracked you down one more time."

"We drove in from camp this afternoon," Gretchen explained. "So, tell me why you sent it."

Jessie let her gaze trace the back of Kale's neck once more as she wished her sister, just once, could keep track of a chain of events. "You told me to send it, Gretchen. I met Pancho, got the package and mailed it to you, just as you asked me to do."

Kale lifted his concentration from the chess board and Jessie saw the spark of interest in his expression.

"Didn't you like Pancho?" Gretchen asked. "He's so...Latin-American. If he were a little older..."

"You'd better go slow, there," Jessie cautioned. "He's crazy about you already, Gretchen."

Gretchen's sigh carried a thousand regrets. "The young ones always are. So, tell me about the sweater."

"Pancho sent it . . . to keep you warm."

"How thoughtful. I'll wear it under my parka. What about the computer disk in the pocket?"

A funny feeling coiled in Jessie's stomach. "Weren't those the ones you wanted?"

"I asked Pancho to get the three floppy disks from my desk, but there was one in the pocket of the sweater and I don't know where it came from."

Jessie couldn't keep her gaze from colliding with Kale's. He couldn't have heard Gretchen's words, but Jessie knew he was paying close attention to what she said. "I . . . didn't know about that. Does it have anything written on it?"

"No. It may be blank. I could use it, I suppose. Reformat and—"

"Don't do that."

Kale's expression changed and he no longer pretended to be interested in the chess game.

Jessie wondered what to do next. "What does it look like?"

There was a moment's pause, then a puzzled note in Gretchen's voice. "It's a blue, cardigan-type sweater. Didn't you pack it in the box, Jess? Don't you remember?"

"Not the sweater. The floppy disk."

"Are you serious? It looks like every other floppy disk in the world. Five-and-a-quarter size, double-sided, double-density. What else is there to say about a floppy disk?"

A lot, Jessie thought. A whole heck of a lot. "Gretchen? Do you believe Pancho would steal anything?"

"No! For heaven's sake, Jess. Where did you get an idea like that? Pancho's such a kid and he's completely dedicated to getting his degree and returning home to be—"

"—a rich farmer," Jessie inserted. "I know. But you see, something has been stolen and it, well it looks like he might have . . ."

"Not Pancho," Gretchen stated. "No. He wouldn't—"

"She has it, doesn't she?" Kale scooted back his chair, cutting through Gretchen's voice in Jessie's ear. "I knew it. Pancho sent her my research."

"—and besides, why would he send it to me?" Gretchen continued to speak and Jessie tried to hear what her sister was saying. "You're not thinking clearly, Jess. There's no way that Pancho—"

"Where is it?" Kale demanded.

"—besides that, I can't visualize—"

"Let me talk to her." Kale reached for the phone. Jessie glared and turned out of his reach.

"Gretchen—?"

"I mean, why would he do that? It's so ridiculous that—"

"Tell her that if anything happens to that floppy disk—"

"Stop!" Jessie yelled.

The ensuing, stunned silence lasted less than five seconds.

"What?" Gretchen said. "I thought you wanted to know about Pancho."

"Does she have my research disk?" Kale wanted to know.

Jessie answered with a heavy frown. "Would you sit down and shut up for a minute so I can find out?"

Kale took a step back. Gretchen raised her voice. "How can I sit down? I'm at a phone booth and I'm trying to tell you—"

"Gretchen," Jessie interrupted. "I wasn't talking to you. There's someone here with me and I can't hear you for all the questions he's asking."

"Grandad Joe?"

"No. Grandad Joe is here, of course, but there's someone else. Maybe you know him. Dr. Warner. Dr. Kale Warner, from the university at Fayetteville."

"Dr. Warner." Gretchen rolled the name. "He's a professor?"

"Yes. He teaches—" Jessie realized she didn't know what exactly Kale did teach. But now that he was quiet, she didn't want to ask and get him going again. "I don't know. He works with chickens. Does that ring a bell?"

"Chickens? At the experimental farm, you mean. But that's Pancho's job. He takes care of some of the test animals. He and I have had long talks about the humane treatment of laboratory animals. Ask Dr. Warner if he knows Pancho."

"He knows him," Jessie said flatly. "He thinks Pancho stole his research."

"What?" Gretchen was outraged. "That's ridiculous."

"Well, you do have the diskette and it was in the pocket of Pancho's sweater."

Kale was on his feet again. "I knew it. He sent her the information. Ask her who she's working for. Tell her she can turn over the research and I'll ask the court to go easy on her."

Jessie shot him another frown. "Gretchen had nothing to do with your—"

"Now wait just a minute." Grandad Joe pushed back his chair. "I don't understand this."

As if anyone could, Jessie thought. "Don't worry, Grandad, no one—" she stressed the words with a deliberate glare at Kale Warner "—is going to jail. This is just a misunderstanding."

"Jail!" Gretchen shouted. "What are you talking about, Jess? Who's going to jail? He can't send Pancho to jail."

"Jail?" Grandad looked concerned. "Who said anything about jail? I thought we were looking for a chicken."

"We are looking for a chicken," Kale explained. "And a missing computer disk. Your granddaughters each seem to have one part of my stolen research in their possession."

"Are you accusing my—"

"Jessie, what in Sam Hill is going on?" Gretchen's strident question tore Jessie's attention from the men.

"It's Dr. Warner's research." Jessie bunched the phone cord in her fist. "He lost his chicken and the computer disk somehow got in Pancho's pocket and now you have it and..." It was futile to attempt to explain this mess, Jessie decided. It was impossible to believe she was in the middle of it. "Look, Gretchen, just send the floppy disk back to me, okay? That'll take care of—"

"No!" Kale reached for the phone and this time Jessie wasn't quick enough. With a shrug, she let him have it...the receiver, that is. "Is this Jessie's sister? Dr. Warner, here. Don't...do not...send back the disk. I'll come and get it. Understand?"

Jessie settled into one of the chairs with a half smile. Gretchen might be a trifle absentminded, but she wouldn't put up for two minutes with Kale's patronizing tone. By the look of consternation creeping into his expression, Jessie figured Gretchen was giving him a piece of her mind at this very moment. A well-deserved piece, too, Jessie thought. How could she have been fooled by one little kiss into thinking this man had charm? For two cents...or even a penny...she'd give him a piece of her mind, too. Just as soon as Gretchen finished with him.

"No." Kale didn't sound cowed and Jessie looked up curiously. "You put it in a safe place until I get there to retrieve it," he continued. "Don't give it to anyone else. Please. This is very important."

"I thought he was after a stolen chicken." Grandad Joe shook his head as he deliberated a move of his castle. "Just goes to show you can't believe everything you hear."

Jessie narrowed her eyes in her grandfather's direction. "If you move that, I'm going to beat you," she said, still listening to the phone conversation, still wondering what was going on. Had Pancho stolen the disk? He'd sent the sweater and the . . .

"How will you recognize me?" Kale shrugged. "I'm six-foot, one inch, about a hundred and seventy-five pounds, dark hair, blue eyes." There was a pause and Jessie glanced over her shoulder to look at him. "Well, yes, there might be some other guy who has the same description, but— How am I supposed to know that?" His voice sharpened with impatience. "Look, I'll show you my driver's license when I get there. Does that satisfy you?"

Jessie bit back a smile. Gretchen was asking the right questions for once, she thought, and it was kind of nice to see Kale Warner on the defensive.

"All right, all right. I'll bring your sister along to vouch for me. Will that do it?"

Jessie straightened. Her smile disappeared. "No," she said. "Don't get me into this—"

"That's right. We'll get a car at the airport and drive out to the camp." Kale went right on making plans without her approval and Jessie couldn't believe his gall. "Tomorrow or the next day. Depends on when we can get a flight. We'll have to get off this mountain first and get to an airport with a connecting flight, so—"

Jessie was on her feet again, yanking the receiver from his hand. "Gretchen? This man is crazy. I'm on vacation and I'm not going to Seattle."

"He wants this floppy disk," Gretchen said.

"Well, give it to him." Jessie turned her back to the men. "You won't have any trouble recognizing him, Gretch. I'll tie a hangman's knot around his neck and you'll know who he is right off."

Gretchen's throaty laughter echoed over the wire. "You must be really taken with this guy, sis. Sure you don't want to fly out here with him? It seems dumb to go to all that trouble for a computer disk, but the trip would probably do you good.''

It would do her a world of good to kick the daylights out of Kale Warner, but she was too adult to do something so juvenile. "I'm spending my vacation on the farm with Grandad Joe. Period. End of discussion.''

"Okay by me." Gretchen's attention began to fade. Jessie could tell and it occurred to her, along with a sly smile, that Kale wouldn't have the faintest idea how to find Gretchen in Seattle or anywhere else.

"Well, I'll see you," Jessie decided to end the conversation and get off the phone before the same thought occurred to Kale. "When will you be home?''

"I don't know. The cleanup is slow, tedious work. Poor animals. Covered in crud. It's pathetic." Gretchen's voice grew distant. "What? Oh, all right. Jess? I've got to go. They've found a restaurant with a salad bar.''

"Goodbye—''

"Wait a minute." Kale took the phone away from Jessie. "Gretchen? Does Jessie know where to find you? No? Then you'd better give me directions.''

Jessie sighed and moved back to the table. So much for hoping Kale wouldn't remember to ask for the details on how and where to find her sister. It was probably better, anyway. Now Kale could just go recover the misplaced research, and let Jessie get on with her vacation.

"Checkmate." Grandad Joe cackled his delight. "Beat you, again, Jess. You should have let Kale finish the game for you. He might have won.''

"Yes," Kale spoke into the receiver. "Got it. We'll be there, don't worry. And don't give that disk to anyone but me. No matter what they tell you.''

Jessie watched as Kale hung up the phone and stared at the notes he'd made in the margin of the evening newspaper. "I hope I wrote this down right," he said. "Seattle airport. Then west toward Puget Sound on the expressway and..." He murmured and mumbled through the rest of the directions. Gretchen giving directions and Kale taking them down was akin to the blind leading the blind, Jessie thought with a sudden return of good humor.

"Do you know how to find her now?" Jessie put her tongue in her cheek before asking the question.

Kale looked up. "I think so. Some guy was telling her and she was passing the directions on to me, so we'll just have to hope he knew what he was talking about."

"Yes," Jessie said. "You'll just have to take your chances."

"It shouldn't be that difficult to find an oil spill." Kale tore off the penciled notes and tucked the piece of paper into his shirt pocket. "Between the two of us, we shouldn't have any trouble at all."

"I am not flying to Seattle to introduce you to my sister." Jessie pressed her palms flat on the table, tried to keep every ounce of irritation out of her tone. "I'm going to stay right here and play chess with Grandad Joe until I beat him."

Grandad made a shuffling noise as he put away the chess set. "You may as well go to Seattle, then, missy, 'cause you ain't going to beat me at chess."

Jessie frowned at his lack of support. "I might," she said. "I'm improving all the time."

"Play a game with Kale while you're in Seattle. Then come back and we'll give it another go." Grandad turned to Kale. "I take it you're leaving?"

"Yes. Tonight. I'll have to find out where and when I can get a flight. But chances are, Jessie and I will have to drive to Little Rock tonight in order to catch a plane out in the morning."

Grandad nodded and adjusted the straps of his overalls, as he always did just before retiring. "All right, then. What about the chicken?"

Kale glanced at Jessie and received only an annoyed frown in reply. "I'll come back for it," he told Grandad Joe. "In the meantime, just collect any eggs she lays as payment for her room and board."

"Aren't you taking quite a chance, Kale, leaving Jennifer here with me and Grandad?" Jessie asked. "We might have chicken and dumplings while you're gone."

"That was crude, Jessie." Kale gave her the full weight of a disapproving glare. "Besides, you won't be here to do anything with my chicken. You'll be with me."

"Don't worry." Grandad yawned. "I eat eggs, but I don't eat my laying hens."

Kale's stomach turned with the thought of CTA #43 ending somewhere in a frying pan. Wherever Jessie had put her, Kale hoped the chicken was safe from that, anyway. "Thanks for all of your hospitality, Grandad Joe. I do appreciate your help."

"Anytime." Grandad dropped his usual good-night kiss on Jess's cheek and shuffled off to his bedroom.

The silence in the kitchen was as thick as chicken stew. Kale groaned at the thought. He had chicken on the brain. And it looked as if he were going to have to do some heavy persuasion to get Jessie to come with him. But he'd be damned if he was going to leave her here. No telling what she'd do with CTA #43 in his absence. "So, Jessie" he said. "How soon can you be ready to leave?"

Obviously that was not the right approach. Jessie simply got up from the table and walked out of the room. Kale pursed his lips and followed her. "Don't you think it would be best to drive to Little Rock tonight? I'm sure we could get a flight out in the morning."

"Why don't you try calling the airline and finding out," she suggested none too sweetly. "And if I were you, I'd try Tulsa. It's a little closer than Little Rock."

"You're from Tulsa, aren't you? That's where your business is, isn't it? I remember you telling me that."

Jessie lifted a dainty shoulder in a careless shrug. Kale found the action appealing. He wondered what she'd do if he kissed her now? But no, that was probably not the wisest course in her present mood.

"Could we stay at your house tonight?" he asked. "If we leave now, we could be in Tulsa a little after midnight."

Jessie raised her delicately shaped eyebrows. "We? There is no 'we' in this conversation, Kale. *I* am not going with you to Tulsa or to Seattle. You are on your own."

The old clock on the mantel ticktocked loudly in the quiet living room. Kale pondered his options. Jessie picked up a magazine. "All right, if that's the way you feel." Kale turned toward the kitchen doorway and paused for effect. "But you really should go along, if only to be on hand in case your sister needs to be bailed out of jail."

Jessie didn't even glance up. "My sister is not going to jail. You didn't even report this supposed theft to the Fayetteville police."

"I didn't?" Kale inserted a note of surprise into his voice and managed to pull her attention from the magazine. "What makes you think I didn't inform the proper authorities?"

"I haven't seen any sign of Colonel Sander's S.W.A.T. team." She went back to flipping the magazine pages.

"You don't seem to be able to take this very seriously." Kale moved across the room to where she sat. He felt awkward standing there, towering above her while she pretended not to notice. So he knelt in front of her chair. "Look, Jessie. The research I've done may be unimportant to you, but there are people who would pay a lot of money to get their hands on it. You can sit here and tell me your sister had nothing to do with stealing it, and you can explain your part in it as coincidence, but from where I sit, you have my chicken and your sister has my computer disk. And one way or another, I intend to get both of them back.''

Her eyes met his fully, sending a little jolt of awareness through him. She was questioning him, looking for a hint of insincerity in his expression, in his words. He gave her back gaze for gaze . . . and wished he could have figured out a way to work in another kiss. Of course, any move like that on his part would ruin his efforts. He knew that and still his gaze wanted to drop to the soft outline of her lips, to see the moistness there, to dwell on the thought of how soft, how sweet that one kiss had been. He tightened his lips and his resolve. He had no business kissing Jessica Day. He had no business even thinking about kissing her.

''What do you want, Kale?'' she asked softly.

''I want you to help me recover the computer disk. Your sister said she wouldn't give it to me unless you were there. I guess she thinks I might be a kook or something.''

''I guess so.'' The slightest smile tipped the corners of Jessie's lips. ''It's hard to imagine how she could have reached that conclusion, isn't it?''

''Yes,'' he said truthfully. ''I need your help, Jessie. We can fly up there, get the disk, and fly right back. I'll even deliver you right here to Grandad's farm. I'll set up the chess game for you, give you a few tips on how to win. You'll hardly know you were gone. Just please come with me.'' She was wavering, he could tell, and he pressed his advantage. ''It's the least you can do after you've kept me cooling my heels here on the farm for the past couple of days.''

''I've kept you . . . ? Do you mean to tell me you've been waiting around here for me?''

''Well . . . yes, kind of.''

A new thought occurred to her. "Or were you waiting around for Gretchen to call?"

He drew back, puzzled. "Of course not. I didn't know until just now that Gretchen had the computer disk. How could I? You convinced me it wasn't in the package you mailed to her."

"I didn't know it was. I was as surprised to find out she had it as you were, probably more." Jessie narrowed her eyes in suspicion. "So, if you didn't suspect that Gretchen had the disk, why did you say you were cooling your heels waiting for me?"

Kale put a hand on the arm of the chair. "I figured that sooner or later you'd say something, let something slip about where and what you really did with CTA #43." It was not the right thing to say, he saw that immediately. If he'd been made of flammable material, he would at this moment, be a smoking cinder.

"Dr. Warner, you have a dangerous mind and the thought that your research might benefit mankind scares the living daylights out of me. If you paid the slightest attention to detail, you wouldn't have lost your chicken in the first place and in the second place, if you'd listened to anything I said, you'd have figured out I was telling you the truth."

"Truth?" Kale struggled with the implications. "I can't believe you'd think I would believe that you had put that chicken in the henhouse with all those other..." A huge knot of apprehension lodged in his chest. "You didn't put... You're not serious, Jessie. CTA #43 isn't really out there in Grandad's henhouse."

Jessie derived some satisfaction from his pained expression. "The chicken I brought with me from Fayetteville, the one Pancho 'rescued' and gave to Gretchen as a pet, is most certainly out there... with all the rest of the chickens."

His hand came up to his forehead in a gesture of gloom. "I really wish you hadn't told me that."

"Life is full of disappointments." Jessie stifled an impulse to reach out and pat his head. Why did this crazy man bring out these protective instincts in her? She usually had better sense. "So all the time I thought you were trying to figure out how to pick out Jennifer from the rest of the flock, you were actually waiting for me to make a mistake and admit I stole your chicken and handed her over to someone else, right?"

He met her gaze with some degree of apology. "Not entirely. I did spend some time thinking about what kind of tests I could do and how long it would take...if CTA #43 really had been in the henhouse. And I enjoyed being here. With you."

The caution light flashed in her mind and Jessie regarded him pensively. "So now what are you going to do?" she asked.

He settled back on his heels. "I'm going to Seattle. A disk in the hand is worth a chicken in the henhouse. At least for the time being." He paused, offered her a pleading look. "Will you come with me? It'll make things easier all the way around."

For who? Jessie wondered. Not for her. The easiest thing for her to do would be to stay where she was and let Kale Warner walk—or fly—out of her life. And good riddance. He wouldn't have Gretchen arrested. How could he? Gretchen would hand over the computer disk and everything would be hunky-dory. Unless something happened and Kale made Gretchen mad and she refused to give him the disk and then... Jessie didn't know what might happen in that scenario. She didn't want to know, either. That was Kale's problem. And Gretchen's problem if she decided to be contrary. In which case, it would then become Jessie's problem. With a sigh, Jessie resigned herself to making the trip. "How soon do you want to leave?"

His slow smile melted her resignation into something like anticipation. The warm pleasure in his azure eyes touched her heart . . . and Jessie straightened in the chair, trying to move her heart out of reach.

"Fifteen minutes," he said. "Is that too soon?"

She shook her head. "If we're only going to be gone one day, it won't take long to pack."

"I only have one change of clothes, anyway. And a toothbrush."

"And a tie. Don't forget the tie."

"No, I won't. Anything else?"

Jessie pushed up out of the chair, forcing Kale to move backward out of her way. "You might want to call the airlines and check on flights. It would help to know if we need to go to Little Rock or Tulsa."

"Tulsa," he said decisively. "It's about the same distance and that way we can stay at your place tonight. Unless of course, you object to me staying with you."

"Oh, no. Why would I object to that? You've been sleeping in the next bedroom for the past three nights."

He smiled charmingly. "I wasn't sure you'd noticed."

Jessie decided she'd made enough concessions for one night and she headed for her bedroom without answering him. There was no need to admit, not even to herself, that she was disappointed by the current turn of events. She'd believed for a day or so that Kale was enjoying her company. But now, regardless of his persuasive words, she knew he'd been waiting for her to admit that she had stolen his chicken.

She didn't now why it bothered her. After all, it had been obvious from the first time she laid eyes on Kale Warner that he had one thing, and one thing only, on his mind. She'd been silly to have entertained any thought that he might see her as anything except a means to that end.

And it wasn't as if she was interested in him. Good grief. He was the last man she needed to think of in terms of romance or relationships.

So she'd go with him to Seattle, keep the meeting between her absentminded sister and this absentminded professor civilized, and then she'd settle down for a restful, uneventful vacation.

And she'd beat Grandad Joe at chess, too. Just as soon as she'd ironed out a few details for Kale Warner and saved his research for the benefit of mankind.

Jessie smiled ruefully as she threw a few things into her bag. If there was any justice in this world, she would have a zero cholesterol count at her next checkup.

Chapter Eight

It was after midnight before they reached Jessie's apartment...way after midnight. And her blood pressure was high and rising.

Jessie wasn't quite sure when deep-seated annoyance nudged aside her slight irritation, but she knew who was at the root of both. It might have started as they were walking out the door at Grandad's house, when Kale had said he hoped his station wagon would make the trip okay. He'd been meaning to take it in for a tune-up, but hadn't as yet had the time. Deciding dependable transportation was high on her priority list, Jessie volunteered her car. After some deliberation, Kale agreed and promised that he'd help with the driving as well as pay for the gas.

It wasn't so much that she minded taking her car instead of his. But she was somewhat alarmed when he said it had been years since he'd driven a five-speed. He was sure he hadn't forgotten how. Which was probably true. Still, the sports car had been her reward and one indulgence when Day Dreams began to show an annual profit. She wasn't about to turn it over to a man who studied her every move when she shifted gears. She told him not to worry, she'd drive.

He'd scrunched his legs between the seat and the dash— Jessie considered the space adequate even for a six-footer—

and complained about foreign-made automobiles. He said if she didn't mind, he'd catch a few winks and then, he'd promptly fallen asleep. Jessie thought the least he could have done was snore and keep her awake.

But he didn't snore. He just slept. From Crow Mountain through Russellville and Fort Smith and Sallisaw and Muskogee, Kale slept like a man with the sweetest of dreams. Why wouldn't he have sweet dreams? Jessie thought. After all, she was taking care of life's details for him at the moment. She was driving him to Tulsa. She was taking him to her apartment. She was going to accompany him to Seattle and help him retrieve his computer diskette. And why was she doing it?

That was the Sixty-Four-Thousand-Dollar Question.

And Jessie couldn't even come up with a twenty-five cent answer.

"Are we in Tulsa, yet?" Kale said when he roused just outside the city limits. He yawned, stretched a little in the confines of the car, and gave her an appealing smile that swept right past her annoyance and stirred a warm response inside her. A response she tamped down by sheer willpower.

"Why didn't you wake me?" he asked. "I could have talked to you or sung to you or done something to keep you from getting sleepy."

"I managed to stay awake on my own, thank you."

She felt the weight of his questioning gaze in the still interior and kept her chin high.

"You're too independent for your own good, Jessica Day," he said after a minute. "And stubborn as well. Has anyone ever told you that?"

"No," she said stubbornly. "And you're pretty critical for a man who's dependent on my largess for a place to sleep tonight."

"Hey, I can sleep anywhere."

"That's obvious."

A puzzled expression took the place of his earlier smile. "I offered to drive, Jessie. You're the one who insisted on taking your car and you're the one who said you preferred to drive. I don't know why you're suddenly so upset with me."

He wouldn't, she thought. "Did it occur to you that I might be upset at the changes you've made in my plans? Did it occur to you that I don't care what happens to your research? Did it occur to you that I might not want to be here?"

He considered that as he shifted position in the bucket seat and Jessie felt a twinge of guilt for dumping all her annoyance in his lap. But, damn it all, it was his fault.

"You could have said no."

She could hardly believe he'd said that. "Arguing with you is just like arguing with my sister."

"Watch out there, Ms. Day. I think you may be getting altogether too comfortable with me, comparing me with your family and all. The next thing you know you'll be asking me home for Thanksgiving dinner."

Jessie decided not to dignify that with a denial. It would serve him right if she did ask him to share the chaos of a holiday in the Day household. Of course, being like the other members of her family, he probably wouldn't notice chaos if it hit him in the nose. And besides, by Thanksgiving, Kale Warner would be buried in his research. These few days were an interlude for him, forced upon him by circumstance and his own negligence. As soon as he'd recovered the computer disk and the chicken, he wouldn't even remember Jessie's name...or whether or not she'd invited him for Thanksgiving Dinner.

That thought only increased her irritation, but she put up what she thought was a good front until they reached her apartment. Kale waited politely until she'd unlocked the door and invited him inside before he carried in their respective bags and placed them on the floor. He whistled softly as he looked around. "Pretty nice. Doesn't look ransacked at all."

Jessie smiled despite her mood. "Unlike my sister, I enjoy a certain amount of order in my life...and my apartment."

"Hmmm." Kale wandered further into the living room and stopped beside the chintz sofa. He ran his hand over a striped piece of velvet fabric before picking it up and examining it more closely. "Do you live with someone?"

"No." She frowned at the robe he held in his hands. "Oh, Anthony must have left it. He's always leaving something over here."

Kale's fingers tightened on the robe. He had caught the scent of a man's cologne lingering on the fabric. "Oh, well, I don't feel so badly about forgetting my toothbrush then. Who the hell is Anthony?"

Jessie glanced up from the stack of mail she was looking through. Her brown eyes met his in surprise. "He lives in the apartment next door. Don't you like his robe? I admit it's a bit pretentious, but then he can afford it."

"No one can afford to have taste like that." Kale dropped the robe and felt some satisfaction when it slipped from the back of the sofa and crumpled to the floor. "What does he do for a living?"

"Litigation. He's an attorney."

"Is he a nice guy? Do you...like him?"

"Yes." She straightened the stack of mail. "What is this, Kale? Do you think Anthony might have some of your stolen research, too? Is everyone a suspect? Maybe we should take him with us to Seattle, just in case."

"I don't believe that will be necessary. Unless you feel you need his protection."

"Protection from what? Chickens and their irate owners? I don't think Anthony would be much help in that regard."

Kale met her saucy smile with a frown. He didn't know what it was about the robe and the next-door neighbor that irritated him. He wasn't sure he wanted to know. "Where do you want me to sleep?"

Her gaze met his for just a fraction of a moment, and he knew she was aware...as he was aware...that they could sleep together...if they chose to, which of course, they wouldn't. He wouldn't. At least, he didn't think he would. Unless she asked. And then...

"The guest bedroom is the second door on the right," Jessie said firmly, decisively, as if there never had been a question in her mind about where he might or might not sleep. "The bathroom is across the hall. Towels in the cabinet under the sink. Is there anything else you need?"

He opened his mouth to apologize for whatever he'd done or said that had made her angry. Ever since they'd left Arkansas, she'd acted as if he were a virus or something. He'd done his best to persuade her to come with him, true. But he hadn't kidnapped her. And damn it all, she was to blame for taking CTA #43 in the first place. "No," he said tersely. "I think I'll go to bed."

He hadn't taken two steps before there was a knock at the door and then the sound of a key turning in the lock. "Jessie?" a man's deep voice called. "Are you home?"

"Anthony?" Jessie turned toward the door and the man standing in the doorway. "Hi. I'm sorry, did we wake you?"

"We?" Anthony came into the room and closed the door behind himself. He sought out Kale, assessing the situation. "I didn't expect you back," he said to Jessie, while he kept an eye on Kale. "Is something wrong?"

"A change of plans," she said. "Anthony, I'd like you to meet Dr. Kale Warner. Kale, this is Anthony Adams."

Anthony moved forward, hand outstretched, mouth curved in a ready smile. Kale watched him and wondered why he had a sudden urge to deck the guy...smile and all. The robe wasn't really all that bad. Forcing the corners of his mouth into a suitable response, Kale offered his hand.

"M.D.?" Anthony asked. "Or D.O.?"

"D.O.A." Kale said without a blink. "It's after midnight, you know."

Anthony looked confused, but ready to laugh at the joke...as soon as he figured out what it was. He was about Kale's size, had thinning sandy-brown hair, and expressive brown eyes. It was probably the eyes that could sway a jury, Kale thought. On the other hand, it might be the silly look on his face.

"We were just about to go to bed." Jessie stepped forward with an explanation. "We drove all the way from Grandad's."

"Actually Jessie drove." Kale watched the shifting of Anthony's gaze, enjoyed the consternation in those expressive eyes.

"I thought I heard someone in your apartment," Anthony said. "That's why I came over. To check on things."

"You're a good friend, Anthony." Jessie fiddled with the top button of her blouse and Kale wondered if the nervous action had any significance. "I see you've watered the plants and collected the mail for me. I really do appreciate it."

Anthony's smile became whole again, self-confident and winning. "You know there's nothing I wouldn't do for you, Jessica. Nothing."

She nodded. "Well, I'm leaving again in the morning. Do you think you could—"

"Anything."

Kale decided he was too tired for this saccharine exchange. "She's a devious woman, Anthony." He said in a man-to-man tone. "Watch out or she'll ask you to wash her car."

"Jessica doesn't ask me to do near enough for her, Dr. Warner. I keep offering, hoping that someday she'll let me take care of her."

Jessie yawned. She couldn't help it. Anthony was nice. Really nice. And about as exciting as a mattress pad. "I do appreciate your coming over to check on me, Anthony." She took a purposeful step toward the door. "But Kale's right, we're both just about dead on arrival. And we do have a plane to catch in the morning."

Curiosity was eating away at Anthony, but Jessie didn't feel up to giving explanations now. She took Anthony's arm and escorted him to the door.

"Where are you going?" he asked.

"Seattle. I'll tell you all about it as soon as I get back from my vacation, okay?"

He leaned forward to kiss her . . . briefly, but warmly on the mouth. "All right, sweetheart. I can wait. If you need me, just call. Understand? Just call."

Jessie smiled her thanks, knowing he was absolutely sincere, knowing she wouldn't call him no matter what. Anthony was exactly the kind of man she'd always told herself she wanted. He loved to do things for her. Taking care of her gave him pleasure. But he didn't strike any sparks. Not so much as a flicker. With a sigh, she closed the door and turned to face Kale. Now, what was wrong with him, she wondered?

"That was Anthony," she said, because it seemed like the best thing to say.

"He forgot his robe," Kale pointed out.

"He can get it later."

"Undoubtedly since he has a key to your apartment."

"He's taking care of things while I'm away."

"So he said."

Jessie frowned and fought back a second yawn. She was too tired for this. Anthony had loaned the robe to her one night when the electricity had been off all day and her apartment was freezing. He'd told her it would keep her warm and he'd get it later. Later hadn't arrived as yet, but Jessie was damned if she was going to explain all of that to Kale at this time of night. "I'm going to bed," she announced. "Feel free to borrow Anthony's robe, if you want. He won't mind."

"I have better taste." Kale said to her retreating form. "If I'd known how much you liked robes, I'd have brought my own."

Jessie stopped, looked back over her shoulder. "What are you talking about?"

"Anthony, the lawyer, your neighbor."

"What about him?"

"How can you like someone like that? He was almost begging to be allowed to wash your car."

"Is there something wrong with that? Frankly I find him a refreshing change from the total self-conceit of most of the men I meet. You might take notes on how to treat women."

"I thought he acted like an ass."

Jessie raised her eyebrows. "If anyone has behaved like an 'ass,' Dr. Warner, it is you. Now, good night."

Kale watched her go, watched her bedroom door close between them and he pursed his lips in perplexity. What had gotten into him? He *had* behaved like an ass...and he didn't understand why. Unless . . . no, that was just too ridiculous. How could he be jealous of Anthony's relationship with Jessie? Just because the man had left a robe in her apartment was no reason to assume . . .

And even if the assumption was correct, why should it make any difference to him?

The clear memory of Jessie's voice speaking softly on the other side of the wall in Grandad's house came to mind.

He'd liked the conversations they'd had. He'd liked the husky vibrations of her voice, the gentle thread of laughter, the soothing tones of her reminiscences. He wanted that camaraderie back. He wanted Jessie to enjoy this trip to the West Coast. He was glad she was coming along.

The thought drew him up short and he analyzed it as he brushed his teeth and prepared for bed. How long had it been since he'd been glad for someone's company, actually wanted a particular woman to be with him? Longer than he could recall. It wasn't that he didn't have contact with other people, even other women. He did. But Jessie was different.

Somehow.

With that ambiguous answer, Kale decided to retire for the night. So what if there was another man's robe in her living room? So what if the man next door had a key to her apartment? So what if...? Kale tossed and turned for the next thirty minutes. It had been a mistake to nap in the car but, well, Jessie hadn't seemed in the mood to talk and she hadn't seemed at all happy to be with him.

Close on the heels of that thought, his feet hit the floor and he headed for the kitchen and something to eat. Jessie hadn't offered, but he didn't think she'd mind if he had a snack of some kind. Halfway across the living room, he realized he was only wearing his underwear and, of necessity, grabbed Anthony's robe and slipped into it. It fit a little loosely across the shoulders and that bothered him. The velvet fabric and lambs wool lining was a bit... lascivious for his taste, but then it was the only piece of clothing handy. And he was only going for a snack.

Halfway through a glass of juice and a packaged brownie, he began to wonder if he owed Jessie an apology. He had acted like a jerk, dragging her along on this trip. If he were one hundred percent positive that she wasn't a go-between for the thieves and whoever had commissioned the theft, maybe he could have let her out of his sight.

Maybe not.

Still, the question was, did he owe her an apology? No, he decided. He'd done nothing except protect his interests. On the other hand, she was angry. No doubt about that. So perhaps a simple, ''I'm sorry'' would restore her good humor. It might, also, soothe his troublesome conscience and let him get to sleep. Tomorrow was going to be a long day.

Decision made, Kale headed down the hall to Jessie's room. He hesitated before tapping lightly on the door. When he heard no reply, he turned the knob and quietly pushed at the door. The room was dark and it took a moment for his eyes to adjust. Jessie was curled beneath the covers, sound asleep. Kale started to close the door again, to leave her to a well-deserved rest, but he couldn't resist standing for another minute, watching her, wondering if she was dreaming and what she might be dreaming about and if he, by any chance, figured into those dreams.

He wasn't sure what caused him to approach the bed. Perhaps it was the idea that she wouldn't know he was there. Perhaps it was the realization that he had no right to be seeing her like this. Whatever the reason, he was drawn closer. Until he could see the soft shadows of sleep on her face, the tousled repose of her hair on the pillow, the slow rise and fall of her shoulder as she breathed in and out...in...out. He was mesmerized by the sight and, unbidden, he reached out to touch a strand of gold-dust hair. He caught his hand back, pushed it deep into the pocket of Anthony's robe—and wondered if Anthony's robe had ever been in Jessie's bedroom before.

The feeling that spun through him was complicated, composed of one part jealousy and several parts envy. He would have liked *his* robe to have had the honor of being discarded in Jessie's bedroom. But, of course, he hadn't brought his robe. And even if he had...

Jessie moved. Her arm stretched over the top of the covers, pulling down the sheet to expose the curve of her shoulder and a creamy V of skin. He stared, enchanted by the little hollow in her throat and the beginning of a shadowy cleft between her breasts. Her nightshirt and the covers blocked further investigation, but he could imagine.

Oh, yes, he could imagine.

A sigh echoed in the stillness and Kale's gaze moved to her face. Had she sighed? Or had it been he? Her eyelids wrinkled, her lashes fluttered, and then suddenly, she was looking back at him. Sleepily, at first, her eyes closing, then opening again.

Kale was startled. He hadn't expected her to awaken and thought he'd better back gracefully to the door and leave her bedroom. It was one thing to watch her when she was asleep, quite another to be caught at it. She might think he was a Peeping Tom or something. How could he explain? Apologize, he recalled. He'd come in to apologize.

"I'm sorry," he said.

The drowsy look began to fade from her eyes. "What for?"

"For whatever I did to make you mad. For behaving like an ass this evening."

Jessie nodded and then, as if cognizant, all of a sudden, of where she was and where he was, her hand groped for the covers and brought them up over her shoulder to her chin. "You could have told me that in the morning."

"I couldn't sleep," he started to explain. "I thought maybe you were still awake so I came in to tell you I...I don't know what I intended to tell you."

"Whatever it is, let's consider it said and you can go on to bed. Your bed."

She didn't think he'd come in here to—? "Look, Jessie, I came in here to apologize. I shouldn't have insisted that you come with me and . . . if you don't want to go to Seattle . . . I'll understand."

Understand? Jessie didn't think she would ever understand Kale Warner. Was this an apology because he really had acted like a jerk? Or was this an apology intended to manipulate her feelings and get his way . . . one more time? And what was he doing in her bedroom? At—she squinted at the clock—2:21 a.m. "I accept your apology," she said. "Now, good night."

He nodded. "So are you coming with me?"

"I'll tell you in the morning."

"Oh." He took a couple of steps back. "I hope you will. I'd like for you to. I'd enjoy having your company."

That had been a little hard for him to admit. Jessie could see that and a sudden warm affection curled through her body. Despite every reason not to, she liked Kale. "You're wearing Anthony's robe," she said, thinking it looked even worse on Kale than it did on her. "Were you desperate?"

He glanced down. "Sort of. I figured it might upset you if I walked around in my underwear and since I didn't bring my robe, I—"

"I get the picture." Jessie was grateful for the shadowy darkness in her room. The setting was too intimate, the conversation too personal. She never talked to men about their underwear. It was just one of those things she didn't want to know. And the fact that Kale was so matter-of-fact about it . . .

"I guess I should let you get some sleep."

"I guess you should." It seemed a silly thing to say, a dumb way to end a conversation that had had little substance and yet seemed somehow important. Jessie didn't know how Kale was able to arouse this tender feeling in her. She would have been embarrassed and annoyed, probably even angry, if Anthony had come into her bedroom in the middle of the night with no more explanation than that he'd wanted to apologize. But she believed Kale. It was, after all, just like him to do something like this with so little fore-thought. She was getting used to it. "Good night, Kale," she said. "See you in the morning."

"Good night." In several careful backward steps, he reached the doorway. The light from the hall pooled into her room and she thought she saw him smile. "You know, Jessie, I think I was lonely. I missed having you on the other side of the wall. The mattress on the bed in your guest bedroom is firmer than at Grandad's, but the conversation leaves something to be desired."

A silky pleasure wrapped around her. "Do you want me to move my bed over against the wall?"

"No. I'll just use my imagination."

With that, he was gone and Jessie lay back against her pillow...the soft, polyester-filled pillow. *Imagination,* she thought. It must be her imagination. For a minute there...a fraction of eternity...she had imagined asking Kale to climb into bed with her. She'd imagined that he would kiss her and hold her in his arms and—

Jessie turned over and pounded the pillow into a neutral lump. There were worse things than imagination, she sup-posed. But at the moment, she was grateful that the walls of her bedroom were thick and decently soundproofed and that Kale Warner was safely on the other side of them.

Chapter Nine

"We made it." Kale's voice was rich with satisfaction as the plane climbed into the skies over Tulsa. "In no time at all we'll be landing in Seattle."

Jessie cast him a skeptical glance. Making the plane had been no small feat. She'd slept late and he hadn't wanted to wake her until it was almost time to leave for the airport. It had been a thoughtful gesture on his part, she admitted. Unfortunately she'd have preferred to have had a little more time to get ready and a bit less of a rush. But, as he said, they'd made it.

"Do you fly much in your work?" He pushed his carry-on bag more securely under the seat in front of him.

"Yes, I have to do some traveling for Day Dreams to meet with the distributors. It's still a small enough business that I can handle most of that myself. Someday, maybe I'll just travel for the pleasure of it."

"I'd enjoy that myself. The only travel I get to do is the drive between my house, the university, and the experimental farm."

She could believe that, no problem. "Well, look at you now, Kale. You're a long way from Fayetteville and your normal routine."

"You're right. I should make the most of this." He took her hand in a move slick enough to impress Casanova. And he made no move to let go, either. "As soon as I have that research in my hands again, you and I will celebrate. How does that sound?"

Like a bribe, she thought. "Great," she said, knowing that the chances he would remember making the offer, once he had possession of the research again, were probably a hundred to one. Maybe a thousand to one. "What kind of research were you doing with Jennifer? You never have told me, precisely."

"I thought you knew." His deep blue eyes questioned her. "It seemed logical that you wouldn't have helped to steal the—" He stopped at the warning lift of her eyebrows. "I mean, when I thought you were the go-between for Pancho and whoever is behind the theft. But I suppose it doesn't make much difference now if I tell you. It stands to reason that whoever wants the research knows almost as much about it as I do or they wouldn't have gone to the trouble to steal it, right?"

"Do you always make everything so complicated?"

He smiled. "It's one of the hazards of having a scientific mind. Does that bother you?"

"I'm used to it. Complications are a hazard of being born into my family."

"Like having a sister who runs off to save the whales?"

"And a brother who writes comic books and having a mother who lives in a world of science fiction and having a father who knows the ancient languages of Asia, but can't communicate in regular English. It's enough to make me a bit gun-shy about complications."

"I see." Kale smiled at the young flight attendant and requested a cup of coffee. "I think I'd probably like your family, Jessie. They sound interesting."

"Wait until you meet them."

"I'm looking forward to it . . . starting with Jennifer."

"You mean Gretchen. Gretchen is my sister. Jennifer is your chicken."

"Right. That's what I said, wasn't it? I'm looking forward to meeting Gretchen today or tomorrow." He ran a thumb over the back of Jessie's hand, sending a heated pulse up her arm and straight to her heart. "She's not going to corner me about the use of animals in laboratory testing, is she?"

Jessie laughed softly. "She might. With Gretchen, with any member of my family, you just never know."

"I certainly don't know where I am with you, Jessie."

Her stomach jumped and her heart stopped for a second. "You're right where you want to be, Kale. On a plane bound for Seattle and your research."

"With you," he said as if that were the only part that mattered. Kale was, she discovered, full of charm when it suited him.

"I thought you were going to tell me about Jennifer and your research." Jessie leaned back and let her gaze turn to the window and the powder-puff clouds below.

"Are you really interested?" His tone became suddenly serious.

Her gaze swung back to him. "Of course. I asked, didn't I?"

"Yes, but then, you're not without complications yourself, Jessie."

She didn't reply and he began to tell her about his study of chickens, how he hoped to find a genetic trait that would result in lower-cholesterol eggs, and how he'd discovered the mystery of CTA #43. He explained how a dentist had brought a young hen to the lab, saying it had been an Easter chick given to his daughter. Since the dentist had no place to keep a chicken, he'd decided to give it to the experimental farm. Kale said it wasn't the usual way they acquired animals, but since he was testing at random anyway, and he suspected that the dentist might find some less acceptable way of getting rid of it, he accepted the chicken and promptly labeled it CTA #43. After several tests, he'd discovered that CTA #43 laid a much lower-cholesterol egg than the other test birds. He was now in the process of trying to figure out why and if the trait would be passed to her chicks.

Jessie was captivated. It wasn't just that what he told her was fascinating, but it was the way he talked about it. His eyes became a deeper blue...if that were possible...his expression was animated and appealing, his gestures became broad and encompassing.

Jessie loved watching him. Something inside her responded to Kale on a purely physical level. Something about him made her happy. And somewhere over the Rocky Mountains, she stopped fighting all the very real, very valid reasons for not getting involved with Kale Warner. It would turn out to be a mistake, she was sure. But for the next couple of days, she decided she might as well enjoy being with him.

At least he hadn't confused her with the chicken. So far he hadn't called her Jennifer. And he hadn't, as yet, referred to her by number. She decided to be thankful for small favors and not expect too much. After all, in twenty-four hours or so, she'd be back in her world and he'd be immersed again in his.

"DID THAT SIGN say Dusken Beach?"

Jessie tried to see the Interstate sign, but wasn't quick enough. "I don't know. I missed it."

Kale frowned and signaled to move into the right-hand lane. "We ought to be close by now...unless we misread those directions."

"What do you mean, 'we'?" Jessie glanced once again at the scrap of newsprint in her hand and the scribbled directions in the margin. "You're the one who copied down the directions."

"And a fine job I did, too, considering how far we've come in just a couple of hours."

"You did get us out of Seattle," Jessie admitted with some grudging admiration. She would not have done nearly so well in a rental car in a strange city. "Dusken Beach has to be somewhere nearby. Maybe we should stop and ask."

"As soon as I can work my way to an exit, I'll do that. But I'm almost positive that sign said Dusken Beach. I just wasn't in the right-turn lane."

"I hope Gretchen is keeping a lookout for us at the camp. Otherwise, we may never find her." Jessie had visions of other times, other places when she'd been supposed to meet her sister. It was a scary thought. "She's easily distracted."

"Don't worry. I'm sure we won't have any trouble." Kale glanced meaningfully at Jessie. "Unless I get cornered about using animals in my research."

"You're worried about that, aren't you?"

"Walking into a group of animal rights' activists strikes a note of fear into my heart, yes."

"But you don't mistreat the animals in your lab. I mean, you don't use them to test cosmetics or anything like that. Do you?"

"No, of course not. Nothing like that." He sounded offended that she'd even asked. "The chickens I use in my research are fed better than many humans and all they have to do in exchange is lay eggs and have blood samples taken every so often. It's a cushy job...for a chicken...and very few of them 'cackle' about it. But there are some people who cannot accept any compromise. No animals in the laboratory, period." He turned on the blinker, indicating another lane change. "I hope your sister and her friends are a bit more open-minded than that."

"I can't recall Gretchen being adamant about it. That doesn't mean she isn't, you understand, but I can't believe she would be upset with you for studying chickens and chicken eggs."

"Thank you, Jessie. It's good to know that if I'm to be tarred and feathered, you'll stick with me in there."

"You can rest easy, Kale. If anything happens to you, I'll make sure none of Jennifer's feathers are sacrificed to the cause."

"That's a load off my mind. Now will you look at those directions again? Does it say west from the exit for Dusken Beach or should we turn east?"

Jessie spent the next several minutes interpreting the hastily scribbled notes and trying to read roadside signs. After two service-station stops for directions, they arrived at the end of the road and a camp for the volunteers who helped with the cleanup operations. It wasn't difficult to find someone who knew Gretchen, but finding anyone who knew where she might be was a different story. There were differing opinions, but finally there was a consensus that Gretchen had left with a group that morning for a town on the Oregon coast. There had been a report of a chemical spill and possible environmental danger to the sea lions. No one knew when the group would be back or if they'd be back at all.

"I knew it," Kale said as he got into the rental car. "I knew something like this would happen. Your sister isn't going to get away with this."

"Away with what?" Jessie snapped her seat belt and looked out the car window to the choppy and beautiful waters of Puget Sound. "I warned you that the members of my family are not always dependable. You should have listened to me and had her mail the diskette. Then you would already have it in your hot little hands."

"I doubt that. She'd have mailed it to the wrong address and it would have wound up with the people who stole it in the first place."

"If you're accusing Gretchen of—"

"I'm not accusing her of anything. I just want to get my research back." He pulled on his seat belt and looked out at the water. "Pretty place, isn't it? Now, how long do you think it will take us to reach Oregon and your sister?"

"More than twenty-four hours," Jessie pointed out.

"You're right. But what difference does it make? You're on vacation, aren't you? You're on this trip for the fun of it, aren't you?"

She was on shaky ground. "But, Kale, the chances of finding Gretchen are not good. There's no way of knowing when we'll catch up to her and even if she'll still be there when we do. She may have mailed the diskette or thrown it out with the bath water. This is probably another wild-goose chase."

"I beg your pardon. Jennifer would not like to be lumped into a class of common geese. Get your terminology straight, Jessica. We are on a tame chicken hunt and Jennifer and I would appreciate it if you would remember that."

"Goose or chicken, Kale, you're ignoring my point, which is, you're probably not going to find Gretchen or your research disk if you search from here to Mexico. We may as well go back to Tulsa."

"We know the name of the town where she's gone. We know it's right on the Oregon coast. It's an easy matter to change our airline tickets and secure this fine rental car for a few more days. I can be away from the university for another week before anyone screams and so I intend to drive down old Highway 101 to see what I can see and find who I can find. Now you can fly home if you want, but you're missing the opportunity of a lifetime. The Washington/Oregon coast is one of the most beautiful areas you'll ever see."

She was tempted. She'd never seen much of the West Coast and, he was right, this was a good opportunity. After all, she was already here. And she was on vacation. And she might find inspiration for new linen designs on the ocean drive.

She might also find herself in love with the wrong man. The time already spent in his company had shown her she was vulnerable to Kale's charm, even though he was not her type, not the kind of man she was looking for. On the other hand, maybe a few more days with him would solve the problem and convince her of how very right she was. Maybe when it was over and he returned to his laboratory, she could return to her remaining days of vacation, glad for the interlude and heart-whole. It was a risk, she realized, but she felt a little reckless. What were vacations for?

"All right, Meriweather Lewis," she said. "Lead on."

He grinned and put the car into gear. "First, we need a map and from there—who knows what we may discover."

"I hope we don't discover the average rainfall in the area. I didn't think we'd be here long enough to fool with bringing an umbrella."

"Don't worry, Jess. I'll make sure you stay dry and warm."

He meant it, she thought. He really meant it. Not that she believed him. No, she'd better plan on buying an umbrella at their first stop. But it was nice to know he had good intentions and that he wanted her to be comfortable. "Then let's get on the road," she said with a smile. "Look out, Gretchen, here we come."

"Do you suppose she still has the diskette with her?" Kale asked as he waited a moment before turning the car onto the highway. "She wouldn't really have mailed it, would she? Not after I specifically told her to keep it?"

So much for general conversation, Jessie thought. They were not even five minutes into the trip and Kale was back to thinking about his research again. She sighed and settled into the car seat. "As I've said, with my sister, you never know."

"MAY I BORROW your umbrella?" Kale gave her the wry shrug and easy smile she was becoming accustomed to, maybe even a little fond of.

Jessie reached down to the floorboard and silently handed over her umbrella, the one she'd purchased in a town named Elma. It had been the only umbrella for sale in the shop and it had enormous blue flowers painted all over its orangy-red surface. Kale had called it 'Amoebas by Dali,' but Jessie had ignored his comments and told him she, at least, would stay dry.

They'd hit rain about twenty miles on the other side of Seattle and it hadn't let up yet. The windshield wipers beat a steady rhythm, pausing just long enough between swipes to allow the raindrops to streak and run in jagged patterns before wiping the glass clean and beginning again. With darkness the dance became one of liquid and light, interspersed with the swish of the diligent blades. Headlights of approaching cars splashed the drops of rain with gold and moved away in the ongoing shower. Highway 101 might be the most scenic route along the Pacific, but so far Jessie could see little except a dark, rainy highway and a rain-splashed windshield. Wasn't it just like Kale to tell her how gorgeous the view would be and then drive at night?

"This won't take long." Kale positioned the umbrella just before he reached for the handle of the car door. "This motel looks all right to you, doesn't it?"

Jessie glanced at the warm, well-lighted interior of the Coastal Inn and nodded. At this point, a park bench would have looked all right to her. Providing that it was out of the bone-chilling rain. "I just hope that sign really means vacancy. I don't think I can stand riding in this car any longer."

"Well, hang in there. You'll be tucked up in bed in no time." He opened the door and the umbrella bloomed like a mushroom as he stepped outside. "Be back in a minute or two."

A burst of chilly air rolled in through the open car door before Kale pushed it closed and Jessie shivered as she watched him walk briskly toward the building. She was beginning to notice little things about him, like the way he walked, the habit he had of letting one arm swing freely while the other lodged in his pocket...front or back, it didn't seem to matter. She had started to watch for the tightening of his jaw just before a smile tugged at the corners of his mouth. And she was learning to appreciate his subtle humor and gentle teasing.

The truth was she was a little in awe of Kale. When he spoke about his research and described the work he had done and the problems he still wanted to solve, she was struck by his intensity and intelligence. He might be absentminded at times, but there was no doubt that he knew who he was and what he wanted to accomplish in his lifetime. It took a big man to dream big dreams and Jessie had no choice but to admire him.

Unfortunately she didn't seem to have a choice about this growing attraction she felt for him, either. To her thinking, the very qualities she admired made him unsuitable for a relationship. And yet...

There had been moments during the past few hours, the past few days when, if he'd made a move to touch her or kiss her, she knew she would have responded. But he hadn't made a move so she was left to wonder what she might have done...if he had.

"Jessie?" Kale was back, leaning in through the door, holding the gaudy umbrella over his head. "They have to have a credit card and I don't have one. Do you—?"

She'd reached for her purse the moment she saw him returning from the motel office. With some resignation, she handed him her card. "Did you forget yours?" she asked.

"I don't use them. Never saw the need to get one." He paused, offered her his one-sided grin, and won her rueful smile in return. "Until now. I'm paying for all of this. Just keep track of the expenses and I'll reimburse you when we get back." He moved away from the car, then leaned down again. "Thanks, Jessie. You're a real sport."

Sport? After traveling together for the past fourteen hours, all he could say was "you're a real sport." She ought to take away her umbrella for that. Let him get wet. Let him sleep in the car. After all, it was her credit card. She was the one prepared for this trip. If it hadn't been for her, he would have left his bag on the floor in her apartment. She'd pointed out the fact that he might need a change of clothes on the trip and he'd gone back for the bag, saying he had planned to borrow the extra toothbrush he knew she was taking.

That had been the first time she'd seen the shrug and the smile.

And if anyone had told her she would find either one appealing... Well, she couldn't quite believe it herself. But there was something so undeniably attractive, so entirely charming about him when he did that.

With a soft sigh, she settled back to wait for him and the key to a room and a nice warm bed. She'd been ready for this for an hour or more, had even hinted earlier that perhaps they should stop for the night, but he had waited for the motel with the Best of the West emblem. There was no point in having accommodations that weren't first-rate, he'd said. She was too tired to care and she supposed she ought to be glad that he did. If it had been left up to her, there was no telling what rate the accommodations would have been.

"Here we go," Kale said as he got into the car and shook raindrops from the umbrella. He handed her a room key. "We're around back and downstairs. I was specific about that. Downstairs."

"There's only one key." She'd noticed that right off.

"You only need one. Now, look on this drawing the clerk gave me and see if you can tell where we're located."

She glanced at the piece of paper, brought her frown to bear on him as he backed the car and turned toward the rear of the long L-shaped motel. "What's your room number?"

"What? Read the number on the key I handed you."

She wasn't getting good vibes from this. Being attracted was one thing. Sharing a room was another. And on her credit card, too. "One-fourteen," she said.

"Right and it should be right around here. Look for the number. Darn, it's hard to see in this rain. There it is and, lucky you, the parking space in front of the door is ours." He turned the car into the space and turned off the ignition. He seemed pleased with himself and with this turn of events.

Jessie debated whether to tell him now or later that he was not sleeping in the room with her. She couldn't believe he'd believed that she would fall for such an old ploy. No other hotel rooms, he'd say. This was the only one. And then he'd shrug that shy little shrug and smile that courtly smile.

Irritated, Jessie opened the car door and dashed for the motel. Beneath the overhead porch, she fiddled with the key and finally pushed open the door. The room was typical motel fare . . . brown and gold with worn, lackluster carpet, two appropriately colored and framed prints, and the standard bed, chest of drawers, table and two chairs. Crisp, white towels were stacked like a pyramid by the sink and the usual plastic ice bucket was surrounded by paper wrapped glasses. Jessie wouldn't have called it first-rate, but it was neat and clean.

Kale closed the door and dumped their bags. "If you'd waited a minute, I'd have come around with the umbrella so you wouldn't get wet."

"I won't melt."

His eyes met hers. "Is something wrong with this room?"

Her chin came up. "It's a bit small for two people, don't you think?"

He said nothing for a minute—a long minute—and then...damn him...he shrugged and smiled. "Well, it's not as large as your grandad's chicken house, but I think it's probably standard size for a people motel." He brushed raindrops from his sleeves before taking off the jacket and draping it across one of the chairs. "Don't worry, Jessie, you won't even know I'm here."

Not know he was in the same bed? She prided herself on being self-disciplined, but she wasn't that good. Not even close. "I think you made a mistake, Kale. I mean if you were trying to cut costs, there are other ways to—"

The lift of his brow, the slightest tilt at the corner of his mouth stopped her. "Does that mean you don't want to share a room?" he asked, his voice light and teasing. "You'd rather I cut your rations to a cup of bouillon every other day? I mean, Jessie, think about it. We could hang a blanket from that lamp there—" he pointed to illustrate the light on the wall "—then we could tack it to the ceiling there and, voilà, that would be just like at Grandad's."

"Not just like." She fiddled with the gold chain at her neck. "This isn't—"

"What?"

What an awkward situation. "Look, Kale, I—" Her voice broke, to her chagrin, and a warm and spiraling pre-science wrapped its way around her as Kale took the first step toward her.

Rooted to the floor in front of the bed, Jessie wished she hadn't started this. But then, it was his fault. He should have known— Then he reached her and his hands went to her shoulders, slipped beneath the cardigan she wore and slid down her arms, discarding the sweater in one polished move. He threaded his fingers through hers and pulled her inexorably closer to him. Her breath clung to her lungs, her heart thudded rhythmically against her chest. He could probably hear it. She moistened her lips and kept her chin high. "I think you need to understand, Kale, that I..."

"And I think that you need to understand something, Jessie." His mouth laid claim to her lips so quickly, with such devastating softness, that she lost track of what she thought he ought to understand. It was embarrassing to be a strong, principled woman one moment and a weak-kneed, breathless female the next. Kale wasn't supposed to have this effect on her. She wasn't supposed to be so vulnerable. A kiss wasn't supposed to make her feel so... good.

She'd have to stop this, have to take charge, inform Kale that, kiss or no kiss, he could not share her bed tonight.

But she didn't stop anything. Kale held her hands tightly in his and kissed her until he decided to stop. She opened her eyes to see a challenge in the depths of his and she saw, too, an element of pleased satisfaction in the indigo blue of his eyes. Jessie sighed. For a woman with a valid credit card and an umbrella, she had lost a lot of ground in the past thirty seconds.

"Kale?" She swallowed and groped for just an inch or so of that solid ground. "You shouldn't have—"

He stole the rest of the sentence from her lips in a brief, but debilitating kiss. Then the devil smiled at her. "*You* shouldn't have, Jessie. Here, let me show you something." He guided her hand to his leg and pressed her palm flat against his upper thigh. "Feel that," he said.

Her fingers refused to move. He was being very forward. Possibly even crude. She tried to pull back, but his hand kept hers captive. And slowly, she registered a familiar shape. A blush flamed in her cheeks and she wondered if she'd ever been more embarrassed. "What's in your pocket?" she finally asked in an agonized whisper.

He released the pressure on her hand. "A room key. I'll be sleeping right next door, Jessie. Shame on you for thinking I'd take advantage of you like that. You may have stolen my research, but I do still have my principles. When I share a bed, it's an invitation-only affair."

Chapter Ten

Invitation only.

Jessie came very close to issuing that invitation several times during the night. Luckily she came fully awake before doing anything really stupid. The last thing she needed was to make a mistake like that and end up actually in love with the man. Emotion was such a subtle deceiver, luring one into believing the impossible was not only possible, but wonderful as well. Nothing good could come of inviting Kale to share her bedroom and her bed and intimacies she didn't share lightly. She couldn't deny the chemistry between them. It would be self-delusion to pretend she didn't respond to him physically, and on a few other levels, but that was not a good reason to bridge the buffer zone of common sense.

Kale Warner was not for her. He might wow the world someday with a revolutionary discovery, but it would be at the expense of any relationship he had. She was smart enough to understand that...and smart enough to know she didn't want to be the sacrifice. Unfortunately she was also smart enough to recognize the ache of loneliness inside her and to wish there was some way her sane, rational behavior could diffuse it.

And so she tossed and turned, wondering—for some ridiculous reason—if he'd meant at her invitation or at his.

FREE BOOKS!

FREE GIFTS!

PLAY THE "LUCKY 7" SLOT MACHINE GAME!

AND YOU COULD GET FREE BOOKS, A FREE VICTORIAN PICTURE FRAME AND A SURPRISE GIFT!

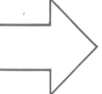

NO COST! NO OBLIGATION TO BUY! NO PURCHASE NECESSARY!

PLAY "LUCKY 7"
AND GET AS MANY AS SIX FREE GIFTS...

HOW TO PLAY:

1. With a coin, carefully scratch off the silver box at the right. This makes you eligible to receive one or more free books, and possibly other gifts, depending on what is revealed beneath the scratch-off area.

2. You'll receive brand-new Harlequin American Romance® novels. When you return this card, we'll send you the books and gifts you qualify for *absolutely free!*

3. If we don't hear from you, every month we'll send you 4 additional novels to read and enjoy. You can return them and owe nothing but if you decide to keep them, you'll pay only $2.74* per book, a savings of 21¢ each off the cover price. There is **no** extra charge for postage and handling. There are no hidden extras.

4. When you join the Harlequin Reader Service®, you'll get our monthly newsletter, as well as additional free gifts from time to time just for being a subscriber.

5. You must be completely satisfied. You may cancel at any time simply by sending us a note or a shipping statement marked "cancel" or returning any shipment to us at our cost.

*Terms and prices subject to change. Sales tax applicable in NY.
© 1990 HARLEQUIN ENTERPRISES LIMITED.

This lovely Victorian pewter-finish miniature is perfect for displaying a treasured photograph— and it's yours absolutely free—when you accept our no-risk offer.

PLAY "LUCKY 7"

Just scratch off the silver box with a coin.
Then check below to see which gifts you get.

YES! I have scratched off the silver box. Please send me all the gifts for which I qualify. I understand I am under no obligation to purchase any books, as explained on the opposite page.

(U-H-AR-01/91)154 CIH NBBW

NAME

ADDRESS   APT

CITY   STATE   ZIP

7	7	7	WORTH FOUR FREE BOOKS, FREE VICTORIAN PICTURE FRAME AND MYSTERY BONUS
🍒	🍒	🍒	WORTH FOUR FREE BOOKS AND MYSTERY BONUS
●	●	●	WORTH FOUR FREE BOOKS
🔔	🔔	🍒	WORTH TWO FREE BOOKS

Offer limited to one per household and not valid to current Harlequin American Romance® subscribers. All orders subject to approval. Terms and prices subject to change without notice.
© 1990 HARLEQUIN ENTERPRISES LIMITED.

PRINTED IN U.S.A.

(left margin, vertical text) **DETACH AND MAIL CARD TODAY**

HARLEQUIN "NO RISK" GUARANTEE
- You're not required to buy a single book—ever!
- You must be completely satisfied or you may cancel at any time simply by sending us a note or a shipping statement marked "cancel" or returning any shipment to us at our cost. Either way, you will receive no more books; you'll have no further obligation.
- The free books and gifts you receive from this "Lucky 7" offer remain yours to keep no matter what you decide.

If offer card is missing, write to:
Harlequin Reader Service, 3010 Walden Ave., P.O. Box 1867, Buffalo, N.Y. 14269-1867

DETACH AND MAIL CARD TODAY

BUSINESS REPLY MAIL
FIRST CLASS MAIL   PERMIT NO. 717   BUFFALO, NY

POSTAGE WILL BE PAID BY ADDRESSEE

HARLEQUIN READER SERVICE
3010 WALDEN AVE
PO BOX 1867
BUFFALO NY 14240-9952

NO POSTAGE
NECESSARY
IF MAILED
IN THE
UNITED STATES

Her mind wrestled him in silent conversation, telling him he was crazy to think she would invite him, answering his invitation with the firm, but gentle information that she simply wasn't interested. Still, even in the solitude of her room, in the seclusion of her own thoughts, he bested her on every angle . . . by smiling that crooked smile and giving that little shrug and by taking her in his arms and putting his lips . . .

Jessie rolled over onto her stomach and bunched the pillow under her forehead. Who would have believed Kale would cause her so much trouble and cost her so much sleep?

Invitation only.

Who did he think he was?

INVITATION ONLY.

How could he have uttered such a smug, egotistical statement? Kale punched his pillow and frowned at the ceiling. He couldn't believe he'd said it. He'd sounded like Clint Eastwood issuing a challenge to some deadbeat in a cops and robbers movie. *Make my day,* he could just as well have said. *Invitation only.* Jeez.

Rolling to his side, he prodded the pillow into shape beneath his head and stretched his legs to the foot of the bed, liking the scratchy feel of the motel sheets. If he'd thought for a minute that she would have shared this bed with him, he would have invited her. Hell, he'd have tripped all over himself inviting her.

The funny thing was, he hadn't even considered getting only one room. He'd entered the motel office like the Lone Ranger, thinking he was taking care of Jessie, knowing she was tired and in need of sleep, feeling good about the way he was handling things. Then, he'd had to ask to borrow her credit card. The Lone Ranger shot himself in the foot.

Kale rolled over onto his back again. What was it about Jessie that brought out these bumbling, little inadequacies in him? He was a capable, intelligent, caring, and—he liked to think—interesting man. Women didn't run away screaming at his approach. Children and animals liked him. He had philosophical discussions with educated, insightful people, both men and women. Some of them even sought his advice. He'd won awards from his peers for his scientific studies.

So why did this petite little blonde have him lying awake worrying about what he'd said to her in a moment of high tension? The memory of the reason for that high tension flooded him with a new wave of restlessness. Kissing Jessie had been a mistake. The first time he'd kissed her had been a deliberate, if misguided, act on his part, designed to throw her off guard. But the kiss tonight had been impulsive and motivated simply by the desire to kiss her and hold her close against him.

A mistake.

But the memory was just as sweet, just as tantalizing and promised to interfere with his sleep just as much as if it hadn't been a mistake at all. One way or another, he'd be better off not to kiss her again. Otherwise he might end up trying to figure out some way to get her to invite him into her bed.

Maybe if he'd brought Anthony's robe along—no, wrong train of thought. Anthony's robe was not the issue here. Kale was confident that he was the better man. Why, a few more days with him and Jessie would kick that ugly robe right off the balcony of her apartment with its owner wrapped in it.

Kale groaned. What was wrong with him? He wasn't on this trip to win Jessie's favor or to worry about some mangy old bathrobe she chose to allow in her life. He was here to retrieve a valuable collection of scientific data. How could he have forgotten that...even for a minute? Why wasn't he barreling down the highway in search of Jessie's sister at this very moment? He probably would have found her by now, retrieved his floppy disk, and headed for home. Instead he was lying in a motel room, all alone, wondering if Jessie was lying on the other side of the wall, thinking about him.

Kale turned, and a cool draft of air hit his shoulder. Tucking the sheet and blanket back around himself, he hoped Jessie was comfortable. He sincerely hoped so. It might have been her credit card, but he had a feeling he was going to pay a high price for this night's lodging.

"I SLEPT like an angel," he said when she opened the door to his knock the next morning. "How about you?"

Jessie regarded him with a frown. "Ask me after I've had a cup of coffee."

"That's why I'm here. I thought we might get a bite of breakfast at the coffee shop before we hit the road." He glanced at the sky. "You can put your umbrella in the trunk today. It's going to be gorgeous weather."

He seemed to be in a jolly good mood, Jessie thought as she turned to pick up her purse. But then, why wouldn't he be? He'd slept like an angel, while she'd tossed and turned and wondered if it was possible that she was falling for him. "It is beautiful." She tried for a rested, amenable tone of voice. "The air here is so...rich, somehow."

Kale pulled shut her door as she stepped out and they walked across the parking lot to the restaurant. "Probably has something to do with the moisture content of the air."

Jessie didn't like his response or the unreasonable burst of annoyance it evoked. "Only someone like you would think of that, Kale."

He stopped in the middle of the parking lot. "Now what did I do?"

"Nothing."

"That makes a lot of sense." He caught up with her and jerked open the restaurant door. "If I didn't do anything, then what's wrong with you?"

"Nothing is wrong with me!" Jessie slipped past him, yanking the purse strap up her arm to secure it against her shoulder. "What is wrong with you?"

"Two for breakfast," Kale said politely to the waitress in the brown-and-gold uniform. "Non smoking—I think."

He glanced at Jessie, who struggled to tamp down her inappropriate irritation. "Non smoking," she confirmed.

"Good." He smiled at the hostess, then at Jessie. "I was afraid I saw a little puff or two coming from behind your ears."

"Very funny." She took off after the waitress, not at all sure why he was being so annoying or why she was letting him get to her.

Kale followed slowly, toying with the reason for Jessie's bad mood. Was she that devoted to caffeine? "Coffee, please," he said as he slid into the booth. "Two cups, and make hers a double."

Jessie narrowed her eyes and pursed her already tight lips, but she didn't look at him. Instead she nodded pleasantly at the waitress. "Yes, coffee, please, with cream, but no sugar."

"No sugar?" Kale asked.

"No sugar."

The waitress left and Kale pretended an acute interest in the restaurant. It wasn't crowded, indicating to him that the tourist season on the northwestern coast didn't extend into late October. On the other hand, he supposed it might be a little late in the morning for the breakfast crowd. "Did you sleep all right, Jessie?"

"Fine, thank you."

There was still an edge to her voice, but he could tell she was fighting to overcome it. He thrummed his fingers on the tabletop. "I thought the room was quite comfortable. In fact, I slept like—"

"—an angel. I know. You mentioned it."

Was that what was wrong with her? Was she upset because she thought he'd slept . . . and she hadn't? He looked closer, but couldn't make out any dark circles under her eyes or other signs of sleep deprivation. Now, what could have kept her awake? And why did the idea make him feel better? "You didn't have any trouble getting to sleep, did you?"

She lifted a meaningful ash-brown gaze and practically burned a hole in his nose. "No," she said. "I didn't have any trouble getting to sleep or staying asleep. In fact, I would have liked to sleep a lot longer than I was able to."

"Probably jet lag."

"No? Do you really think so?"

His annoyance rose to match her. "Look, Jessie, I'm just trying to be nice. You could put out a little effort, yourself."

"I warned you I needed coffee."

"So you did. All right, conversation is suspended until after the coffee arrives. I hope your disposition improves after that."

"It will."

It didn't. Coffee came and then breakfast and then more coffee. But Jessie couldn't get over her peeve. She couldn't even figure out why she was upset. Kale didn't ask to use her credit card. He paid cash for the meal and the tip without a word. And he didn't say anything else about sleeping like an angel. In fact, he didn't say another word to her until they were in the car and ready to leave.

"We'll stop at the front office to check out." He ran his hands over the steering wheel before sending her a cautious glance. "You'll have to go in and sign us out."

"I know...it's my credit we're using." She twisted around in the seat and pulled on her seat belt. "I can handle that."

"Is there anything you can't handle, Jessie?"

She was feeling guilty about her ill temper. Breakfast, coffee, and a little bit of quiet had done her some good. She was still out of sorts with him, but she thought it was probably more a form of self-defense than true annoyance. She offered a slight smile as a peace offering. "Well, I'm not very good with chickens."

"You're being modest." He picked up the offering and the tension in the small car began to ebb. "How are you at handling a camera?"

"Pretty good. Why? Did you bring one?"

"No. Did you?"

Jessie shook her head. "Bringing a camera just wasn't on my priority list. I didn't think we'd be anywhere where I might want to take a picture."

"What about your sister?"

"I have pictures of her already."

"Well, what about the redwoods? Wouldn't you like to have a picture of me standing in front of one of those huge trees? It could be a collector's item someday...when I'm famous."

Jessie turned toward him, searching his face for the purpose-filled scientist she knew was there somewhere. "What about your research?"

"It will probably be a collector's item, too."

"Really, Kale. You can't be serious about stopping to see the redwoods when you're frantic to find Gretchen and the computer diskette."

"I'm not frantic. We have all day to find Gretchen and I want to see the redwoods. When in Oregon..."

He was up to something, Jessie thought. She just didn't know how it affected her. "How are you going to take pictures without a camera?"

"Something will turn up." He put the car in gear. "Somebody's bound to sell postcards."

"Postcards will be best," Jessie said. "Considering that the redwood forest is in northern California."

"Darn. You're right. Well, we'll find some tourist attraction. I'm sure of it."

MANY MILES, several stops for information, a state forest, and at least two dozen postcards later, Jessie was still wondering what he was up to. The morning had sped into a pleasant afternoon and miles of Pacific coast. Sea lions sunbathed on rocks within sight of the highway. Ponderosa pines reached for the sky, leaving a nest of shade and shadows and primeval quiet below. Jessie drank in the sights, breathed in the smells, shivered with the cool, damp air, and loved Kale for taking the precious moments to show it all to her. He had his faults, but today she forgave him everything and simply enjoyed his easy company and his knowledge of flora and fauna.

By the time they reached Clemson, Oregon, the town where Gretchen was supposed to be, Jessie had mellowed into a rather nice person again. And oddly enough, Kale had become one, too.

It took several tries before they found anyone who knew about the environmentalists and several more tries to find the right place. But finally, they found the group and Gretchen.

It was a small step from introductions to recovery of the computer disk. Kale held the floppy disk in his hand as if it held the secrets of the ages and Jessie felt a pang that the moment marked the beginning of the end for her acquaintance with him. Only one small, leghorn hen stood between him and his laboratory and Jessie didn't think it would be long before Jennifer, too, was in his hands and he was back in the laboratory. Then Jessie would be back where she started.

"So," Gretchen said over a steamy cup of vegetable gumbo. "Now that you're here, why don't you explain why?"

Jessie glanced at Kale across the table from her and at Gretchen beside her. This could be the showdown. Kale could accuse Gretchen of treachery and Gretchen could tell him to put his theory of thievery where the sun didn't shine. Jessie wondered how to head them off at the pass. "It's a long story," she began.

"And gets longer by the minute." Kale swallowed a mouthful of coffee and made a face. "This is the real stuff, isn't it? You need to try a cup of this in the morning, Jess. I can't believe it would do much for your mood, but it certainly would keep your eyes open."

Gretchen's eyebrows rose. Jessie could almost see the sibling radar go up. "Did you two stay in Seattle last night...together?"

"We missed you in Seattle," Jessie said, pointedly ignoring the question. "You might have waited for us, Gretchen."

"Tell that to the sea lions, Jessie." Gretchen tossed her long, straight, silvery-blond hair and turned to Kale. "Tell me how your computer disk got into Pancho's pocket."

Kale ran a hand over his jaw before launching into an explanation of how he'd discovered the disk was missing and how he came to the conclusion that Pancho had stolen it. Jessie sampled the gumbo as she looked around at the large room that served as temporary headquarters and lunchroom for the Save Our World organization. Gretchen often spoke of the professional way in which the group could move from place to place on a moment's notice. It must be true, since the community center where they were now looked more like a commando outfit than a country club. There were cots, coffeepots and several portable computers. Home away from home, Jessie thought and hoped she wouldn't have to occupy one of those cots tonight.

"That's the most ridiculous thing I've heard in a month." Gretchen shook her head and lifted her thermal cup to her lips. She blew softly at the steam and then took a sip. "Pancho did not steal that computer disk. He wouldn't do anything like that. It's more likely that it was put in his pocket by mistake and he never even knew it was there."

"How does a computer disk get into a pocket by mistake?" Kale asked. "He stole it and he stole CTA #43, too."

Gretchen propped her chin on her hands. "What is a CTA #43?"

Jessie restrained a sigh. Here we go.

"A chicken," Kale explained. "A chicken from my laboratory. It was taken at the same time as the disk."

"You use chickens for experimentation?"

Kale's blue eyes flicked to Jessie and she rallied to his defense. "He doesn't hurt the chickens, Gretchen. He just tests them."

Gretchen leaned across the flimsy, card table. "Around here, those are fighting words."

Kale pushed restless fingers through his dark hair. "Before you jump to any conclusions I'd like to say, for the record, that the experimental farm is both humane and careful with its animals. From insects to cattle, nothing is mistreated, maimed, or in any way disfigured for the sake of science. The chickens I test are happy campers . . . every last one of them."

"One of them is happier than the rest at the moment." Jessie smiled at the thought of Jennifer making a place for herself in Grandad's henhouse.

Gretchen looked suspiciously at Jessie. "Are you acquainted with the 'happy campers' in Dr. Warner's laboratory?"

"One of them. Jennifer."

"That's CTA #43," Kale said. "Pancho stole it from the lab and Jessie obligingly took it to your Grandad's farm."

"It's a present for you, Gretchen. Pancho said he rescued it and asked me to keep it until you got back from this trip. I thought it was a kitten or a puppy or something like that, but when I found his 'gift,' it was a chicken. Kale's chicken, as it turns out."

"I still can't believe you turned it loose with the other hens." Kale's attention swung fully to Jessie. "How am I ever going to figure out which one—"

"Are you trying to tell me that Pancho stole a computer disk and a chicken? Why would he do that?" Gretchen's forehead wrinkled with thought as she took another sip of coffee. "The only reason Pancho might take the chicken was if he thought it would be hurt. He's extremely sensitive and absolutely moral."

"And crazy about you." Jessie felt her sisterly affection stir. "If you're not careful, Gretchen, you may find yourself on a truck farm in Ecuador."

"Pancho's just a kid."

"He could be a very rich kid if he'd been able to sell the information." Kale downed the last of his coffee.

"Maybe he did." Jessie scraped the last bite of gumbo from the thermal cup. "Who's to say he didn't copy the disk while it was in his pocket?"

"That's a cheerful thought," Kale said. "I thought you were Pancho's staunch defender."

Jessie shrugged. "I think Gretchen's probably right and that the disk got into his sweater pocket by mistake, but that's not to say someone else didn't copy the disk before it got into the pocket."

"Thank you, Jessie, for that uplifting idea. I'll sleep better tonight."

She glanced up, surprised at his curt tone. But after all, it was his own fault for not taking more care for the security of his research. "Oh, you'll sleep like an angel, Kale. You always do."

His eyebrows shot up. "I don't know why my sleep patterns bother you. It isn't my fault you were awake all last night."

"I was not awake—" Jessie realized the intensity with which Gretchen was listening and decided to back out of this discussion with Kale. "I'll sleep all the better tonight. Which brings up a good point, Gretchen. Where do I bunk?"

Gretchen smiled. "There's a very nice motel a couple of miles down the road. I'd ask you to stay here, but we're a bit limited on space and you'd be more comfortable at the motel. It's a Best of the West." She sized up Kale with sisterly appraisal. "Did you say you're a professor at the university? Why haven't I met you before?"

"It's a big university and I stay at the experimental farm most of the time."

"I see." Gretchen continued to regard him with a measured gaze. "Jessie didn't tell me that."

"Jessie doesn't know much about me yet. But she's learning."

Gretchen's expression softened with astonishment. "Really? I wondered why it took you so long to make it from Seattle to Clemson today."

Jessie shifted in the folding chair. "Kale wanted his picture taken in front of a redwood tree, but he settled for a postcard of a ponderosa pine."

"You stopped to look at trees?" Gretchen asked. "I thought this computer information was important."

"It was. It is." Kale floundered with the affirmation and Jessie's mood took a sudden upward shift. He was defensive and she realized he had made something of a sacrifice in sightseeing on the drive down instead of rushing to recover the disk. Had he done that for her?

Kale cleared his throat. "Jessie wanted to see the sights and I wanted to show them to her and, well, one thing led to another and we stopped to see the trees. And the seals."

And a couple of interesting points on the coast. And an inn where they'd had a leisurely lunch. And a whole row of stores that sold postcards. Jessie began to feel better...a lot better.

Chapter Eleven

The Best of the West sign flashed a neon welcome as Kale drove into the parking area of the Sea Star Inn outside the town of Tillamook. Clasping his hands on the steering wheel, he leaned forward and peered up through the windshield at the marquee. "What do you know?" he said. "Gretchen gave us the right directions."

"Don't get too excited. She did have some help."

"True. I thought for a while a couple of those guys were going to run us out of the camp on a rail." He grinned at Jessie. "Did you see how the whites of their eyes turned red when I said I worked on an experimental farm?"

"I'm beginning to think you did that on purpose, Kale. What a turn of phrase to use in a group like that. Luckily for you, Gretchen was able to explain."

"You didn't do too badly, yourself. I'm honored that you rushed to rescue me from my folly."

Her glance slid to him in the soft darkness. Was he teasing? She had made a few comments in his defense, thinking he needed someone to provide a buffer between him and the zealous Save Our World activists. But Kale had proved later that he was capable of defending himself. She'd heard him in conversation with a couple of the men in the group and he hadn't appeared to need a champion at all. "I'm not sure you needed rescuing, Kale."

His jaw tightened and then the corners of his mouth lifted in tandem with the slight lift of his shoulders. "That might depend on who's there to rescue me. I got the idea from Gretchen that you're the 'mother hen' type."

"Not by choice, believe me. Sometimes I think I got mixed up with another baby at the hospital and wound up in the Day family by mistake. I love my family, don't misunderstand, but they do require a lot of care."

He stretched his arm along the back of her seat and played with a strand of her hair. Her stomach made a curious jump and a spiral of warmth tingled along her nape. "You're a very caring person, Jessie. Your family is lucky someone switched babies in the hospital."

It was a nice thing to say. And Kale said it in a nice way. And Jessie felt pleased and, somehow, a little embarrassed. "Thanks, Kale. But I've never felt particularly special. Someone's got to take care of the details, you know. I've always thought it would be wonderful to find someone to do the same for me."

He wrapped the strand of hair around his finger, brushing her temple with the palm of his hand. The warm tingle trickled down her spine and pooled in delicious whirls around her heart. Jessie concentrated on keeping her breathing regular, steady. What would she do if he discovered his touch interfered with her breathing? Even in the dark, she could see the smile in his eyes, hear the barely audible catch in the deep breath he drew.

"I've always thought it would be wonderful to find someone who..."

He stopped and Jessie had to keep herself from leaning forward and asking, *What? Someone who—what?* For the space of a dozen heartbeats, the atmosphere inside the rental car was as taut as a violin string...and as fragile. Silence echoed, tantalizing Jessie with words not said, thoughts not voiced. Then Kale moved. His hand went back to the steering wheel, his attention returned to the motel sign. "I'm very fond of mother hens," he said with a smile. "If I wasn't, I couldn't enjoy working with the chickens in my lab, now could I?"

Disappointment—a completely irrational disappointment—wrapped around Jessie like morning fog. What had he started to say? And why had she thought even for a second, that he might be going to say something personal, something unrelated to his work and his precious chickens, something pertaining to her? That would be like expecting Gretchen to start talking about the best cleaning fluid on the market or the most efficient way of organizing a room.

Jessie held back a sigh and chided herself for feeling let down. "It's getting colder. I'll go in and get the rooms this time. Any preference as to location?"

"Do you think they might have a room in Fayetteville?" Kale laughed and Jessie's heart sank. Of course, he wanted to be home. Now that he had the floppy disk, now that he had accomplished his goal, there was no reason to want to stay. "Just kidding," he said. "Just kidding. Actually I'm sort of partial to sleeping on the other side of the wall from you. I think it might be becoming a habit."

His grin was light, teasing, and Jessie wondered if he knew how to be serious with a woman. She wondered what it would be like if he suddenly became serious with her. "I'll try to get you a room as close to Arkansas as possible."

"Anything will be fine." Kale maintained his smile until Jessie entered the lobby of the Sea Star Inn. Then he decided to wrestle the lump of sentiment lodged in his throat. He'd almost said something really dumb. Something about finding someone like Jessie. Finding someone who laughed like she did, smiled like she did, talked like she did. Someone who had an alluring little dimple in her chin. He was beginning to wonder about the feelings she evoked in him. He'd never thought so much about someone else's comfort and well-being. And he'd never been able to do so little about it.

She had the credit card. She remembered little things that he forgot. She wanted someone to take care of her.

Jessie was so dad-blasted independent. Why didn't something go wrong for her? Something he could fix? But so far, no opportunity for rescue had presented itself. He wondered if he should have gone ahead the night before and paid for the room in cash. But then, if he ran out of cash to pay for food and other incidental expenses of traveling, wouldn't that be worse? Having to eat crackers and water hardly qualified as taking good care of Jessie. Not in his book . . . and certainly not in hers.

Kale couldn't figure out why the whole situation bothered him so much. He had his research disk back. He had a reasonable hope of recovering the stolen chicken. So where was the problem? What was the source of his anxiety.

Jessie.

Okay, he could admit that. She bothered him. She appealed to him. He wasn't sure why and he sure as hell didn't know what to do about it.

Jessie pulled open the door and shivered as she got into the car.

"Where're the rooms?" Kale turned up the heater. "Point me in the right direction."

Silently she handed him the key and he tried to decipher the expression on her face. "Are we upstairs?" He glanced at the key in his hand. "One-oh-five. All right, that ought to be easy enough to find." Still she said nothing, just sat there looking oddly stricken. "Is your room next to mine?" Kale asked. "It's all right if it isn't. I was just kidding about not being able to sleep without being on the other side of the wall."

"There was only one room," Jessie said tightly. "We'll have to share."

On a Richter scale, his reaction would have measured about a six-point-five. All sorts of tantalizing scenes and ideas flooded his mind. Jessie in the same room. Jessie in the same bed. He held down a smile. "Is the motel that crowded? Are you sure there's nothing else available?"

Her brown eyes singed through the dusky light. "Do you think I would lie about it?"

Obviously not. His enthusiasm died to a new concern. "I guess I could go back to the Save Our World camp and try to find an empty cot."

"Don't be silly. You'd wind up tarred and feathered...or worse. We're adults. We can share a room without going crazy."

Kale thought she was overly optimistic. "What kind of room is it?"

"I don't know. The usual, I guess."

"Let me be more specific. What kind of bed is in it?"

She sniffed, looked out the side window, away from him. "King-size. There'll be plenty of room. You won't even know I'm there."

"Grow up, Jessie." He reached for the door handle, wishing he didn't have to be gallant about this. "I'll go in and ask about a roll-away bed. Surely they have those."

"No." Jessie's gaze swung to him. "No. I—asked."

Her quick denial and subsequent hesitation caught Kale's attention. Her eyes pleaded with him. But why? Had she asked about a roll-away? Or—was it possible?—would she have gotten one room on purpose? Would she go to that much trouble to share a room, a bed with him? His heartbeat picked up speed, but logic reined it in. Stupid idea. Last night, Jessie had made it clear what she thought of sleeping with him. One day wouldn't have changed her mind. He was thinking like some young stud instead of like a mature and sensitive man. "We'll find another motel," he said firmly.

"There's bound to be something else in town. A bed-and-breakfast inn, maybe."

"Gretchen said there wasn't much in the way of accommodations here," Jessie pointed out. "She said the cleanup operation had strained the few resources in the town. We're probably lucky to have found an empty room at all. It'll be okay, Kale. I can stand it if you can."

Stand it? Oh, yeah, he thought he could stand it all right. If he had an ounce of good sense, he'd be driving around looking for another bed as if it were the Holy Grail. But why the hell should he fight with her? He hadn't had a good night's sleep since he met her. What was one more sleepless night? "It'll be tough," he said finally. "But, hey, I survived an evening in the Save Our World camp. After them, you look like a piece of cake."

"Thank you, Kale. Do you think we could get on with it, now? The room's on the south side of the building."

There was an edge to her voice and the thought crossed his mind that she could hardly have sounded more thrilled about going to an execution. So, if she felt that way, why hadn't she let him at least try to find a better arrangement? Kale put the car in gear. Whatever amount of effort it took, however difficult, he was going to behave with sensitivity and control. As far as he was concerned, there was an imaginary wall down the center of that bed. Just like at Grandad Joe's. He would be a pillar of restraint, the Lone Ranger protecting a lady's honor. Jessie had nothing to worry about. Nothing at all.

"This will be fine." Kale deposited his bag beside Jessie's on the green shag carpet and surveyed the motel room. "I think this is nicer than the motel we stayed at last night. Was the rate about the same?"

Jessie glanced up from her position on the edge of the mammoth bed. Kale's presence filled the room. He was too tall, too broad shouldered, too masculine to ignore. A strand of dark hair shadowed his left temple and she wanted to brush it back. Jiminy, but she was nervous. "What? Oh, the rate. I think this one's a little more expensive."

He nodded. "This will be fine, Jessie. Just fine. Do you want the bathroom first?" He tucked the fingers of one hand into the back pocket of his slacks, a gesture she found endearing and as sexy as hell. She swallowed. Would it be better to be the first in bed and lie there waiting for him to get in? Or should she get into the bed after he was in it?

And the answer was—she should not get into a bed with Kale Warner at all.

"I'll go first." Grabbing her satchel, she headed for the bathroom and a moment of serious meditation. There was no mirror in the room, just a stool and a tub. Not even a sink to wash her face. That was in the other area. Sink, glasses, ice bucket, electric plugs and Kale were all in the room with the bed. It was a big bed, to be sure. But if it had been wall-to-wall, she didn't think it would have been big enough.

Jessie sat on the edge of the tub and turned on the cold-water tap. This was the dumbest, most irresponsible act she'd ever committed. But standing there in the office, listening to the clerk tell her he did not have two rooms next to each other, she'd panicked. She didn't want Kale sleeping somewhere clear across the way. She wanted him nearby. She was used to thinking of him on the other side of the wall. And so, she'd done the unthinkable. She'd asked for one room. True, she'd thought she could get one room with two beds, but that hardly made any better sense. And now, look where her crazy impulse had taken her.

She could understand Gretchen getting herself into a fix like this. Gretchen was always doing things that defied explanation. But she was Jessie. Sane, sensible, think-it-through Jessie. What was she doing in a Best of the West motel getting ready to jump into bed with a stranger?

Ah, but wasn't that the rub? Kale wasn't a stranger. Sometimes she felt as if she'd known him forever. Sometimes she thought she wanted to know him at least that long. So now the question was: What did she want to happen once she was in that big bed with him?

The water ran icy cold over her hand and Jessie reached for the other faucet. She'd run herself a bath and ponder the question, she decided. But once immersed in a steamy bath, she had to admit that the answer was simple. Somewhere in her subconscious, she'd already made the decision. How else could she stand in a motel lobby and state that she'd take one room...no matter how big the bed.

No, she had to stop kidding herself. Despite her better instincts, despite the fact that she knew a relationship with Kale could not last forever, she had gone ahead and fallen in love.

It was not what she'd planned, not what she'd wanted...but there it was. She was in love with a man who needed her. Worse, he didn't know he needed her. He had a laboratory, a career and a vision that didn't leave much room for her. In a matter of days, he might be referring to her as CTA #44. To his credit, she did believe he'd change the acronym to something like Chicken Tracking Assistant before he assigned a number. But in the overall scheme of life, what he called her later wouldn't make much of a difference.

Jessie held up the washcloth and dribbled warm water across her stomach. It pooled around her navel and ran back into the bath. She could hear noises from the other room. The radio. Then the television. Then silence. Then a decisive knock on the bathroom door.

"Jessie? I'm going to get some ice. Be right back."

"All right."

Footsteps receded and then came the sound of the door opening and closing. Jessie sighed and decided she might as well get out of the tub. In five minutes or less, Kale would be back and she'd need to let him in. He wouldn't, she suspected, have remembered to take the key.

After a quick toweling, Jessie pulled on the one sleep shirt she'd packed . . . a long-sleeved T-shirt with a screen-print picture of her brother and sister on the front. Hardly a garment for seduction, she thought. She hurriedly brushed her teeth, ran a comb through her hair and debated on wearing blue jeans and socks into bed. But she didn't want Kale to think the situation bothered her, and the sleep shirt reached past her knees and putting too much emphasis on clothes would—

The door opened and he walked in, glancing up to see her, then turning his attention to getting the key out of the lock, and the door closed. "Have a nice bath?" he asked and wished to high heaven he could have thought of a more interesting comment. "You'll probably sleep like an—" he caught the swift arching of her brow "—a charm. Nothing like a warm bath to relax the body, is there?" *Body.* Gee, he wished he hadn't mentioned that.

"Traveling is tiring." Jessie hesitated between the wash area and the bedroom area, making it difficult for Kale to decide what to do. If he moved toward her, she'd probably shy away like a skittish calf. If he stayed where he was, the ice was going to melt in his sweaty hands. Why had he ever agreed to this? He should have stuck by his "invitation only" principle and not have gotten himself into this impossibly platonic situation.

He stepped forward, holding the ice bucket in front of him for security. "I know what you mean," he said in his most buddylike voice. "I'm beat. Seeing all the tourist attractions along the coast really wore me out." He reached the counter and set the bucket beside the plastic-covered glasses. "There was a soda machine beside the ice maker and I bought a couple of cans of soda. Would you like one?"

"Sure." Her hands went wide in a nervous gesture before she tucked them safely, arm over arm, across her waist. "That'd be great."

Kale tossed her what he hoped was a nonchalant smile and told himself not to pay any attention to the way she looked...all fresh and damp and seductive. "I'll fix the soda for you. You can go on and get into bed, if you want."

"Oh, no, thanks. I can wait."

"No reason to do that. You'll just get cold. Go ahead. I'll be there in a minute." It could hardly have sounded more intimate if he'd rephrased the words a dozen times. They were going to get into that bed together, but not to do the normal things a couple might do in bed.

Oh, no, Kale thought as he took the cans from his coat pockets, popped the flip top and poured soda into the plastic glasses. He and Jessie were going to get into that bed, drink a soda, act as if they were completely unaware of each other and then lie awake until morning...as close to the edges of the bed as was humanly possible. But if that's what she expected, then that's what he'd do.

If it killed him.

"Here you go." He handed her the glass, then took it back. "Oops, forgot the ice." Two plops later, he handed it to her again and almost spilled it, he was trying so hard not to look at the soft outline of her breasts beneath the sheet she had tucked around her. "Comfortable?" Taking her agreement for granted, he walked around the foot of the bed and approached the situation from the opposite side. If Jessie was under the covers, he figured the best place for him was on top. Once settled there, fully clothed except for his jacket, he took a sip of fizz and chanced a shy smile.

"Are you going to sleep like that?" she asked. "Won't you be uncomfortable?"

Kale stared at the carbonated bubbles in the soda. He had a strong urge to put the glass down and show Jessie exactly how uncomfortable he already was. There was only so much gallantry in him, after all. "This is not a comfortable situation, Jessie. But since it's unavoidable, I intend to make the best of it. And if that means sleeping on top of the covers, then that's what I'll do."

She looked miserable and Kale wondered how he could make her feel better. This wasn't her fault. She was unhappy and embarrassed about the whole thing. But, damn it, he wasn't getting under the covers with her to prove some idiotic point. He moved restlessly, positioning a pillow behind his back and dragging on the covers as he scooted up against the headboard. The sheets slipped down over the slope of her breasts and he saw the picture on her sleep shirt. "Who is that?" He leaned closer to investigate.

"What?"

"On your shirt." He indicated the print by moving his finger closer to her. A mistake, he realized as he came within an inch of touching her gently defined breasts. "Who is that?"

She frowned, looked down. "Oh. Gretchen and Eric. They gave it to me for Christmas last year." She pulled down the sheets so he could see the grinning faces of her brother and sister. "They said they didn't want me to sleep by myself. Really thoughtful, huh?"

"I'll bet Anthony loves that."

"Anthony?" Jessie flicked her fingers at a minuscule speck on the garment and then smoothed the fabric against her skin. "I don't think he's ever seen it."

Kale felt better instantly, until it occurred to him that there could be a lot of reasons Anthony hadn't seen Jessie's nightie. Jealousy uncoiled annoyingly in the pit of his stomach as he fought the image of Jessie with Anthony and without the nightgown....

"I wear it a lot," Jessie went on, blessedly unaware of his turmoil. "It's silly, I guess, because Eric and Gretchen give me so many headaches, but I suppose I'm more sentimental than I like to admit."

"I, for one, am glad your sister and brother are in bed with us...in a manner of speaking, of course. It might be harder to stay on my side of the bed if you were wearing something less family oriented."

Jessie stared at him and, to save his life, Kale couldn't interpret the expression in her ash-brown eyes. Maybe he shouldn't have said that. Maybe he should turn out the lights and pretend to be asleep. Could he lie that still?

"I'm surprised you don't have a sleep shirt with Jennifer's picture on it." Jessie slid down under the covers and turned onto her side...away from Kale. She struggled with a sigh, not wanting him to know she was disappointed in the conversation so far. She'd been unsure of herself, a bit uncertain about the wisdom of making love with him, but it was no help at all for him to act like he was sharing a bed with his buddy. As far as Jessie could tell, he didn't even realize she was female, let alone that at odd moments during their acquaintance, there had been a definite attraction at work between them. What was wrong with him? Couldn't he keep his mind off those dumb chickens for one night?

"Jessie?" She felt his hand on her shoulder, his breath against her temple, experienced an increasing heat that wrapped around her with all the titillating sensuality of a forbidden pleasure. Finally, she thought, he was making a move.

She rolled slowly to her back and lost her reason in his delicious indigo eyes. "Kale?" she replied.

He was in serious trouble here, Kale realized. He'd meant to ask her if she'd mind if he turned on the television, but somehow he didn't think he ought to follow through with that idea. It had been purely survival instinct, anyway, and he wasn't sure now that he would survive this. Her lips were just a whisper away and as he watched, they parted. Was that an invitation? Did she want him to kiss her? What would happen if he did? What would happen if he didn't?

And who the hell cared? He'd done his best to be the Lone Ranger, but he was all out of silver bullets. Without further hesitation, he bent and captured her mouth, pulling out all the stops and unleashing the severe self-restraint he'd been exercising. If Jessie wanted platonic, she shouldn't have looked at him like that. And she definitely should not have wrapped her arms around his neck, as if she wanted to hold him close, as if she didn't want the kiss to end.

Kale groaned against her lips and shifted position to pull her into his embrace. He ached in every nook and cranny of his body. Desire rose in him with the force of a hot-air balloon catching the wind and rising, rising. This was not in the script, he thought. Not the wisest course he could follow. But, oh, Jessie tasted good. He slid a little farther down on the mattress to gain greater access to the flowering kiss.

Jessie, pinned by the bedcovers and the contours of Kale's body, lay quietly while wild sensations raced through her body. She felt sensuous and wicked, as if she knew a thousand and one ways to seduce a man, but had suddenly discovered one more. Kale's kiss was deep, his tongue teased hers, evoked curling tendrils of delight inside her. His hands splayed on her back, one up close to her shoulders, the other down close to the hollow of her spine. Her palms pressed against this chest, her fingers nudged at the cotton fabric of his shirt.

She was going to regret this. She regretted it already. For the past couple of days, her better judgment had been tossing out warnings like life preservers. And she, drowning in a sea of illogical emotion, ignored the life rafts and swam straight for the sharks. Not that she considered Kale a shark.

He was too gentle, his touch too tender, his body too warm against hers. And she was in love.

It was crazy beyond any stunt Gretchen had ever pulled; as irresponsible as any action ever taken by a Day family member. Jessie didn't know why her heart had chosen Kale, but there it was. With resignation and a wealth of satisfaction, she moved her hands around his neck and pulled him closer.

Kale became aware of a change in Jessie. Even with the covers pulled taut and restrictive between them, he felt a new intensity in her response. What was happening here? What was happening to him? How did Jessie get him into these situations? If things had gone according to his plan, she'd be asleep on her side of the bed and he'd be on his side of the bed, patting himself on the back for his restraint. She hadn't wanted to share a room with him, much less a bed. She'd been nervous and uptight—feelings he could identify with—and so, he'd promised himself nothing would happen. She'd trusted him! He'd coerced her into coming on this chicken hunt and now that it was practically over, he was taking advantage of an unavoidable situation. And only the night before he'd been bragging about his principles.

Kale forced back his natural inclination to continue holding and kissing the woman in his arms. He established a small, but important, distance and promised himself that the next time he kissed Jessie, it would be something he wouldn't need to apologize for later. An apology was hardly appropriate at the moment, either, but he felt sure she would think of it tomorrow morning. He hoped there was a coffee maker somewhere nearby.

With a calming stroke of his fingertips across her brow, he kissed her cheek and struggled to come up with a smile. She looked into his eyes with a question and he almost . . . almost . . . kissed her again. Her lips blushed with the pressure his had bestowed. Her cheeks were tinted with the pale pink of awareness. Her eyes held a dark realization of the passion they had almost shared.

And Kale felt about as honorable as a lizard with half a tail. How the hell was he going to get out of this?

Chapter Twelve

"Oh, shoot! I forgot." Kale snapped his fingers. "I meant to call Grandad Joe and make sure CTA #43 is all right."

A quart of Freon couldn't have cooled Jessie any faster. She stared unblinkingly into his devastatingly blue eyes and told herself she should have expected something like this. A kiss. A kiss she considered to be beyond the ordinary. A kiss that made her forget all the reasons she should not have fallen for this man at this time. A kiss that in a matter of minutes would have led to something deeper, more intimate and satisfying.

A kiss that reminded him of a chicken.

"It's too late," she said. "He'll have been in bed for hours by now. And he doesn't know which chicken is yours anyway."

Kale frowned . . . a little desperately, Jessie thought.

"Oh," he said. "Well, I guess it can wait until tomorrow, then."

Yes, Jessie thought, it most certainly could. "I'm sure your chicken is fine. What could happen to her on Grandad's farm?"

"She might catch a poultry virus or be lovesick over Joe's fickle rooster."

"Don't be silly, Kale. She's better off there than in some cage in a laboratory laying eggs on demand."

"Do I hear a note of activism in your voice?" He propped his head on one hand and managed to establish an inch or so of important distance between his body and hers. Did he think she wouldn't notice?

Jessie refused to give him the satisfaction of knowing she not only noticed, but felt suddenly, incalculably chilled. "What you hear in my voice is weariness, Kale. It's late. I'm tired. Good night."

He held steady . . . smile and position . . . and she turned onto her side and presented him with a view of her motel-blanketed back. So much for being the hero, he thought. No wonder there wasn't a waiting line for the job. Jessie hadn't appreciated his efforts, his tremendous efforts, to save her from tomorrow's regrets. What had he accomplished by denying his true and aching desire to make love to her? Another sleepless night, that's what. It wasn't fair. Not after the way she'd kissed him.

"Good night," he muttered and rolled away from the memory and from close proximity to her tempting lips. He would lie still if it strangled him. She wasn't going to know the restless disappointment that coursed through him with each heartbeat. She wasn't going to guess the regrets multiplying in his head with every breath he took.

He tried to distract his thoughts from Jessie with complicated theorems and experiments. But the only image to stay in his mind for more than a few seconds was the image of Jessie; talking to her sister; talking with him; standing in the never-never land between motel bed and motel bath, wearing that too-big, but sexy sleep shirt, honeyed hair tousled and enchanting, her expression . . . He dozed off trying to figure out the emotions behind her expression.

As the sound of his breathing grew steady and even, Jessie's anger gave way to wounded pride and then to genuine hurt. This was not a night she would write about in her diary. The femme fatale had fallen flat on her face in the sheets. And it sounded so easy when her friends talked about it. Be honest, they'd advise. If you want to go to bed with a guy, say so. The odds of rejection are slim, they'd said. Take a chance.

Yeah, well, what did her friends know? She hadn't said she wanted to sleep with Kale, but how he could have misinterpreted her actions? Even she wouldn't have fallen for the line about there being only one room with one bed in the whole town. She'd initiated the setup, so why hadn't he followed through with a bit of initiative of his own?

Jessie masked a sigh and rolled a bit closer to the edge of the mattress. It wasn't even as if he'd given her an out-and-out rejection, either. He'd simply stopped kissing her and thought about his chicken. Or had he thought about the chicken and then stopped kissing her? Which came first—the chicken or the thought? And who really cared? The result was the same. She was on her side of the bed, he on his, and the mattress between them might as well have been the length of ten football fields.

As she lay in silent misery, listening to the in and out rhythm of Kale's breathing, she comforted her aching vanity with the knowledge that at least she'd saved the price of an extra room.

From that dismal thought, Jessie went to laying blame and Gretchen became a handy and deserving target. If Gretchen hadn't befriended Pancho; if Gretchen hadn't encouraged him to rescue any and all animals; if Gretchen hadn't run off to Seattle and then to Oregon...

A full-blown sigh escaped. If only Gretchen hadn't given her this nerdy sleep shirt...

JESSIE AWAKENED to the sound of Kale's voice and a heaviness of body and spirit. She glanced over her shoulder in time to see him replace the phone receiver and give her a smile.

"Good morning," he said.

She pulled the pillow over her head to muffle the too-loud, too-cheerful, and disgustingly rested tones. The mattress tilted as he leaned across and lifted one corner of her protective cover. "Rise and shine." His breath tickled a warm place close to her ear. "We're going home, Jessie. *H-o-m-e*. I was just making the reservations. We'll catch a flight out of Portland about noon, but we'll have to hurry to make it. We've got a couple of hours of driving to do. Oh, and you can congratulate me, I'm a grandfather this morning. I called my office and was told the first incubator of chicks hatched last night. Jennifer's chicks."

"Congratulations." Jessie grabbed for the corner of the pillow and repositioned her head under it. "Now, go away, Gramps."

He patted her on the back. "What you need is a cup of coffee. Maybe two cups. I'll go to the office and see what I can find."

Jessie needed sleep, not coffee, but she didn't want to talk to him, either. So she stayed where she was until she heard the door close. Then, with an effort, she ducked out from under the covers and blinked into the smiling eyes of Kale Warner.

"Good morning, bright eyes," he said. "Good to see you moving around."

She pushed a tawny lock of hair from her face. "I thought you went to find some coffee."

"I forgot to pick up the room key. Were you waiting for me to leave before getting up?"

Jessie had no answer. Her mind felt thick and fuzzy. In fact, now that she thought about it, she pretty much felt that way all over. "Yes," she said, and hoped that was the answer that would get him out of the room for a while.

"Okay, then. I'm on my way. Can you be ready to leave in thirty minutes?"

Jessie slid into a sitting position and massaged her temples. She would be ready if it killed her... and at the moment, that seemed like a distinct possibility. "I'll be ready."

"Good, so will I." He walked to the chest, picked up the room key and dropped it into his pocket. "Hang in there. I'll be back with caffeine before you know it."

This time, Jessie watched the door close to make sure he was really gone. Then she headed for the bathroom and a cold shower. She needed something to open her eyes.

By the time Kale placed the hot paper cup in her hand, she felt better. Not great, but considering her night had been filled with intermittent flurries of wide-eyed wakefulness and pointless mental conversations punctuated by short periods of restless dozing, it was not surprising that she wasn't feeling up to par. After a two and a half hour flight, she'd probably sleep for days. Unless of course, Kale kept her awake.

But once they reached Tulsa, she'd drive him out to Grandad Joe's to get his car. Then Kale would go on to Fayetteville to see his baby chicks and that would be the end of that. She sipped the coffee and told herself she'd be better off when he was out of her life. She'd come to her senses then; forget this love nonsense. It had to be a bad case of infatuation anyway brought on by a strong physical attraction.

He lifted his bag and hers and started for the door with an easy gait and a sensual swing to his hips. Definitely a physical attraction, she thought. Still, once he was in his laboratory, he'd forget about her and she would forget about him. It wasn't meant to be. That's all.

"Are you all right?" Kale stopped by the door. He'd been unusually quiet since returning with the two cups of coffee. And he kept looking at her. Her khaki slacks and turquoise sweater were nothing to be ashamed of, but they didn't exactly inspire instant respect, either. Her hair was damp from the shower, but it wasn't doing anything spectacular. Makeup. Kale must be noticing the imperfections of her face without makeup. Funny, though, she hadn't thought he would notice...

"Jessie?" He set down the bags and came to sit beside her on the bed. "Are you all right?"

"Fine." She returned the cup to her lips and swallowed the last of the strong coffee. "I'm fine and ready to go." She tossed the cup into the trash and glanced at her watch. "Only fifteen minutes late, too."

"And counting." His smile lacked the full-blown cheerfulness of earlier. "You seem...preoccupied about something."

She summoned a brighter look. "No, no. Everything is fine. Or will be when we get home."

"I thought you might be anxious to get back."

"Not as anxious as you, I'm sure. I don't have baby chickens waiting for me."

"It will be a while before these chicks will be of much use to me, but they're the next step on the genetic ladder. I can't wait to see if Jennifer passed on her valuable hereditary traits." Kale's eyes never left Jessie's as he spoke and she began to feel restless, uneasy.

"We'd better shake the dust of the Sea Star Inn from our feet, then. I wouldn't want to keep science waiting." She started to rise, but he put a hand on her arm and she stopped cold.

"When I was getting the coffee, I heard the desk clerk reporting to a supervisor. He said there were seven vacancies last night."

Jessie swallowed. Could this possibly get any more embarrassing? "What? But he told me—"

"Why did he tell you there were no vacancies, Jessie, when there were?"

The jig was up. She might as well confess with whatever grace she could muster. "Okay. I asked for two single adjoining rooms and all he had was one room here and one room clear across the parking lot and I... well, I took this one, instead." There she'd told him. It was too late, but she'd been honest. He could make what he wanted of it.

Kale stared at her for one excruciatingly long minute before he put his head in his hands. *"Heigh Ho, Silver. Away,"* he said.

Jessie didn't know whether to run for cover or pull the pillow back over her head. So she sat and waited, wondering if he would say something about Chicken Little and Turkey Lurkey next.

When he lifted his gaze again, Jessie saw new purpose there... and he was starting to smile. He had no right to look like that and make her feel like this. "Look, Kale, let's just forget about the Sea Star Inn and go to Portland. I think this vacation peaked somewhere outside of Seattle."

"Oh, I don't know." He gathered her into his arms with such precision that it could have been a scientific experiment. But there was nothing scientific about the way he reached for her hands and placed them around his neck. And there was nothing technical about the possessive way he bent to capture her lips. And there was certainly nothing technical or scientific about the response that sprang up inside of her like a scolded puppy suddenly returned to its master's good graces.

Jessie savored the kiss, didn't even think of resistance, and developed a serious weakness of character when his lips moved in slow, tantalizing nibbles from one corner of her mouth to the other. His tongue followed the path his lips had made, gliding lightly over the full inner curves, never quite pushing past the entrance.

Then on one supple move, he took her mouth in a complete and soul-stealing kiss and somehow—though Jessie didn't remember falling—they were lying side by side, chest to breast, on the bed. True, her feet were still touching the floor. She thought his probably were, too. But that was merely a technicality... at the moment she hardly knew she had feet. Her pulse thrummed with a fevered desire. She felt hot, cold, hot again. The hands, her hands, nestled in at the back of his neck. She hadn't intended to do that, but the feel of his dark hair around her fingers was sensual delight. She even dared to let her hands drift down, just inside his shirt collar, and stroke the muscles of his back.

Jessie didn't want to seem overimpressed with this after-the-opportunity effort. But it was difficult not to be impressed as his hands massaged the length of her spine with the same sentient pleasure with which he manipulated her lips. Spools of wonder curled tightly inside her and then began to spin slowly into myriad circlets of anticipation.

She would not give him the satisfaction, or herself the complication of anticipating anything more. Determined as her mind was to be logical, though, her body acted like a private contractor and kept right on anticipating. More of his touch, more of his kiss, more... more...

When Kale removed temptation and sat up, Jessie was breathing hard and felt flushed. She lay, exhausted and energized and wanting, and wondered why he'd come alive now... at the least opportune moment of their whole vacation. She tensed when his hand rested lightly, and oh so tantalizingly, on her stomach.

"I just wanted you to know, Jessie, that I'm not always so slow on the uptake. Now, let's get this stuff in the car and hit the road."

With one long, shuddery sigh, Jessie pulled herself out of her inertia and onto the edge of the bed. "Whatever you say, Kemosabe."

"How about two aspirin and a soda?" Kale asked as their connecting flight waited for takeoff clearance from the Denver Airport. "Or maybe they'll have some cans of soup on board. I'll ring for the attendant and—"

Jessie caught his finger before it reached the call switch. "I'm fine, Kale. I don't want aspirin or soda or an angry flight attendant. She's already told you she can't get anyone a drink until after takeoff. Now will you settle down?"

"You don't look fine and you don't sound fine." He'd developed this protective attitude after they'd left the motel, and if Jessie had felt better she'd have nipped it in the bud. But the truth was, she felt awful. Even the hairs on her head ached and she'd started sneezing just outside of Portland. Kale had stopped at a drugstore and emerged with a sackful of remedies . . . none of which were able to do more than soften the outward symptoms. Consequently she was groggy, her mouth tasted like the residue in a two-day-old coffee cup, and the only thing she cared about was getting home to a familiar bed.

"I'll just ask one of the attendants for some more aspirin." Kale patted Jessie's arms and started to unbuckle his seat belt. "I have time before the plane—"

"No," Jessie said as firmly as she was able. "You don't have time and besides, if you keep giving me stuff I'm going to get sick."

"You're already sick. That's why I'm giving you stuff."

"Yes, well, stop it, okay? If I'm going to die, I at least want to be semiconscious."

"So you admit it. You are sick."

Why he found some perverse satisfaction in making her acknowledge the beginning of a cold, she didn't know. But he'd been pestering her for miles now. *You're sick,* he'd said as they'd left the motel. *I think you're coming down with something,* he'd said five miles out of Tillamook. *Have you had your flu shot?* he'd asked in Portland. Jessie had denied each allegation with grace and patience. She didn't like to be sick and worse, she didn't like to be fussed over when she was. Still, it was nice of him to ask; nice of him to be solicitous; nice of him to buy her a thousand and three sure cures. Now, if she could just persuade him it would be nice if he'd shut up.

"I'm fine," she said one more time. "But I think I'll try to nap as soon as we're airborne."

"I'll get you a pillow."

Jessie's hand on his arm stopped him from getting up again. "Please, Kale. Let me do this my way. I've been getting my own pillows for years now. I can take care of myself."

"You told me you wanted to find someone to take care of you," he pointed out in self-defense. "I'm only trying to take care of a few details for you while you're not feeling well."

A faint smile graced her lips. "Thank you, Kale. I appreciate it, really. But I'm all right. You can work on your research theory—or whatever it is you're working on—and I'll take a nap." She hoped he'd take the suggestion and leave her in peace during the flight, but she didn't like the annoyed expression that deepened the blue of his eyes to indigo.

"All right, Miss Martyr. You handle it." With that, he put his head back against the upright seat, crossed his arms at his chest and closed his eyes . . . ready for takeoff.

Now why was he upset? Jessie turned her aching head toward the window. This was really the last straw. She'd only wanted him to stop fussing, stop being so darned . . .

You said you wanted someone to take care of you.

Kale's words throbbed through her thoughts with a dismal, repetitive rhythm. She had said that . . . many times. She meant it, too. So why did it bother her that he was trying to take care of her now? Since they'd left the Sea Star Inn, he'd been kind and solicitous. In fact, she couldn't recall him being anything else since they'd met, unless she counted that first, unfortunate encounter at Dakota Jack's when he'd acted like a lunatic. Kale certainly had made an effort to ensure her comfort and well-being on this trip, despite the singleness of purpose that made him forget details like credit cards and umbrellas. So why did all his efforts make her uncomfortable?

She ought to be enjoying this. Maybe it was just that his concern came a bit too late. She couldn't help thinking it might be his way of soothing his conscience before he left her in Tulsa and went back to his life on the other side of the state border. That was a depressing thought. Jessie massaged her forehead with pushy fingers, but the realization that she and Kale would soon separate for good would not go away.

The plane vibrated as the engines revved in preparation for takeoff. Beside her, Kale didn't move a muscle. He might have been asleep for all the concern he exhibited now. Jessie sighed. She was too miserable to be happy about anything at the moment, she decided. If she'd felt better, Kale could have taken care of her to his heart's content. But she was sick and she just didn't want to be fussed over.

"GOD BLESS YOU." Kale figured he'd called for consecration of Jessie's sneezes enough times now to be nominated for sainthood. And if the invocations weren't enough, his patience during the past four hours ought to have put him over the top.

Jessie *was* sick. Her eyes were red and watery; she'd gone through a handkerchief and at least a hundred tissues on the flight home; sneezes burst from her every ten minutes, as regular as Old Faithful; her face was flushed and hot. He knew she had a fever. But would she admit she was anything but "okay"? Oh, no, not Jessie...woman of steel.

"Let me fix you some coffee before you leave," she said when they'd been at her apartment approximately five minutes. "It won't take—" A sneeze stopped her right on schedule.

Kale took her by the shoulders and steered her toward the bedroom. "You're not fixing anything for anybody, Jessica Day. You are going straight to bed. Do not pass Go. Do not collect two hundred dollars."

"Don't be silly, Kale. I'm—" Another sneeze.

He stuffed a tissue into her hand. "Where's the thermostat? It's freezing in here."

"It's in the hall, but don't turn it up too high. Sixty-eight will be warm enough."

"I can handle a thermostat, Jessie. I'm good with temperatures. Now while I take care of that, you take care of getting yourself in that bed."

"I'll go to bed after you leave, Kale. At least let me say goodbye."

"I can let myself out, Jess. Get into bed." Turning on his heel, Kale went in search of the thermostat and switched it to a warm seventy-two degrees. What a stubborn woman Jessie was. She denied she was sick; denied she needed assistance; denied that she wanted him to stay.

"Did you find—?" Her sneeze punctuated the question and Kale shook his head. She was going to take some of that medicine if it killed both of them.

He came back to the bedroom doorway. She sat on the edge of the bed, looking about as healthy as a water lily in a drought. When she noticed him, she wiped her nose, tossed away the tissue and pushed lackluster strands of golden hair behind her ear. "Oh, I hear the heater. You must have found the thermostat."

"Yes. It was right on the wall. Easy to see." He stood his ground and remembered a few nights before when he'd stood in this room watching her sleep. His memory supplied a ready image of how the room had looked in darkness, how Jessie had looked in sleep. "I see you need some help getting into bed." He stepped toward the dresser. "Where do you keep your nightshirts?"

"There's no reason for you—"

He pulled out the top drawer—intimate apparel but no gowns. He reached for the next drawer down.

"Kale, quit that. You can't go through my chest of drawers. I can find my own nightshirt."

He continued looking and finally found the sleepwear department. "Here we go. Which one, Jess? This blue thing or the pink..." His voice trailed into a pointed silence as he held up a sheer pink teddy that almost made him lose his balance. He hadn't expected this. Not after the brother-sister screen-print she'd worn to bed the night before. Was this why Anthony had never seen that nightshirt? Lord, he hoped not. Kale stuffed it back into the drawer and pulled out the blue satin nightgown instead. It was every bit as feminine as the pink teddy, but a little easier on the male libido. "Here." He tossed it onto the bed. "Put that on while I fix you a hot toddy."

"Are you trying to be my mother?" Jessie asked with a sniff. "Because if you are, I'll tell you right now that my mother would let me take care of myself. She would not be throwing out orders like some bossy nurse with more bedpans than aspirin."

"I'm bringing some aspirin with me when I come back. And if you need a bedpan, I can probably find—"

"That was just a figure of speech, Kale." She paused for a sneeze. "I'm just trying to tell you that I don't need all this attention."

He moved to stand in front of her and then went down on his knees to be at her eye level. "Jessie, make up your mind. One minute you're telling me about how you want someone else to take care of the details in your life and the next minute, you're telling me you don't need my assistance. Now, maybe you'd prefer to have Anthony fussing over you right now. But Anthony isn't here. I am. So, unless you want me to take care of every little detail of undressing you and tucking you into the bed, I'd advise you to do it yourself.''

She stared at him in a sort of feverish trance, eyebrows arched in a puzzled expression. "Anthony?" she whispered. "What has Anthony—?''

Kale reached for the bottom of her sweater and Jessie pulled back. "I'll do it," she said. "I'll be in bed when you get back.''

With a nod, Kale forced his fingers away from her sweater and rose. "See that you are." Feeling a little like the bossy nurse she'd accused him of being, he started for the door.

"Kale?''

He looked back.

"Where are you going?''

"To the kitchen.''

"Oh." She picked up the blue nightgown and ran her thumb over the lace edging. "You're not leaving?''

"I'm not leaving.''

"Oh." She raised her gaze and, even through the watery misery, he could see gratitude in her eyes. "I'd better hurry then, hadn't I?''

He smiled and left the room, feeling a little less like the hated Sergeant Nurse and a little more like Dr. Kildare.

JESSIE AWAKENED to the sounds of hen scratching and blinked two or three times to clear her head. Sunshine filtered through the apartment window, across the foot of the bed, and across Kale's stockinged feet. With a narrowed gaze, she traced a path from those feet upward to the head of the bed to where Kale sat propped with a pen and a notepad. He looked serious and studious, with his glasses jammed into the thick, dark hair on top of his head. His forehead and mouth were pursed in duplicate lines of concentration as he wrote on the pad balanced in his left hand. A ribbon of warm affection curled through Jessie.

"Wouldn't it be easier to write at the table?" Her voice rasped out in a reedy whisper.

"You're talking in your sleep, Jessie." He continued writing, without looking up.

"I'm not asleep," she said a bit louder.

"Well, go back to sleep then." His pen scratched against the paper for a full minute before he stopped and glanced cautiously at her side of the bed. "Jessie? Are you talking to me?"

"There isn't anyone else in this bed, is there?"

He laid the pad on his outstretched legs. "Should you be awake yet? You're sick."

"I feel better . . . I think." She bunched the pillow under her head and ran a quick inventory of aches and pains. Relatively few. And the stuffed-like-a-featherbed feeling in her head seemed to have passed. "Yes," she said. "I'm much better."

"I'm glad." He smiled, his lips curving in a semi-shy, semi-daring lift. "Think how embarrassed I'd be if you were feeling worse."

A newborn laugh trickled past Jessie's lips. "Embarrassed? Why would you be embarrassed?"

He placed his palm on her forehead, frowned, then placed two of his fingers against the pulse at the base of her neck. A warm sensation pooled beneath his touch and seeped down toward the pit of her stomach. "I've been your doctor and life-support team during the past two days," Kale said. "I'd probably lose my AMA standing if you hadn't gotten better."

"You're not a doctor," Jessie said as she yawned and fought a tempting urge to go back to sleep.

"I beg your pardon. My students don't call me Dr. Warner for no reason."

"All right, you're a professor and, if we stretched a point, you might be called a chicken doctor. Neither title qualifies you to treat humans."

"Thank you very much, Miss Day. You won't be so sure of that when you receive my bill for services rendered."

The sleepy feeling dribbled away. "Services rendered" had such a nebulous sound to it. "What exactly were the, uh, services you rendered, Doctor?"

His smile was pure sunshine. "You'll receive an itemized statement—"

A funny noise broke through his teasing and Jessie tried to place the sound. It was muffled and had all the resonance of a trombone stuffed with cotton. She watched as Kale rolled to the edge of the bed, reached underneath and extracted a pudgy, misshapen pillow. He unwrapped it carefully and the telephone emerged . . . from the fluffy lining of Anthony's robe.

"Hello," Kale spoke softly, as if she were still asleep. He paused and then turned to look at her, before he nodded. "Yes, yes, she is. I don't know. It's hard to tell with a rhinovirus. I'm not sure when she'll be over the infectious stage. It could be another week. It might even last the rest of the year."

Jessie propped her head on the palm of her hand and gave him her most serious regard. What was he up to?

"Yes, well, thanks for calling. Of course, I'll tell Jessie you were concerned . . . just as soon as she's lucid, again." Kale replaced the receiver and rewrapped the phone.

Once he'd tucked it back under the bed, Jessie tapped him on the arm. "What were you doing just now?"

"Muffling the phone so it wouldn't bother you. I've been getting a few calls from the university— I called in the day we arrived and I've received a couple of calls a day since. I didn't want it to disturb your rest, so I wrapped it.''

"In Anthony's robe."

"Your robe wasn't heavy enough and I didn't bring my robe with me. His was handy and so...."

Jessie sighed and laid her head on the pillow again. "Who was on the phone just now?"

"Anthony, your true-blue next-door neighbor. He's called to inquire about you a time or two."

"He hasn't been over? That's unusual for Anthony."

"Well, I did tell him you were quarantined. I just didn't think you should have visitors, Jessie."

"Thank you, Kale, but it's just a cold. And now that I've slept for a few hours, I feel a hundred percent better."

"I'll bet you do. Almost anyone would feel better after a thirty-hour nap."

"Thirty—?" Jessie rolled onto her back so she could see him better. There was something very comfortable about being in this bed with Kale ... even if he was on top of the covers while she was beneath them. "I haven't been asleep for thirty hours, Kale. Anthony may believe all that nonsense about rhinoviruses and talking in my sleep, but I'm not so easily fooled."

Kale picked up his pen. "I didn't tell Anthony that you talk in your sleep."

"Because that would be a lie. I don't."

"Yes, you do. What do you think I've been writing on this notepad?" He flipped it up and held it out of her reach ... if she'd been inclined to reach for it, which she wasn't.

"Chicken scratchings."

"Maybe. Maybe not." He tossed the pad to the floor and straightened the covers across her shoulders. "Your mother called yesterday. She invited me for Thanksgiving dinner."

"Did she ask you to bring the turkey?" Jessie's hand flew to cover her mouth. "Oh, I'm sorry. That was a tasteless thing to say. I mean, that's about as bad as asking you to bring a box of Colonel Sander's best, isn't it?"

Kale merely arched an eyebrow. "I believe you are feeling better, Jessie. Actually your mother only asked me to bring you. I told her you'd been sick and she said to tell you to drink lots of liquids and she'd see you in a couple of weeks."

Jessie nodded and tried not to dwell on the appealing curve of his jaw, or on the muscular shoulder only a few inches away from her head. She was becoming increasingly aware of his nearness and of the intimacy of the bedroom, which could only mean she was definitely feeling better. "I can't believe I slept through Mom's phone call and the calls from your office."

"You slept through those and a half dozen more calls, Jessie."

"Oh, stop teasing. You're making that up."

"I'm not. Your mother called; Anthony's called a few times; your brother called to find out if you wanted a puppy for Christmas; someone from your office called about a special order; your mother called again . . . by mistake, and your sister called last night."

"Gretchen? What did she want?"

He made an unsuccessful attempt to look modest. "She wanted to know if you and I are a 'couple,' I think. She might have just wanted to talk about me."

Jessie shook her head. "I don't believe you."

"She called collect."

That part sounded plausible. "I really slept that long?"

Kale reached over and tapped her on the nose. "You did wake up every once in a while."

"I don't remember any of that."

"You don't remember how I spoon-fed you? You don't remember all the times I placed cool compresses on your head to break the fever? You don't remember how you begged me to crawl into bed with you and keep you warm?"

He'd been on a roll there for a minute, but Jessie leveled him with a look. "Dr. Warner, you are either a compulsive liar or you're developing some incredible fantasies. Even in delirium, I would not beg any man to get in bed with me."

"So how did I end up here?" Kale made a sweeping gesture, encompassing his stockinged feet and long length of leg as well as the rest of him. "You don't think I'm working in here by choice, do you?"

"Yes," Jessie said. "I do. What I can't figure out is why you're not working at your lab in Fayetteville?"

Kale smiled and shrugged. "It's a long walk."

Walk. Of course. Kale didn't have a car. He'd ridden from Grandad Joe's in Jessie's car. Her spirits deflated like a chiffon cake after a thunderous door slam. A sneeze caught her unaware and was followed by a second and then a third. "Excuse me," she said.

"God bless you." Kale rolled off the bed and came around to her side. He sat on the edge of the mattress and fussed with the covers. "You'd better quit talking so much and go back to sleep. It's time for another Nas-O pill, anyway. I'll get it."

"Nas-O?" Jessie wrinkled her nose in disgust. "I don't want anything called Nas-O."

"It's worked wonders for you so far and that's not really the name of the cold capsule. That's just what I call it. And it won't take a minute to get you one."

"Kale, would you stop? I've slept long enough. My cold is almost gone and—"

He put a finger against her lips. "Don't argue with the doctor. And you had the flu, not just a cold."

Jessie decided it wasn't a point worth arguing. And she was beginning to feel drowsy, again. "How about a compromise, Doc? Food instead of a cold capsule. It can't be good to take a pill on an empty stomach."

He smoothed the sheets that lay across her breasts and Jessie experienced a heat wave that had nothing to do with flu or fever and everything to do with the brush of Kale's fingers across her skin. "I'll fix you some soup," he said, his gaze slowly lifting to meet hers. "Vegetable soup. We'll talk about the pill after you've eaten."

"It's a deal. And I didn't even have to mention malpractice."

Kale scoffed lightly and finished adjusting the gray-blue blanket around her. "I wanted to tell you, Jessie, that I like these sheets. They remind me of you."

She glanced down at the abstract designs of the gray-blue linens. "This was my first design and it's still my favorite. It's called Day Dreamer."

His lips tipped at the corners. "My grandmother used to tell me that 'A dream grants what one covets when awake.' What do you dream about when you're asleep on these sheets, Jessica?"

How was she supposed to answer that? Tell him that lately, awake or asleep, no matter what sheets she was on, she dreamed of him? Stupid. Especially since he dreamed of lower-cholesterol chicken eggs. The only reason he was here with her now, was that he didn't have a way to get home without her car. Admit she dreamed of him? No way. "I dream about vegetable soup," she said. "Bowls of steamy vegetable soup."

Disappointment flickered in his eyes but he leaned forward and planted a chaste kiss on her forehead. "You're sicker than I thought. But I'm on my way now to make your dreams come true. Prince Charming has nothing on me."

And with that, he left her with her sheets and a box of tissues and a nagging daydream.

Chapter Thirteen

Despite her protests, Jessie took another cold capsule. Kale
was as insistent on that as he was that she eat every bite of
her vegetable soup. She found his concern overbearing, but
touching nonetheless and she pondered this new side of Kale
Warner as she drifted back to sleep.

She awakened before dawn feeling well and as grungy as
if she'd been ill for a week instead of just a couple of days.
Kale was not beside her in bed and, for the first time since
she'd been sick, he wasn't in the room, either. She found
him asleep in the living room, sitting in the big armchair
with his feet propped on the hassock and a spattering of
papers drifting from his lap to the floor. He wore a navy
sweat suit that Jessie vaguely recalled as belonging to Anthony. The sleeves were too short for Kale and the pants
rode above his ankles, revealing an inch of hairy calves. His
hair was tousled, as if he'd run his fingers through it time
after time before falling asleep.

A rush of emotion caught Jessie by surprise. What was it
about this man that tied her in knots? She'd been so sure of
the type of relationship she wanted, the kind of man who
would give it to her. Kale was not that man and this was not
that relationship, but here she was in love with him just the
same. Was it possible that what she'd always believed she
wanted was not, in reality, what she needed? Was there any

way she could rearrange her daydreams to encompass and nurture the love she felt for Kale?

She wasn't sure, but she recognized the physical ache in her body and knew, at that moment, none of the hypothetical questions made a hill of beans amount of difference. Right now she wanted to be in Kale's arms, to experience the feel of his lovemaking, to taste the passion she expected to find in his embrace.

He slept, unaware of her presence and her thoughts. Finally Jessie turned away with a sigh. She'd take a shower, scrub away the grungies and this crazy impulse to lure Kale into her bed. And if the shower didn't work...

Jessie decided she'd deal with that problem when it arose.

It didn't go away. She scrubbed every inch of her body, from the top of her head to her toes and thought how nice it would be to shower with Kale. By the time she'd roughly toweled herself dry, she'd decided to refuse to listen to further protest. She thought about putting on the pink teddy, but decided against it and slipped into a chenille robe. She was going to make another attempt at seduction, true, but she saw no reason to be totally obvious. She did still have some pride.

Pride deserted her, though, when she stood beside the chair where he slept. Desire took its place in aching waves. Jessie was surprised at herself. It was morning, after all. Early, early morning at that. Not the all-time best opportunity for seduction, but her body didn't seem to recognize that as a hindrance. This might be her last opportunity with Kale. Before the day was out, he'd want to be on his way to Arkansas. Before the day was out, he might be out of her life for good.

All the more reason not to pursue this further, her conscience reminded.

Jessie might have listened, too, if only Kale hadn't opened his eyes then... and smiled.

"Hi. What are you doing up?" He yawned and glanced at his watch. "It's only a little after three."

"I guess I'm through sleeping."

"Then I guess I am, too." He shifted to a more upright position in the chair, putting his feet on the floor and giving his arms a little sensuous kind of stretch. "Your hair's wet."

"I took a shower."

He nodded as he made a visual inspection from her damp, bare toes to the top of her wet head. "You'll probably catch something else if you don't put some clothes on and dry your hair."

Jessie smiled slightly at his concern. "I'll be fine."

He gave another yawn and another partial stretch. "Then the question is, how do you feel?"

"Good...except for a little achiness."

"I think that's normal after a bout with the flu."

"It doesn't have anything to do with the flu, Kale."

He went still. "You probably ought to stay in bed today, just the same."

"Maybe I will."

"You probably shouldn't have gotten up at all."

"I was lonely."

Caution flickered in his eyes. "I came in here because I was afraid I'd disturb your sleep."

"I'm not sleeping anymore."

He paused, obviously casting about for other interpretations of the signals she was sending. "Want a Nas-O?" he asked.

"No, thank you."

He matched her gaze for several pulsing minutes before he offered another tentative suggestion. "Vegetable soup?"

"No."

"Jessie...? You've been sick."

"Been is the operative word, Kale." She shivered for effect and he was on his feet faster than a speeding bullet.

"Come on, I'll tuck you back into bed before you catch something else."

She decided not to mention that she was already caught and turned her attention to the ill-fitting sweat suit he wore. "Nice pj's," she said. "Has my neighbor been taking care of you, too?"

"What do you mean, 'too'? He still thinks you're out with the three-week plague. The man has an unhealthy fear of germs, but he did slide these sweats under the door. Actually he caught me downstairs in the laundry room wearing his robe and offered to let me borrow a few things."

Jessie nodded. "Anthony is a thoughtful guy."

"Especially when it comes to you." Kale touched her elbow as she stepped into the bedroom ahead of him. "If he offered to bring over homemade soup once, he must have offered twenty times."

Nervousness began to slow loop inside her and Jessie wondered what to do next. Could she hope that Kale might make this easier? "You should have let Anthony bring over the soup. He's a very good cook."

Kale jerked back the covers. "Eating chicken soup would have made you sicker and I told him so."

Jessie laughed restlessly and toyed with the sash tie of her fuzzy robe. She was not taking it off. If Kale wanted it— The atmosphere in the room went from friendly bantering to intense quiet in the space of a heartbeat. Jessie glanced up and saw that Kale had picked up the small foil packet of protection that lay beside the clock radio on her nightstand—right where she'd put it after her shower. Just in case.

She swallowed hard. Why were situations with Kale always so awkward? Why didn't seductions in real life happen as smoothly as they occurred in novels? With considerable effort, she made herself stand steady when he turned to look at her.

"Tell me Anthony did not leave this here."

"Anthony? Why would you think Anthony—? No, he had nothing to do with . . . with that."

Kale dropped the packet back on the table and advanced to the foot of the bed where she stood.

"I'm an intelligent person, Kale. A modern woman. I know how to protect myself." Jessie continued talking, saying anything to calm the fluttery beating of her heart. "Gretchen gave them to me. She's a real nuisance about that kind of thing."

Kale's hands went to Jessie's shoulders and her heart threatened to pound right out of her chest. "Remind me to thank her." He drew Jessie into a long and infinitely promising kiss. Then he turned her toward the bed and placed his lips lightly on the slope of her neck before releasing her. "Hold my place," he said. "I'll be back in a couple of minutes."

Great. Jessie's pounding heart slowed to a confused thud and she sank onto the edge of the bed. She had never met a man who could get her going so fast and leave her with no place to go a second later. This was not going to work. In the couple of minutes he was gone, he'd probably remember something about his research and forget all about seduction and her. Another chicken hypothesis would sidetrack Kale and she'd be left to wonder where she'd gone wrong this time.

After an eternity of waiting, probably about eight minutes tops, she felt the mattress give as he leaned toward her from the other side. She felt his fingers brush her nape, just inside the collar of her robe. She felt him lift the honeyed weight of her still-damp hair; felt the warm, moist promise of his lips at the hollows of her shoulder; felt the cool smoothness of his freshly shaven chin. She felt—fine. Oh, Lord, but she felt fine.

"Jessie?" His whisper blew gently against her ear, creating a new, enticing ache low in her stomach.

She tilted her head to one side to allow him greater access to her neck and shoulders. "Kale, if you say the word, chicken, I'm going to do something unladylike."

"Really?" he murmured against her skin just before he traced a sensual path with his tongue from her earlobe to her nape. "I wasn't going to say anything about chick—" He broke off the words and retraced the path along her neck from the opposite direction. "I was going to ask if you're sure you feel all right."

That would be the understatement of all time. Jessie shivered beneath the touch of his lips. "All right" didn't begin to describe the way she felt. "Yes," she said simply. "Yes."

His sigh shuddered past her temple and he pulled her back to lie across the bed. Jessie shied away from meeting his gaze until he stroked his fingertips across her throat and tipped up her chin. She tried for a nonchalant look and failed miserably. This was not casual sex. This was not even a moment of pleasure between consenting adults. She was in love with this man, as crazy as it seemed, and Jessie couldn't remember being in love before. At least, she couldn't remember feeling this hot, aching need that now consumed her.

"It's so early," she whispered as if that fact had some significance.

Kale's smile was slow and tantalizing as he stripped off his sweatshirt and tossed it aside. She had little time to observe the muscles of his chest and shoulders and arms before he'd stretched out beside her. His breath, warm and minty fresh, caressed her cheek. His fingers left her chin to trail downward to where the lapels of her robe crossed. Jessie trembled with the seductive warmth of his hand so near, yet not quite touching, her breast. She longed for him to undo the sash of her robe. She was anxious for more intimacy, for more knowledge of him and for him to have more knowledge of her. But she didn't want him to rush, either. It had taken a long time to get Kale in the mood. She wanted to savor every minute.

He bent his head to kiss the point where her skin met the folds of the robe, then as if he had to find out what lay beneath, he parted the material and slid his hand inside.

"You aren't wearing anything under this, Jessie."

"Premeditation seems to be the only way with you, Kale."

"Give me a chance. I'm only just getting started."

He proceeded to prove his point, untying the sash and laying open the robe. He began moving his hand in lingering circles over her bare stomach. Pinpricks of sensation spread over Jessie's skin; pleasure mingled with a needy ache. When he bent to take her lips in a long, steamy kiss, she couldn't choose between the pleasure and the aching need. They entwined inside her, becoming a flowing band of emotion, binding her to this moment, this man. The more he touched her, the more daring his caress became and the more she wanted to draw him into her arms, into herself, and hold him there.

But Kale didn't let her lure him into a quick consummation. They might have played a game of cat and mouse up until now, but he had changed the rules all of a sudden and become the seducer. She had little control and no desire to stop him. She was weak and yet, in surrender, she knew she wielded a mighty power. Kale wanted her . . . as much as she wanted him. She liked knowing that, even though the power it gave her would never be used. What would she do with it anyway? Demand a gentler seduction? If he were any more gentle, any more unhurried, she'd probably die of anticipation. Jessie couldn't believe he would have been any more careful with a new project in his laboratory than he was with her at this moment. He aroused her desire like an artist applying the master's touch to areas of her body Jessie hadn't known could be brought to such vivid life.

As he discovered her, she grew bolder and explored him with her hands and her mouth. Her fingertips found pleasure in massaging the hard-lined muscles of his upper arms and venturing into the whorls of fine dark hair that dusted his chest. Her lips located a spot just the other side of his collarbone that seemed to evoke a purring sound from him. Jessie liked that, liked knowing she could arouse him. She hoped...oh, how she hoped...he would remember this night two weeks from now. Even one week would do, she decided and made up her mind that, one way or another, she'd make sure he didn't forget too soon.

Kale fought for control through a maze of fevered sensations. He had to go slowly, had to show Jessie that he knew how to take care of her, please her, pleasure her. His instinct was to find satisfaction quickly, but intuition cautioned him to woo her with tender kisses and a thousand caresses. Not that he could count at the moment, but he could read her responses. He would know when she was ready to receive him and the love he longed to give her.

Her fingers at his chest, her lips on his skin pushed him to the edge of restraint and he had to discipline himself to the slow, steady rhythm of seduction. He felt Jessie tense as his mouth cradled her nipple in soft supplication. He drew his hand along the inside of her thigh, allowing his fingertips to flirt agonizingly close, then slide downward and away from temptation. She relaxed, then tensed again as he repeated the action, each time drawing nearer, lingering longer. He wanted her to want him. He didn't think he'd ever wanted anything quite so much. Jessie had invaded his senses the same way she'd invaded his life. One look, one kiss, and he was spinning, searching for reasons in a tumult of emotions over which he exercised no control.

"Kale..."

It was a sigh, a whisper, an entreaty, and like a low-burning flame suddenly turned up, his desire flared high and hot. And still, he took his time in getting back to her lips. Her cool, inviting, and devastatingly sweet lips. He found passion there, heavy and heady and he knew a need like none he'd experienced before. When her tongue curled daringly around his, coaxing a moan from his throat that matched the pleasured sounds she made, he was aware of an ache in his heart as intense as the ache in his groin.

He didn't know much about falling in love, but this had to be it. Then her hand slid down his stomach to loosen the drawstring of the sweatpants and rational thought fled before an influx of new sensations. He'd never believed Jessie would be so... imaginative.

A tremor of longing traced a sensual path down her spine, leaving Jessie hungry for relief. She kissed him with all the ardor and frustration he'd built into her during the past several days. She kissed him long and fully and lost her way in the flood of feelings he evoked when he returned her kiss.

Jessie realized suddenly what it meant to drown in a man's embrace. For she was drowning, grabbing for a life preserver, and finding Kale.

And when, at last, he moved to rid himself of his clothes and to put on the protection she'd provided, she was ready, willing to give to him all that he asked. More than he asked. If only he would ask...

He possessed her body with sure, even advances. He possessed her heart with savagely tender kisses and endearments whispered in throaty passion. Jessie, in turn, possessed the moment in all its splendid sweetness. She took from Kale and gave to Kale and loved him until she burst with the glory of it. Splinters of fire showered through her, leaving her hot, exhausted, and satiated with delight. She'd never experienced anything like it. From the way, Kale held her, she suspected he hadn't, either.

"Ohh." The sigh slipped from her lips and Kale picked it up.

"Oh?" he repeated.

She nestled her head against the curve of his shoulder. "Oh," she confirmed. "Just . . . ohh."

He pulled her close and she somehow knew he smiled. "I can live with that." He lay still for a moment. "But there is one thing that bothers me."

Please, Jessie thought. Keep your mind on me for a little while longer. Don't let it race off to the laboratory just yet. "What?" she asked.

"The next time we make love in your apartment, I want it to be my clothes on the floor, not—his."

"I can live with that." Jessie savored the relief she felt before it occurred to her to wonder what he was talking about. "His? You mean Anth—?"

Kale stopped the name with his hand before it could completely leave her lips. "Shh. If you say his name, he'll probably come right over with a bowl of chicken soup."

"I don't understand what Anth—he—has to do with your clothes being on the floor."

"Humor me, Jessica. The man has terrible taste…except when it comes to you."

She frowned in confusion and settled more deeply into Kale's arms. "The next time we make love in my apartment, you won't be wearing anything, so it won't make any difference whose clothes are on the floor, will it?"

Kale laughed softly in the early-morning darkness and rolled over to place a kiss on the slope of her breast. "I can live with that. As long as you're not wearing anything, either."

"Deal," she said on a sigh.

"Deal," he agreed and kissed her while they were both in naked agreement.

IT WAS MIDMORNING before Kale began to worry.

He couldn't determine how he felt about this new turn in his relationship with Jessie. From the first, he'd found her desirable, but he hadn't thought she felt the same way about him. And then, that night in the motel he'd maintained such strict control of his desires, only to discover she'd gotten the one room, one bed, on purpose. Then she'd gotten sick and he'd decided to demonstrate his caretaking capabilities.

Apparently he'd done all right . . . if his aim had been to get into her bed . . . which it hadn't been. But now that he was there, lying bare and momentarily sated, he worried that she might feel he'd taken advantage of her weakened condition. And he worried that their lovemaking might have been, for her, a way to reward him for his services while she'd been ill. He didn't like either idea, but he didn't quite know how to bring up the subject. If she hadn't thought he was taking advantage, he certainly didn't want to introduce the idea. And if she'd lured him into bed as a reward . . . Well, he didn't want to know.

At moments like this, Kale wished he knew less about the genetic makeup of chickens and more about the intricate workings of a woman's mind. Actually just to know what Jessie was thinking as she lay snuggled securely in his arms would give him some peace.

Or maybe it wouldn't.

Kale slowly released a sigh so as not to disturb her.

If this was love, it certainly didn't fit any equation he knew.

KALE'S CHEST rose with a sigh and Jessie began to worry. Was he regretting what had happened? Did he resent the way she'd lured him into her bed? Was he thinking about her at all? Or was his mind winging its way home even as he held her close?

That was the trouble with playing seductress. A woman could never be sure exactly why the man had succumbed. Sex for men was different. They didn't have to be emotionally involved. They didn't have to worry about the "whys" and "wherefores." They just seized the moment and, when it was over, they thought of other things.

Didn't they?

Why had she never thought to discuss this subject with her brother? Eric could have told her, given her some insight into the workings of a man's mind . . . before and after. Jessie frowned as her memory served up the time Eric had told her how he'd plotted an adventure comic book while spending the night with a girlfriend. Was Kale working on genetic equations while he lay so peacefully beside her? Was Jennifer, the leghorn hen, more real to him right now than she, Jessie, was?

It was a sobering thought and Jessie decided it was time to clamp down on fantasy and get on with life. If Kale was going to be around for the long haul, well, she would like that. And if he disappeared into the netherworld of science and study . . . ? Well, she could live with that.

She'd have to.

"Kale?" she whispered, testing the air with his name to see if he was awake.

"Hmm?"

Now that she knew he was awake she didn't know what to ask. "Kale? Are you . . . ?" No, Jessie thought, she couldn't ask if he was happy. That was too trite and showed too much insecurity on her part. "Are you . . . ready to get back to work?"

His hand moved sensuously along her bare arm. "I'm always working, Jessie, no matter where I am or what I'm doing."

Of course. He'd worked all the time she was sick. He'd probably plotted a whole experiment from hypothesis to conclusions while making love to her. Jessie felt a relapse coming on, but she fought off the heartsick feeling. "I guess I'd better get up then and drive you to Grandad's so you can get your car."

"I'm in no hurry...if you're not."

"Well, I do have a few days of vacation left. It would be nice to spend them with Grandad Joe."

"Are you sure you feel all right? It might be better if you stayed in bed today and finished recuperating."

She wasn't sure there was a cure for what was wrong with her, but she knew staying in bed...with Kale...would only worsen the symptoms. "I'll be fine. I can be ready to leave in an hour. Is that all right with you?"

"We don't have to hurry." His arm tightened around her, but Jessie resisted the urge to nestle closer. No point in prolonging the agony.

She wriggled out of his hold and scooted to the edge of the bed. "If we stay here much longer, Anthony will be back offering chicken soup and sweat suits. Let's go while the going's good."

Kale's sigh was deep and audible. "If you insist."

"I do," Jessie said firmly even though her heart wasn't in it. "We'll make it to the farm before dark."

"WE'RE NOT GOING to make it before dark," Kale said as they drove past Forth Smith. "It's another couple of hours on to Russellville."

"And thirty more minutes to Crow Mountain and the farm." Jessie floored the accelerator and sped into the passing lane and around a slow-moving livestock truck. "If you hadn't insisted on seeing my office at Day Dreams, we'd have gotten an earlier start."

Jessie was irritated about something and Kale had come to the conclusion that he was no match for her in her present mood. He'd kept his own counsel on the drive from Tulsa, but he was beginning to lose patience. She was acting as if this whole trip...not to mention his presence...was a terrible imposition and the only thing that kept him from telling her to let him out at the nearest town with a bus station was the knowledge that she had been ill and wasn't, as yet, back to normal. "I liked your office, Jessie. In fact, I was pretty impressed with the whole Day Dreams operation. I had no idea you were so talented."

"Thank you, Kale. I'll treasure that compliment."

Now what had he done? The cynicism in her voice was unmistakable. The reason for it was unfathomable. "I think I'll catch forty winks, unless you'd like for me to drive a while." He glanced at her, frowned at the stubborn set of her chin. "Maybe you need a rest."

"I'm doing fine," she said tightly. "Just fine. I'll have you in your station wagon and heading back to normal routine in no time. Okay with you?"

Kale didn't answer. He didn't really see the point.

"WHAT—?"

Jessie voice roused Kale from a dream of sunny smiles and warm laughter. She wasn't smiling now. Or laughing. She was slowing down as they approached the farmhouse and Kale blinked into a full-blown wakefulness. "What is it?" he asked.

"Look. The outside lights are on and Grandad's heading for the pickup." Jessie leaned forward. "Oh, Lord help us, he's got his shotgun."

"Tell him he doesn't have to shoot me. I'll do the honorable thing."

Jessie glared at Kale as she jerked the car to a running stop and reached for her door handle. "Will you wake up, Kale? This looks serious."

Serious about summed it up, Kale thought as he caught a glimpse of Joe Day's expression. It certainly looked like someone was going to get a seatful of buckshot. Kale got out of the car. "What's going on, Joe?"

"Damn chicken thieves!" Joe yanked on the pickup door. "They took my chickens and left the gate open. If my bull gets out, I'm gonna shoot 'em twice."

"Someone stole—" Jessie began.

"—the chickens," Kale finished. "All of them?"

"Every dad-blasted one!" Grandad got in the truck and ground the ignition.

Kale tore toward the pickup in a dead run.

Jessie sorted the information a second later and slid into the truck right after Kale. "Let's go," she shouted. "They've got Jennifer."

Chapter Fourteen

The truck rattled and wheezed as Grandad Joe pushed it beyond the limits of age and a well-worn V-8 engine. It was hard to talk over the noise, but Jessie couldn't wait for answers. "What happened, Grandad Joe? Who took the chickens?"

"I don't know, but I'm gonna find out. I just got home from playing bingo at the church and noticed the gate was open. It didn't take much to put two and two together."

"Whoever stole the hens must have a heck of a headstart," Kale pointed out. "We won't be able to catch them."

"I passed a poultry truck on Bowden Road and didn't think much about it. 'Cept to wonder who on the mountain was selling livestock. But when I saw that open gate and the tire tracks, I knew they was haulin' my layin' hens."

"And mine," Kale said.

Jessie reached over and patted his hand. "Jennifer will be fine, Kale. We'll find her."

"I hope you're right, Jess."

"Hang on to your hats, kiddos." Grandad tightened his grip on the wheel as they approached an intersection. "I know a shortcut."

"A shortcut?" Kale's voice rose as the truck made the curve on two tires. "We don't even know where they're going. How can you know a shortcut?"

"Relax, young 'un. There ain't a place on this mountain I can't get to faster'n a crow can fly. Besides, there's only so many places around these parts a truck can take a load of poultry. And I know every one of 'em."

Jessie knew there was no point in arguing with her grandad. Kale seemed to suspect as much, because he stopped talking and stared out the windshield. Her hand found its way into his and his fingers closed tightly over her own. The headlights bounced like jackrabbits, hitting the ruts a second before the truck tires. Jessie was glad she was over being sick. This ride was enough to cause a relapse as it was. And the thought of Jennifer...

It seemed an eternity before they hit paved road. Grandad gunned the engine and the pickup took off like a thoroughbred. An old and winded thoroughbred, true, but the heart was still there. When the lumbering hulk of a livestock truck came into view, Jessie felt like cheering. But when Grandad laid on the horn and laid rubber on the highway trying to get past, Jessie just held on to Kale's hand and the edge of her seat and prayed they'd survive.

"Stop!" Grandad yelled. "Bring back my chickens!"

Kale glanced at Jessie, then he leaned over and rolled down the side window. "Stop, thieves!" he yelled. "You've got valuable University property in there. The FBI will be called in if you transport it across state lines."

Jessie shot him a skeptical look. "The FBI?"

"It could happen," he said with a shrug and started to yell something else. But Grandad pulled in front of the truck carrying the chickens, raced a little way ahead and pulled to a stop...square across the road.

The truck came closer, threatening with its mass and Jessie reached for the door handle. She was getting out of this truck. It was one thing to chase after the chicken thieves and quite another to be smashed into chicken liver under the wheels of a huge truck. Just as she pulled on the door handle, though, the poultry truck screeched to a halt several feet away and two men got out, looking angrier than any men Jessie had seen in quite some time.

"What in Sam Hill are you trying to do, old man?" one of the truck drivers asked. "We oughta call the cops on you."

Grandad was out of his pickup and facing off with the burly guys like a bantam rooster protecting his flock. "I could say the same thing to you, buster. In fact, I've already called the sheriff. He ought to be here anytime now."

"Big talker," the other, less hulking truck driver taunted. "The sheriff's got no business with us."

"You stole those chickens." Kale stepped into the fray.

"Stole? Hey, no, we got a bill of sale right here." The husky truck driver patted his shirt pocket and looked around as if he expected the written authority to appear magically in his hand. "We got it, sure's shootin'."

"Bill of sale, my foot! No self-respecting poultry man is gonna haul away chickens without the owner bein' at home. Bill of sale or no bill of sale." Grandad Joe hitched a thumb in his suspenders and rocked back on his heels. "You boys oughta known better'n that. If'n you've messed up those hens layin' habits, I'll fix it so you two won't he haulin' chickens around these parts ever again."

"Sure you will." The smaller trucker seemed edgy beneath his bravado. "Look old man, we don't care if they're layin' hens or fryin' hens. We're just supposed to deliver them to the guy that pays us. And that's what we're going to do."

Grandad raised the barrel of his shotgun until it pointed, rock solid, at the two chicken-nappers. "Tell that to my friend, here." Grandad jerked his head toward Kale. "Tell him who's paying you to steal a henhouse full of chickens."

The atmosphere changed dramatically and, when the distant wail of a siren cut through the air, the two men became distinctly restless. "We're just doing what we were told. You ain't got a quarrel with us."

"You got my chickens in that truck, don't ya?" Grandad emphasized his point with the shotgun.

Kale moved forward to back up the older man. Jessie followed right behind him. "You said you had a bill of sale. Where is it?"

The two men exchanged looks and then one of them gestured toward the cab of the truck. "It must be in there," he said. "I'll look for it."

"Not a chance." Kale reached behind him for Jessie. "Jessie, go around to the other side of the truck and see if you can see anything inside that resembles an authorization."

"No way." The huskier man puffed out his cheeks. "She's got no business nosing around our truck. We're legit. I told you that already."

Grandad scowled. "And I told you those are my chickens. Now, 'fess up and tell who's payin' you to do this."

"None of your damn business!"

"That's right!"

"We'll see if you like using birdshot for toothpicks."

Jessie couldn't believe her grandad would get involved in a shouting match, but there was no other way to describe the yelling that ensued. By the time the sheriff arrived in a blaze of flashing lights and screaming sirens, the men were red-faced and edging close to a knock-down-and-drag-out fight.

Sheriff Bill Wilson, a big teddy bear of a man, put a stop to that with his first words. "Well, now, what have we got here?"

The explanation was a garbled mass of threats and accusations until Kale stepped forward. "Sheriff, these men have stolen Joe's chickens. As you can see, the evidence is in the back of the truck. Now, perhaps, you could arrest them and take them in to jail."

Sheriff Wilson craned his pudgy neck to see the back of the poultry truck. "Looks like a load of chickens, sure enough, but that's not hard-and-fast evidence of stealin', boy. What've you got to say about this, Joe?"

"They're my chickens, Bill. I'd bet the church offering on it."

"And what do you two fellers have to say for yourselves?" Sheriff Bill turned to the truckers, maintaining his authority simply by his judicious expression. "Did you take these here chickens from Joe's henhouse?"

The larger trucker squared his shoulders. "We got a bill of sale, Sheriff. The man who hired us to pick up the birds gave it to us in case we had any trouble."

Bill considered that bit of information. "If you got a bill of sale, why didn't you pick up the chickens when Joe was there to give the okay? Are you sure you got the right address and the right henhouse?"

"We don't get paid to make that kind of mistake, Sheriff. We just did what we was told." The second trucker got defensive and Jessie shivered in the crisp night air.

"I can see we're gettin' nowhere fast." Sheriff Wilson nodded to each of the defendants in turn. "Let's move to my office where we can get this sorted out in reasonable comfort."

"But what about the chickens?" Kale asked.

The sheriff gave him a once-over look. "And who might you be?"

Jessie stepped forward, sensing another disaster. "This is Kale Warner, Sheriff Bill. He's a professor at the University of Arkansas in Fayetteville. One of those chickens belong to him."

The sheriff smiled. "Well, hello there, Jessie. How have you been?"

She returned his smile and the dimple flashed in her chin. "I'm fine, Sheriff. How's your family?"

"Good, good. Growing like wild onions in a cow pasture. You're visitin' your grandpa, I reckon."

"Yes. It's been kind of a mixed-up trip, though, so far. And now, with the chickens getting stolen..."

Sheriff Bill shook his large head. "I'll get to the bottom of this, Jessie. No need to worry." He narrowed his brows at the truckers. "You two go get in my squad car. Joe, you follow me in your pickup."

"We ain't leaving these chickens out here," one of the truckers protested.

"Yeah," the other man chimed in. "We got to stay with our load."

Sheriff Wilson seemed suddenly larger than his normal six foot five. "You two—", he pointed a finger so there'd be no misunderstanding as to the two he meant "—get in my cruiser. I'll take care of the chickens." Bill turned to Joe and then to Jessie. "Jessie, can you and this professor get these chickens back to the farm? I ain't sayin', you understand, that they belong to Joe, but they can't sit in a truck on the side of the road all night, either. I'm confiscating the poultry as evidence and assigning it over to your custody, Jessie. Agreed?"

"Yes, thank you, Sheriff. Kale and I will take very good care of the evidence."

"See that you do." He started to walk away, then came back to Kale. "Which one of those layin' hens belongs to you, Professor?"

Kale glanced with mixed pride and consternation at the hens in question. "I don't know."

"I'll bet it's the one that lays the golden egg!" Sheriff Bill laughed heartily at his own joke as he ambled toward his squad car. "I'll get the keys to the poultry truck for you." He was back in a minute. "Surly couple of guys, aren't they? You two be careful. Transporting chickens isn't an easy job. You do know how to drive a truck, don't you?"

"No problem," Kale said. "Jessie knows how to do everything. Leave it to us, Sheriff. We'll be as careful as if these chickens were all laying golden eggs."

"Well, eggs are kind of pricey, these days. Once you get the hens settled, bring the truck on down to my office. Don't worry about your grandad, Jessie. He's in good hands with me."

"Just take his shotgun before he hurts someone."

"Shoot, Jessie. I've been huntin' with your grandad. He can hit a mosquito on the wing at a hundred feet. Believe me, if he'd wanted to hurt these guys, they'd be crying by now. He's not going to shoot anybody."

"Not on purpose," Jessie said. "But that shotgun is loaded with birdshot."

"Is that a fact?" Sheriff chuckled. "Well, maybe I shoulda been a few minutes later arriving. Those two men might have 'fessed right up if they'd gotten stung with a little birdshot."

Jessie didn't like to think of how a confession like that would be regarded in a court of law. "Kale and I will be at your office just as soon as we've put the hens back in Grandad Joe's chicken house."

Sheriff Bill hitched up his britches. "I'll get on with my business then."

Jessie watched as the black-and-white cruiser executed a neat turn and drove away, followed closely by her grandad in his pickup.

"Do you know how to drive one of these trucks?" Kale had pulled open the door of the cab and was looking inside.

She turned around with a sigh. "It's not that difficult, Kale. It's not like it's a diesel truck. It's just big, that's all."

"And open. The chickens must be getting pretty cold. The wind seems to be picking up."

He was right about that and, as little as Jessie knew about chickens, she did know they shouldn't be kept in the truck any longer than absolutely necessary. "Do you want me to drive?" she asked.

"I think I can manage. Your feet probably wouldn't even reach the pedals. You can direct me, though. I don't think I could find my way back to your grandad's farm on a bet." He cast an anxious glance toward the crates of chickens in the back. "I sure hope they make it. If I lost CTA #43 . . ."

"That's why they took Grandad's chickens, isn't it, Kale?" Jessie climbed into the cab and slammed the door as Kale inserted the key and started the engine. "Whoever tried to steal Jennifer from the lab followed our trail to Grandad's and then hired those two to steal all the chickens so he could get his hands on the one you're testing."

Kale struggled with the gearshift and managed to get the truck in reverse. "Pray for no traffic, Jessie. I don't think I can turn this baby around, so we'll just have to back down the road until we hit the intersection. Keep an eye on that side mirror and scream if you see approaching headlights."

Jessie concentrated on the mirror, but as soon as Kale had turned onto the crossroad, her thoughts went back to the reasons for the chicken theft. "Do you think that's it, Kale? Did someone hire those two apes to steal Grandad's hens in order to get Jennifer?"

"I don't know, Jessie, but the possibility certainly crossed my mind. They'd have to have some plan for testing…" The truck rocked on the rutted road and Kale fought to keep it steady. "At the moment, all I care about is getting the hens safely in the henhouse. Have you ever unloaded a truck-load of chickens?"

"No, have you?"

"I've moved a few chickens in my day, but never more than a dozen at a time."

They'd hardly done more than open the henhouse door and remove the slats from the back of the truck before Jessie sneezed. From then on the whole process of transferring the hens was punctuated by sniffs and sneezes. Kale seemed in no better shape than Jessie, but they stayed with the procedure until the last hen was back at roost in Grandad Joe's chicken house.

"We'd better get to the sheriff's office." Kale wiped his palms on the seat of his pants . . . and stirred up more dust. "I don't suppose we have time to change clothes."

"I don't suppose we do," Jessie agreed with a glance at her watch and a pained glance at her less-than-fresh jeans and sweater. "So let's get on with it. I'll drive."

"We have to take the truck."

"Oh, that's right. Okay, you drive and I'll give directions."

Kale sneezed. "We're a pair, Jessie. I only wish I had a camera."

Jessie looked at him, from the bits of straw in his dark hair to the dusty patches on his clothes. His appearance was disheveled and unkempt. His face was dirty and his eyes watered from the effects of dust and chicken feathers. And despite all that, her heartbeat quickened. Kale had cast quite a spell on her. "I don't think you want a picture of this," she said. "If I look as bad as you do . . ."

He glanced down, dusted his hands across the front of his thighs, then let his gaze roam over her. "You do, Jessie, and I wish I had a camera to prove it."

She laughed. "We'd better see what's been proven at the sheriff's office instead. It's taken us over an hour to get the chickens unloaded. No telling what's happened in the meantime."

Kale grumbled as he moved, a little stiffly, toward the truck.

"What did you say?" Jessie asked as she fell into step beside him.

"I said I can think of a lot of other things I'd rather do."

She was certain of that. But she could only wonder if she played a part in any of those "other things."

THE SHERIFF'S office was in an uproar.

There were too many people trying to talk in too small of a space. The two burly truck drivers were leaning over Sheriff Wilson's immaculate desktop, trying to outshout the other people in the room. Two more fellows, who looked almost as husky and as dirty as the truck drivers, stood arguing with the deputy. Grandad Joe was sitting on a wooden bench watching the goings-on with disgust. A man in a business suit, which looked as if it had been put on in a hurry, stood beside Sheriff Wilson's chair, trying to speak in a seminormal tone of voice. He slapped the desktop, though, occasionally to make a point. Jessie took it all in in a glance and wondered why it was taking so long to work out the ownership of less than two hundred laying hens.

"Jessie. Professor. Come on in. We've been waiting on you." Sheriff Bill smiled broadly and gestured as if he weren't surrounded by angry men. "Did you get those chickens put up okay? No problems? There's a gentleman here with a bill of sale, sure enough, but Joe says he never signed it and I tend to believe him."

Kale's grip on Jessie's arm tightened as the man in the suit looked across the room at them. "Tom Jensen," Kale muttered under his breath. "I should have known."

Jessie glanced from one man to the other, but decided she needed to be with her grandad. He didn't particularly look like he needed protection, but she thought perhaps he might need some support.

Kale didn't seem to notice as she slipped out of his grasp and made her way to the bench. Grandad Joe nodded as she sat beside him. "Chickens okay?" he asked.

"They seemed fine, Grandad Joe. How are you?"

"I'd be laughin', if it wasn't so far past my bedtime. I'm too old to be playin' ring-around-a-rosy with a young, argumentative pup like him." He nodded at the man Kale had called Tom Jensen. "He's a troublemaker, Jess. A real razorback in a pigpen. Looks like Kale knows him."

It did look that way. Kale advanced on the sheriff's desk for a face-off with Tom Jensen.

"Hello, Dr. Warner," Tom said with a ready smile. "I'm surprised to see you here in Sheriff Wilson's office. How are things at the experimental farm?"

"I wouldn't know, Tom," Kale answered. "I've been out tracking down stolen research for the past week."

Tom laughed. "Who would steal your research, Kale? No one would be able to make heads or tails out of it."

"Oh, I believe someone could." Kale placed a hand on the desktop and leaned forward. "I believe you'd give it the old college try, Tom, if you thought there might be money in it."

Tom's expression hardened for a moment, then relaxed with a rueful shrug. "You might be right. Jensen-Homestead Farms is always looking for a way to make a profit. But I fail to see how your research could be considered lucrative. Let's face it, Kale, you're in this for science. Nothing you discover is going to net the university much return on its investment."

"Hmm." Kale glanced at Sheriff Bill. "Could I see that bill of sale, Sheriff?"

Sheriff Wilson handed it to Kale and then bellowed, "I'm getting mighty tired of refereein' this dogfight." His voice boomed in the office like the Liberty Bell and the argumentative chatter dropped into silence. "It's late and this has been going on too long. Granted, we had to wait for Mr. Jensen, here, and his two 'helpmates' to show up. But everyone's here now and we either get this settled or everybody's spending the night in jail. Get it?''

Apparently everyone did, because there was a respectful hush. Only Kale's voice broke the quiet. ''How many chickens do you have, Joe?''

Grandad Joe shifted on the bench seat and Jessie patted his knee. ''I don't know exactly. 'Bout a hundred fifty, maybe a couple o' dozen more or less. Why?''

''This piece of paper says you sold Tom Jensen here two hundred leghorn hens. Is that true?'' Kale smoothed the crumpled bill of sale and took it over for Joe's inspection.

''Nope. I haven't sold any chickens for the past ten years or so. I sell eggs, but that clearly says leghorn hens and not leghorn hen eggs. And why would I sell two hundred, if I only had a hundred and fifty or so? That fella's lyin'.''

''He's a senile old man.'' Tom raised his voice. ''I talked with him myself, a few days ago, and he signed this bill of sale then. Ask him. Didn't I talk to you one day this week, old man?''

''If'n you don't talk with a bit more respect to your elders, son, you won't be talking to anybody in this county except Judge Henry.'' Sheriff Bill rose, pressing his fists into his husky waist. ''Now, let's start over. Joe, did Tom Jensen talk to you about selling your chickens?''

Grandad Joe shook his head. ''He came to the house one evening, wanting to know where he could buy some layin' hens. I suggested he call Buck Talbot over at Palmetto, but he kept asking about my hens, how many I had, if'n I'd acquired any new ones of late. I didn't think much about it. The corporate farms are always sending someone out to check on the homesteaders. But I didn't sign any paper. I got no reason to sell my hens.''

"Did you mention to Tom that you had acquired a new laying hen?" Kale placed his hand on Joe's back. "Did you tell him about Jennifer?"

Joe looked up. "I suppose I did. That's about the most exciting thing that's happened on the farm this month, 'cept for you and Jessie fussin' and fightin' and flyin' off to meet Gretchen."

Jessie squeezed her grandad's knee. He didn't have to tell everything he knew. "Did he want to buy your hens after you told him about Jennifer, Grandad Joe? Do you remember?"

"Who is this Jennifer?" Tom wanted to know. "We're talking about chickens here. Not people."

"Jennifer is a chicken," Jessie informed him curtly. "And you're lying. My grandfather did not sign that."

"Prove it," Tom snapped back.

Kale snatched the paper from Joe's hands. "We will, Tom. Don't worry about it. We'll tell our side to the judge."

Tom gave a pained kind of laugh. "This is ridiculous, Kale. We don't want to tie up the courts with disagreements like this. We're talking chickens, here. Not life and death."

"So forget about your bill of sale and buy your laying hens from somebody else." Kale put it simply and concisely.

"I want those hens. I paid for them."

Sheriff Wilson stepped in to put a stop to the argument. "We'll let Judge Henry decide whose chickens are whose. Now all of you get out of my office and let me get on with my paperwork. What a day!" He shooed truckers and everyone else toward the door. "You, too, Joe, Jessie. Get on home. We've bandied this back and forth long enough, now. You all do what you want to do. Talk to your lawyers. For now, the chickens are evidence and will stay in Joe's henhouse until the judge rules one way or another."

Grandad Joe got to his feet with no assistance and a smile. "What about the eggs, Bill? Are they evidence, too?"

"You're a troublemaker, Joe. You know that?" Sheriff Bill turned to Tom Jensen. "You got any problem with Joe collecting the eggs every day and selling them?"

It was apparent that Tom didn't like the way this was working out. But he had the good sense not to argue with the sheriff. "He can sell the eggs." Tom stalked from the room, followed by the truckers and the other men.

Kale smiled at Grandad Joe. "I think, for now, you're the man who owns the chicken that lays the golden egg."

"Yeah, well, none of the eggs will be gathered if I don't get some sleep. Come on, Jessie. Let's go home. Thanks, Bill, for your help."

"You're mighty welcome, Joe. Sorry I couldn't just tear up that bill of sale for you and have done with it, but I'm sworn to uphold the law and that just wouldn't be right."

"You did the right thing, Sheriff." Kale stepped forward and opened the office door. "I for one, will be glad to see Tom Jensen hauled into court. It's about time he got called on the carpet for his less-than-exemplary business practices."

"You coming with us?" Grandad Joe asked Kale.

Kale lifted his shoulders in a shrug and pursed his lips in a wry smile. Even with the dust and dishevelment of his appearance, Jessie melted with the appeal in his expression. "My station wagon is out at your place, Joe, so if you wouldn't mind giving me a ride...?"

"That's why I asked." Grandad walked out the door and Jessie followed him to the pickup. Kale was close behind and she wondered how she could possibly feel any kind of attraction for him under the circumstances. They both smelled like chicken feathers and she itched in places she couldn't scratch. But she was aware that she ached to feel his arms around her, his lips on hers. If this had been a virus, she'd have taken a Nas-O capsule and gone to bed. But she had all the symptoms of being in love and she was afraid it wasn't going to go away. Nas-O capsule or not.

Grandad Joe talked on the way to the farm, expressing his opinion of the night's events and the sorry state of affairs when a man's property could be hauled away without his permission. Kale said little. And Jessie said nothing at all. She felt suddenly exhausted and yet, a part of her was certain that Jennifer had been the reason for the theft. She went over the possibilities time and again and kept coming back to that one. Kale's research had been stolen in the first place. He hadn't just misplaced it, as she'd often suspected. And Pancho... What was Pancho's role in the initial theft? Could Gretchen have been wrong about him? Was he capable of stealing?

Jessie couldn't believe that was true. But she knew Kale must be coming to the same conclusion she was. Namely, that whether or not Pancho was the hired thief, he was the missing link in the puzzle. He had answers no one else could give. She wondered if Kale would wait until morning to pursue those answers or if he'd jump into his station wagon the moment they reached the farm.

And what did it mean to her if he did? Would he be back? Or was their relationship over?

A glance at his set and meditative face told her his thoughts were far from her.

As the truck bounced over the road, she concentrated on keeping her balance. It would never do to fall into Kale's lap at this point. There were just too many chicken feathers still up in the air.

Chapter Fifteen

"Jessie?"

Kale's voice carried through the paper-thin wall of the bedroom. Jessie lay still and thought about how close he was...just on the other side of the wall, almost within touching distance, almost near enough for—

"Jessie? Are you asleep?"

"No." She rolled onto her side, facing the wall. It was late. Once they'd reached the farm, Grandad had gone straight to bed, leaving Jessie and Kale to debate who got first turn in the bath. Jessie had been tempted to suggest they go together but, of course, she couldn't. It was her grandfather's house, after all. So she'd bathed first and lain in bed, listening, waiting for Kale, wishing he were coming to her bed...to her.

"Do you think Tom Jensen hired Pancho to steal CTA #43 from the lab?" Kale asked.

A slow sigh rolled from her throat. "He might have tried," she said, forcing her thoughts back to the chicken-napping incident. "But I can't believe Pancho would get involved in theft. Not if he knew it would be stealing."

"But all the evidence leads to him, Jessie. What else am I supposed to think?"

She wished she had an answer. She wished she could kiss him and keep him from thinking at all. "I don't know, Kale. Are you going back to the university tomorrow?"

"Yes. I have to find some answers. I'm convinced Tom Jensen is as guilty as a weasel with an egg in its mouth, but I'll have to have some rock-solid evidence that he planned the theft of my research before I can confront him successfully in a court of law. No attorney would touch this case with the coincidences I have to offer as evidence."

"Anthony could help," Jessie offered automatically. "I know he's tried lawsuits in Arkansas before and he's always interested in unusual cases."

There was a moment of silence from the other side of the wall. "Anthony, huh?"

Jessie frowned. "Never mind. I'm sure you know someone who's an attorney. The university probably has its own legal staff, doesn't it? Forget I said anything."

"No, you could have something, Jessie. I'm not sure who should bring suit. The way things have happened, your grandad may have to initiate legal action since we do have proof that his chickens were stolen. What do you think?"

"I think it's been quite a night. Quite a week."

"A week? Has it only been a week?"

"More like two, I guess. It seems like a lifetime ago that you tried to wrestle Pancho at Dakota Jack's."

"A week," he repeated softly. "A lot can happen in a week, you know."

How well she knew. In the past week, she'd fallen helplessly, irrationally in love. And that sort of left next week in limbo. What would she do for an encore? What would she do if the curtain simply closed?

"Jessie?" His voice dropped to a husky, baritone whisper. "I bet your grandfather is a sound sleeper."

She closed her eyes and half smiled in the darkness. "He's a very sound sleeper."

"But I suppose you wouldn't be comfortable if I came around... Don't answer that. I don't think I'd be very comfortable with it, either. This is, after all, your grandfather's house."

She didn't answer. He was right. They had to sleep on opposite sides of a worthless wall, wishing to be together, kept apart by inhibitions too entrenched to flaunt. Morning would come all too soon, anyway, Jessie thought. And tomorrow promised to be another long day. At least, for Kale. She supposed she would stay on the farm while he tracked down Pancho and found out the answers to a lot of questions.

"Kale?" she whispered. "What time are you leaving in the morning?"

"As soon as I get up. I'll try not to wake you."

Her spirits sank like a shoe into a puddle of mud. "I can always go back to sleep."

"You can?" he asked with some surprise. "Have you got some Nas-O capsules hidden over there?"

She tried for a light tone. "No pills."

Quiet descended like morning fog, seeping through the wall, slipping into the bed with Jessie, chilling her with the knowledge Kale would soon be gone.

"Jessie?"

"Yes?" The word formed a clump of regret in her throat.

"Would you mind very much...if...? Would you, uh, go with me tomorrow? I probably won't be able to get near Pancho if I'm alone. But he'll talk to you. Would you consider—?"

"I'll go." Relief cleared her throat. She didn't care why he'd asked. His ulterior motive—his inability to accomplish the job of interviewing Pancho without her—didn't matter right now. He'd asked her to go and she would, just to be with him a little longer.

"We'd better get some sleep, then." The mattress on his side of the wall creaked as he turned. "Instead of driving both cars to Fayetteville, we could ride together."

"I'll drive," Jessie offered easily. It was a small concession to make to her curiosity, she told herself. Kale needed her assistance a while longer and she...well, she needed some answers.

Like how Kale felt about her. Like what kind of future relationship they might be able to forge from this week-long adventure. Like what she was going to do if she couldn't accept his answers to those questions.

But in the meantime, she'd have tomorrow. Maybe the next day, too. Maybe even—

No, for now tomorrow was enough.

She'd make sure that it was.

THE TRIP to Fayetteville was filled with conversation. Kale talked about his family, his friends, and his reasons for choosing a career in agricultural research. He worried about the upcoming confrontation with Pancho and tried to sketch in the sequence of events that might have led to the theft at the lab. He made plans on how to go about finding Pancho and then plotted out how he would proceed once that objective was gained.

And he held her hand...except for those times when she needed both hands on the wheel.

Jessie drove, listened and offered suggestions or comments, as indicated. But mostly, she just enjoyed being with him and the weight of his hand warmly encompassing hers.

The ride was over all too quickly and Jessie knew a moment of regret. From this point on, she knew Kale's single-track mind would kick into overdrive and research would occupy the lion's share of his thoughts. She wondered fleetingly what had happened to her own determination not to take second place to a chicken. Somehow her perspective had tilted, or been set right. She needed Kale to need her. She wanted him to be able to depend on her support, just as she wanted to depend on his...when she needed to. And she was beginning to understand that a long-term commitment meant being willing to take second place on occasion.

Kale wasn't sure which dormitory Pancho lived in, but on the second try, they found the right residence hall. Pancho wasn't in and Kale decided to try the lab at the experimental farm. They found Pancho there, singing happily as he tended the test chickens.

He saw Jessie first and broke into a wide smile. "Mees Day! I am surprised to see you. What—?" His greeting smile broke when he caught sight of Kale. "Dr. Warner." Pancho tensed, ready for flight if necessary. "Were you looking for me?"

"Yes." Kale's demeanor changed, his tone was gentle, but authoritative. He was a man in charge of himself and his surroundings. "I have some questions for you."

Pancho glanced at Jessie. "You have seen your seester and everything is...okay?"

Jessie wasn't sure what that meant, but she nodded anyway. "Gretchen is fine, Pancho. She received the computer disk you sent to her, and Kale—Dr. Warner—and I flew out to get it back."

Pancho frowned in confusion and ran a hand through his unruly dark hair. "I don't understand."

"The jig is up. We know all about the theft." Kale stepped forward, a menacing note in his voice and in his stance.

Pancho reacted with a jerk and a judicious glance at the door. "I do not 'jig,'" he said defensively.

"Pancho." Jessie took her hand from her jacket pocket and extended it toward the boy in a soothing gesture. "What Dr. Warner means is that he needs to talk to you about what happened the night you took the chicken from the laboratory. Talk. That's all. We—Dr. Warner—wants to ask you a few questions. You won't mind that, will you?''

The dilemma was clearly expressed on Pancho's face. He wanted to get the hell out of there. On the other hand, he trusted Jessie and wanted to help her in any way he could. Finally he crossed his arms protectively at his chest and leaned back against a cabinet. ''If you say so, Mees Day, I will talk.''

Jessie smiled. Pancho smiled. Kale shrugged out of his coat.

''All right, Pancho, let's start at the beginning. Tell me what happened the night you stole the chicken.''

Pancho straightened with a vengeance. ''I do not steal! I saved the chicken from dying. Just like Gretchen told me. Animals should not die for research purposes. That is what she said and that is what I believe!''

''Calm down.'' Kale flipped his coat onto a desk and brushed dark hair impatiently from his forehead. ''No animals in this lab are ever killed for research purposes or for any other reason. You were misinformed if you thought CTA #43 was going to be destroyed.''

''But the instructions on the cage...'' Pancho turned in confusion to Jessie. ''I read English very good. It said chicken was to have autopsy performed. I saved her.''

''I don't believe you stole the chicken, Pancho,'' Jessie said. ''And neither does Gretchen.''

''Gretchen?'' His expression relaxed, grew peaceful again. ''You talked with her? She knows I rescued the chicken?''

''She knows. But she was puzzled about the computer diskette you mailed to her in that package.''

''She asked me to send it. The disks were on her desk in her office. Were they not the correct ones?''

''The three diskettes in the plastic box were fine. It's the one she found in the sweater pocket that concerns us. That disk belongs to Dr. Warner and was taken from this office. It does look like you took it, Pancho.''

''But how can that be? I didn't take Dr. Warner's—'' Pancho straightened, his mouth and eyes growing wide and round. ''Wait. There was a floppy disk. On top of the chicken cage. I remember now.'' He snapped his fingers and Jessie half expected a light bulb to appear in the air above his head. ''I put it in my sweater pocket and forgot it. That is the answer, yes?''

''That is no answer at all.'' Kale paced to the far side of the lab and back. ''Look, Pancho, please try to remember every detail of that night. Think about what happened that day and why you came to the lab that night and what you did once you got in here. That isn't too hard, is it? Just tell us what happened, step by step.''

''Step by step.'' Pancho slumped against the cabinet again and rubbed his chin as if he were rubbing Aladdin's magic lamp. ''I awakened at six-thirty, as always. I got to the doughnut shop. I eat . . .'' He paused, glanced cautiously at Kale. ''This is what you want, yes? Step by step?''

Jessie cut off Kale's frustrated sigh. ''You're doing fine, Pancho. Keep going.''

Pancho nodded and proceeded to outline the events of his day. Each detail was clear and nearly mundane. He attended classes. He studied. He ate lunch. More classes. Jessie suspected he kept such a strict routine that each day duplicated the rest. No wonder Pancho had fallen for Gretchen. Her loosely structured life must have seemed like a whole new culture to him.

Pancho continued outlining his day while Jessie sat quietly and Kale paced the floor. The deviation from Pancho's usual schedule had occurred late that afternoon when Gretchen had phoned to tell him she was at the airport and would be out of town for several days. In Pancho's words, she'd asked him to do her "the big favor" and get some things she'd forgotten to get from her office.

"I was happy to do this," Pancho said. "I would do anything for Gretchen. She asked me to get her notebook and a plastic container with three diskettes inside. I had been to her office many times and knew where these things were kept."

A small miracle in itself, Jessie thought, since Gretchen kept her office in only slightly better order than she kept her house.

"I told Gretchen I would meet you, Mees Day, at Dakota Jack's," Pancho continued. "Friday night at eight."

She nodded her encouragement. Kale looked progressively more impatient. Pancho settled back to recall more minutiae. He'd gone to Gretchen's office immediately after her phone call and from there he'd gone to the library...to find out more about the state of Washington, where Gretchen had said she was going. It had been late, he recalled, when he'd left the library and he'd decided to go out to the lab, to pick up some study sheets he'd left there the night before.

"The lab was dark," Pancho said. "And I remember thinking Joanna must have finished feeding the hens earlier than usual."

"Joanna?" Kale asked. "Is she a student?"

"Yes. Like me. Only she is from Little Rock."

Kale almost smiled. "Do you know her very well?"

"No." Pancho shook his head. "She is very quiet and she works at different times from me."

"So you came into the lab and it was dark and you thought Joanna had left. Right?"

"That is correct. But she was still here. Only in the other room. But I did not know that then." Pancho seemed to be enjoying stringing out his story and Jessie hoped Kale could keep his frustration in check a bit longer. "I bumped into the chicken cage," Pancho continued. "It was not supposed to be on the floor. I never leave cages out when I am on duty." He paused for that bit of solid work ethic to sink in. "So when I see the chicken and see that she is upset because she is not in her usual place, I start to pick up the cage. It is then I see the floppy disk on top of the cage."

Kale stopped pacing and the room got very still. Pancho seemed to sense that this was his moment in the sun. "I must have put the diskette in my sweater pocket, but I didn't mean to forget it was there. I worried about the chicken, especially when I saw the tag attached to the handle. I look, but there was no identifying band on the chicken's leg. I did not understand why. And I could not believe a chicken from Dr. Warner's lab was going to be destroyed. But I knew what autopsy meant and I decided I would rescue this unfortunate bird for Gretchen. In her honor."

"What did you do then, Pancho?" Jessie asked, wondering if she would ever inspire Kale to that sort of devotion. "Did you take the chicken out of the lab?"

Pancho shook his head and proceeded to tell how Joanna, the lab assistant, had come into the room then and told him to leave. They'd argued about him taking the chicken and Pancho said Joanna was most upset with him. "But I could not let her take the chicken," Pancho concluded. "I had to do it. For Gretchen."

Kale picked up a piece of paper and scribbled on it. "So you left the lab that night with the chicken in the cage and the diskette in your sweater pocket."

"Yes. That is true. But I did not remember the diskette in my pocket."

Kale made another scribble. "What did you do with the chicken?"

A pained expression crossed Pancho's face. "I had no place to keep a bird. Dormitory rules are strict. So I put the chicken in Gretchen's garage and decided to ask Mees Day to keep it for a while.''

''And you just happened to put your sweater, with my disk in the pocket, in the box you gave to Miss Day, here, to mail to her sister? That sounds farfetched to me, Pancho.''

''It is true, *señor*. I read about the state of Washington in the library and it is sometimes very cold there. So I sent Gretchen my sweater.''

It sounded entirely plausible to Jessie, the sort of romantic gesture Pancho would make. ''I think that pretty well explains Pancho's involvement, Kale.'' She pushed up from the edge of the desk, satisfied that Pancho had done nothing wrong.

''It doesn't explain how the chicken cage got in the middle of the floor. Or who took off the identification band. Or why Pancho thought the hen was going to be destroyed. We don't do that sort of thing here. University animals are treated like royalty. They're not destroyed unless they're sick or badly injured.''

''Autopsied,'' Pancho corrected. ''It said autopsied. Not destroyed. And I was surprised to see it, Dr. Warner. I knew you do not usually hurt your chickens in any way. So for this reason, I decide to save the chicken. But then you start following me like a shadow and I get scared and run away from you. I did not want to be forced to tell you where the chicken was.''

Kale ignored the interruption. ''Look, Jessie. Maybe Pancho is telling the truth, but that still leaves a lot of unanswered questions. Someone around here must know the answers.''

''Perhaps Joanna could help.'' Pancho made the suggestion tentatively, as if he were afraid of getting the girl in trouble. He cast a doubtful glance at Kale and Jessie decided to support his suggestion. After all, it made sense to talk to the only other person they knew had been in the lab that night.

"Do you know how to find Joanna?" she asked.

"She's a student. She can't be that hard to locate." Kale picked up the phone and dialed a number. "I only wish locating CTA #43 were this simple."

Pancho looked startled. "Isn't the chicken with you, Mees Day? Didn't you keep it safe, as I asked?"

"The chicken is fine, Pancho. She's in a henhouse with a bunch of other chickens and she's very happy there." Jessie avoided Kale's scathing frown. "The problem is, she blends in so well with the other hens that Dr. Warner can't pick out which one she is."

"I could do it." Pancho's smile returned with Latin warmth.

Kale put his hand over the mouthpiece of the phone. "You could pick out my chicken? Out of a hundred and fifty other chickens that all look alike?"

"Yes."

"You want to tell me how you propose to do that?"

"Simple," Pancho said. "I will sing."

IT WAS NOT SO SIMPLE to track down a reluctant Joanna Holmes at her dormitory, but once found, she pretended innocence and ignorance for less than ten minutes before she burst into tears and confessed. She was an awkward coed with bright red hair and an adolescent body that hadn't as yet reached full maturity. Her tears touched Jessie's sympathy and made Kale uncomfortable, but he finally was able to get enough information from her to piece together her story with Pancho's and complete the puzzle.

Joanna tearfully explained her financial problem and her efforts to get aid. She apologized to Kale and to Pancho a dozen times for being "lured" into helping "that" man get his hands on the chicken Dr. Warner had been testing. It took a few minutes and several questions to discover that Tom Jensen had approached Joanna and offered to pay her next semester's tuition if she would help him.

Joanna's account of what happened in the lab the night the chicken disappeared corroborated Pancho's story. Following Tom's instructions, she had substituted one chicken for another and had typed out a tag to give herself an alibi in case she was stopped while leaving the lab with the chicken. She'd planned to cover the cage and indicate that the hen inside had died and was being taken to another lab for autopsy.

Locating the diskette with the research hadn't been difficult, but she'd run into a snag when she'd tried to copy the research files. Since she couldn't access Dr. Warner's files on the computer, she'd decided to take the diskette. And that was when Pancho had arrived to play the hero, leaving her with neither one of her objectives. She'd had to search for the missing diskette and to wonder how she'd explain the theft, not only to Dr. Warner, but to Tom Jensen as well.

Kale made Joanna intensely aware of his displeasure with her conduct and yet he surprised Jessie by showing a generous understanding of her problems. By the time they left Joanna, she was still tearful, but not without some hope.

"That was extremely kind of you, Kale." Jessie slipped her hand into his as they drove away from the dorm where Joanna lived. "You could have had her kicked out of school."

"I probably should have, but I can't see that denying her an education here will accomplish much. Besides she said she'd testify against Tom Jensen, so doing any more than relieving her of her duties at the lab would be cutting off my nose to spite my face."

"Still it was a nice thing to do."

His smile thanked her. Then he glanced over his shoulder where Pancho was hunched into the tiny back seat. "Pancho, if I drop you off at your dorm, you won't run off, will you? I want you to go with Jessie and me to Russellville in the morning. If you think your singing will separate CTA #43 from the rest of Grandad Joe's flock, I'm willing to give it a try. Maybe I'll get lucky and you actually do know more about the behavior of domesticated birds than I do."

"No luck to it, Dr. Warner. She will come to me when I sing 'Sweet Lolita.'"

Kale raised his eyebrows. "I can hardly wait to hear that."

Jessie laughed. "I'm surprised we're not heading for Crow Mountain at this very moment."

"Tomorrow is soon enough to make the trip. Pancho needs to rest his vocal cords. Isn't that right, Pancho?"

"Whatever you say, Dr. Warner." Pancho's bony arm shot past Jessie's head as he pointed at a building. "That is my residence. You can leave me at the corner."

"Where should we pick you up in the morning?" Kale asked as he got out of the car to let Pancho climb out.

"How about the Daybreak Donut Shop? I go there for breakfast every day."

Kale made a face and climbed back into the car. "Daybreak Donuts, it is. Seven o'clock?"

"I see you then." Pancho placed his hands, one over the other, over his heart. "Mees Day, I live for tomorrow and the chance to be a hero for you."

Jessie waved as Kale shifted into gear and drove down the street. "His mood certainly made a one hundred and eighty degree turn," she said. "He got over his fear of you pretty quickly."

"It's my worst fault as a teacher," Kale said. "I'm not ruthless enough to scare my students into a healthy terror."

"Joanna was scared."

"I hope she was scared badly enough not to ever contemplate theft again. I could have pressed charges against her, you know."

"I know. She knows, too." Jessie thought for a minute. "What will you do now, Kale? Do you have enough evidence to file charges against Tom Jensen?"

"I'm going to have a talk with an attorney first. Do you still think Anthony's the man for the job?"

"He's a good lawyer, Kale. I know he's helped Gretchen and some of her special-interest groups before. Besides, he's a nice guy."

"And he's crazy about you."

"All the more reason to believe he has an outstanding IQ."

"Ah, but can he sing 'Sweet Lolita'?"

"If Anthony thought that would sway the jury, you bet he'd sing."

Kale cleared his throat and tapped his fingers against the steering wheel restlessly. "Are you hungry? Let's get something to eat."

"At Dakota Jack's?"

"I had someplace a little more . . . refined, in mind."

Jessie brushed back the loose strands of her blond hair and hooked them behind her ear. Her heart was beating faster at the idea . . . the possibility that Kale was actually planning an evening around her and not slipping into his one-track train of scientific thought. She didn't quite know what to say to ensure he wouldn't get distracted again. "I can get us into Gretchen's house with a minimum of trouble," she volunteered.

He offered a patient smile in reply. "As I said, I was thinking of someplace a bit more refined. Trust me. I occasionally slip the bonds of academe and venture into society. You may not believe this, Jessie, but around here, I'm considered quite a desirable dance partner."

"I'm not surprised, Kale. I'll bet you do a mean Turkey in the Straw."

"I might just show you."

"My palms just broke out in a sweat."

"Well, don't get too excited. If you eat a doughnut for breakfast tomorrow, everything is over between us."

She didn't know exactly what was between them, but she knew she didn't want it to be over. Not tonight or tomorrow or ever. She wouldn't have traded these past several days with Kale for...well, for all the silk in Japan. And she loved silk.

But she loved Kale more.

"I'm not crazy about doughnuts," she said.

"A woman after my heart. Would you like to see my place? I don't have any etchings, but . . ."

"You're going to sing 'Sweet Lolita,' right?"

"I can think of better things to do when you're with me, Jessie."

The moment shimmered with possibilities and her pulse tripped into double time. "In that case, Dr. Warner, lead the way."

Chapter Sixteen

Jessie dreamed of feathers.

Feather pillows. Feather beds. Feather touches.

Kale didn't have feather pillows. They were made of soft synthetic fiberfill. His mattress was spring coiled with a tufted, pillow top. But his touches... Ah, his touches. Even in her dream, they were as soft and tantalizing as the brush of a feather against her skin.

She awakened to a kiss that enhanced the dream, letting her drift between sleep and wakefulness on a cloud of pleasurable sensations. It was the nicest morning in recent memory and she savored every moment, just as she had savored every moment of the night before.

Kale's idea of a "refined" restaurant had turned out to be his kitchen in his house on the edge of town. And he'd cooked a fine meal...eventually. But he'd done finer things first and those were the moments Jessie thought about as she drifted into morning and the sweet awareness of his lips pressed to hers.

"Hmm," she said.

"Mmm to you, too." Kale brushed his hand through her hair and let his fingertips mingle with the sungold strands. "Don't you hear Daybreak Donuts calling you?"

"Ooh." Jessie moaned and kept her eyes closed. Maybe if she pretended to sleep, Daybreak Donuts and Pancho and

Jennifer and Kale's research would disappear and nothing would be real except this moment with Kale beside her in bed, touching her, kissing her...

"You have forty-five minutes to get ready," he whispered as he teased her earlobe with his tongue.

She smiled, lazily turning her head, letting the slow-building heat inside her catch a spark of desire. "I'll only need fifteen."

"Really?" His lips trailed the slope of her neck, reached the sensitive hollow of her throat. "Then you can go back to sleep for thirty minutes."

She opened an eye and cocked an eyebrow. "Not on your life, Dr. Warner. You should know better than to stop an experiment before its completion."

He reached out a hand to cup her breast. He poised his lips a breath away from hers. "You're absolutely right. Let me know when you're completed."

But she didn't have to tell him.

He just seemed to know.

"HERE, CHICK, chick, chick." Pancho clicked his tongue against the roof of his mouth in a fair imitation of a chicken's cluck. "Come, chick, chick, chick."

"I thought he was going to sing." Kale gave the zipper of his jacket another tug, inching it up to the top. "Didn't he say he would find CTA #43 by singing?"

"Shh." Jessie pushed her hands deeper into her coat pockets. The chill in the air felt more like early morning than midday. "He's establishing a rapport with the flock, so he won't startle them." She glanced over her shoulder at Kale. "I thought you knew all this stuff about chickens."

"I know scientific stuff. The real inner workings of birds." He frowned as he watched Pancho walking around the henhouse, calling "chick, chick" and clucking. "This is right out of a Foghorn Leghorn cartoon. I certainly hope it works.''

''Grandad Joe said he's seen stranger things happen.''

Kale's lips tightened. ''So have I, but I'm not staking my reputation on this exercise. If it doesn't work, I'll be spending a great deal of time tagging and testing every single one of those hens.''

Time. Jessie knew that her time with Kale was running in short supply. Even if Jennifer's tiny chicken brain recognized Pancho's singing voice and associated it with food, Kale would be spending a great deal of time in his laboratory from now on. There would be no more impetuous flights to Seattle, no more hurried trips between Fayetteville and Russellville, no more mornings to awaken to the sweet pressure of his kiss. Jessie sighed. She hoped Kale had enjoyed their days together enough to remember them...and her.

''Here, chick, chick, chick.'' Pancho walked through the chicken house, hardly stirring the straw on the ground as he moved. He glanced at the entrance, where Kale and Jessie stood, and grinned. ''I think we are ready.''

The strains of ''Sweet Lolita'' began softly, but gradually increased in volume. Beside her, Kale gave a hearty sigh. ''Just think, we got out of bed and took allergy pills for this.''

''You'll be glad when Jennifer comes running out of the flock.''

Kale gave Jessie a doubtful look before slipping his arm across her shoulders and drawing her against his warm body. ''Come on, Jennifer,'' he said softly to the chickens. ''Listen to this glorious rendition of 'Sweet Lolita' and go to Pancho.''

Jessie had mixed emotions, but she seconded his request. ''Come on, Jennifer. Remember Pancho.''

"Sweet Lolita" entered the second chorus and Pancho switched to Spanish. His voice got stronger and he moved a bit faster down the center of the henhouse. At the end of the third time through the song, Pancho stopped close to Jessie. "I think there is too much distraction in here," he said. "Does your grandfather turn the chickens out into a pen?"

"There is a pen. Maybe it would help if we put them out a few at a time," Jessie suggested.

"This is not going to work." Kale lifted his shoulders in a shrug and released Jessie from his hold. "I'm going to join Joe in the house. Anyone care for a cup of coffee?"

"No, no, Dr. Warner." Pancho protested. "You must believe. The chicken will come to me. It will take time is all."

"I appreciate your effort, Pancho, but I've got to make some contingency plans in case the chicken doesn't come to you. Or in case more than one chicken comes to you. The possibilities are endless. Chickens aren't known for their intelligence, you know."

"Jennifer is smart chicken." Pancho tapped his temple as if that proved his point. "I taught her trick. You will see."

"Stay, Kale." Jessie placed her hand on his arm. "Give Pancho a chance to work his magic."

It was Jessie's magic that had Kale worried. He didn't believe there was a one in one hundred and fifty chance that CTA #43 would respond to Pancho's song. But Jessie's voice was full of promise and memories and magic that evoked a strong response from him. There was a one in one chance that he was in love with her. And he'd never been in love before. He didn't quite know what to do about it.

"I'll be back," he said, taking the easy way out. "I need to talk with your grandad. If Jennifer has forgotten her 'trick,' I need to make arrangements with Joe and the sheriff to move all of the hens to the experimental farm for tagging and testing."

"I'll stay with Pancho." Jessie took her hand from his arm and immediately, Kale missed its trusting weight. "When we find Jennifer, I'll let you know."

"You do that, Jessie, and I'll fix a cup of coffee for you."

"Thanks."

He turned toward the house, noting the reluctance in his feet and in his heart. What was going on with him? He did have some things to discuss with Joe. He didn't need to be standing in the henhouse tossing negative thoughtwaves at Pancho and the flock of chickens. He'd be away less than thirty minutes, not forever. So why was it so hard to leave Jessie behind? Did love make every decision more difficult?

IN THE COZY COMFORT of the kitchen with his feet propped on the connecting slat of a nearby chair, Kale dialed the number Jessie had given him earlier and waited for Anthony, the Wonder Attorney, to answer the phone. The leap from "hello" to "sure, I'll take the case" was swift and broad, but Kale found some relief in the fact that Anthony perceived the setup with a relatively small amount of information.

"Joe got his chickens back?" Anthony asked.

Kale could hear the scratching of pen against paper. "Yes. It's my chicken that is still missing. Well, we know where she is, we just don't know where she is."

"Is Jessie there with you?"

"Yes," Kale said firmly. "She's here with me."

"May I speak with her then?"

"No."

"No?" Anthony must have been caught offguard, because Kale could no longer hear the scratchy pen marks.

"No, she's here, but she's not here. She isn't a part of the lawsuit anyway."

"Didn't you just tell me she could verify your story? Didn't you say she took your chicken to her grandad's farm? That she was at the sheriff's office the night the flock of chickens was taken? That makes her a witness. An important witness." Anthony made a few more pen-scratching sounds. "Look, Kale—I can call you Kale, can't I? After all, I did loan you my sweat suit. That ought to put us on a first-name basis."

For a moment, Kale thought seriously about the wisdom of letting Anthony handle the case. Maybe a complete stranger would be better. Maybe not. But if he changed his mind now, he'd have to explain the "whys" and "how comes" to Jessie. And he didn't want to admit to her that he was jealous. "Sure, Anthony," he said. "First names are fine. After all, we may be working on this case for quite a while."

"Maybe." More scribbling noises came over the wire. "If we approach this as an infringement of your patent—do you have a patent pending on this, uh, chicken?"

"No. I didn't develop the breed or the chicken, itself. I only discovered that this particular hen lays a lower-cholesterol egg. And that's what I'm researching."

"Hmm." Anthony held the hum and the pause for half a minute. "Still, I think that might be the best way to go. If Joe files charges against Tom Jensen for stealing his chickens, it will be hard to prove. Jensen-Homestead Farms will claim it was a misunderstanding and, even if a jury could be persuaded it wasn't, Tom would get a slap on the wrist. Probably a minimal fine and thirty days in jail. I can't believe that stealing chickens can win a very stiff sentence. It's just one of those things that doesn't stir people's emotions, you know."

"Getting my chicken stolen stirred my emotions," Kale said. "A few other people got a little ruffled along the way, too."

"That's my point. We need to play up your side of this, stir sympathy for the researcher who's given his life to a project only to have it yanked out from under him just as he's about to tell the world of his discovery."

It sounded dramatic when put like that and Kale decided not to correct Anthony's embellishment of details. "How can I sue Tom Jensen, though? What grounds?"

"I'll research it and we'll aim the suit at the corporation, rather than at one individual. Technically, infringement might be not accurate, because you don't have a patent, but I think I can make a solid case. Especially with what you told me about the girl. It will make quite an impression on a judge if she identifies Tom as the man who approached her about stealing the chicken and copying the research diskette. Jensen-Homestead will have a hard time explaining that."

"You're the attorney." Kale shifted his feet to the floor and started to rise. "I'll do whatever you say."

"Good idea. I think I can swing some pretty heavy publicity for the case. Tom Jensen is a well-known man in Arkansas and the media won't let a case like this slip by unnoticed. He'll pay a penalty one way or another."

"I'm not out for revenge, Anthony. I don't want to put Jensen-Homestead Farms out of business. But I don't want them to profit from research done at the university with university funds."

"Don't worry. I'm good with this type of case. Ask Jessie."

"I already did." Kale couldn't keep a proprietary tone out of his voice. "She's the reason I called you in the first place. Left to my own devices, I'd probably have used a local lawyer."

"You've done the right thing by contacting me, Kale. Bringing in someone from out of town usually shakes up the other side a bit and I do have a good reputation in your area. I've won my share of cases there.''

Kale appreciated the other man's confidence and hoped it was grounded in experience. ''I know you'll do the best you can for us, Anthony. I trust your judgment.''

''Jessie's judgment, you mean. She's one of my biggest fans.'' Anthony cleared his throat, as if something distressing had lodged in it. ''Speaking of Jessie brings up a couple of points we ought to discuss. First of all, from now until this thing comes before a judge, you should concentrate all your efforts on completing this research and getting enough documentation to establish your claim on the chicken that lays the lower-cholesterol egg. Maybe publication of a paper on the subject would be sufficient. I'm not sure. But whatever, time is of the essence in this case. We don't want Jensen-Homestead coming to court claiming you stole the idea from them.''

''They couldn't do that,'' Kale said, suddenly defensive. ''I have the chicken . . . sort of.''

''Proof, Kale. You need solid evidence that what you're researching could benefit Jensen-Homestead and Tom Jensen in particular. And the sooner you can produce that evidence, the better chance we stand in court. Get the picture?''

''You're telling me to get my chicken and head for the lab.''

''Right-O.'' Anthony hesitated and Kale didn't like the wait. ''The, uh, second thing is . . . stay away from Jessie. Now wait, before you say anything. I knew when you were next door at her apartment that there was more than a friendly relationship developing. That part is none of my business, but what is my business is getting you through a lawsuit and to a successful judgment. If Jensen-Homestead can cast doubt on Jessie's testimony, which will be a corroboration of your testimony, the outcome may not be what we want it to be. All a smart attorney needs to do is get across the idea that you and Jessie are a 'couple.' In a few words, he'll be able to put a whole different slant on the case."

"That's ridiculous." Kale pressed his palm against the tabletop and hoped Joe Day didn't walk back into the kitchen right then. "What difference does it make if Jessie and I are a couple? That has no bearing on what Tom Jensen tried to do."

"It makes a difference," Anthony said firmly. "We don't want any mention of collusion. Not between you and Jessie. Not between you and the young lab assistant. Not between Jessie and the student who gave her the chicken. The law itself is straightforward, Kale, but the people who interpret it are human and they're influenced by impressions. If you want to win this case and protect your research, you'll do just what I've said. You'll get back to your lab and work like there's no tomorrow and you'll put Jessie out of your life until the case is closed."

Kale wasn't at all sure the other man's advice wasn't self-serving. After all, Anthony seemed very fond of Jessie. Fond enough to leave his robe at her apartment. "Maybe you're not the right man for this job, Anthony. I'm not sure I agree with your ethics." Kale almost hung up the phone, but Anthony's words were too quick and caught him.

"Fine. Talk to any attorney. He or she will tell you the same things. Cases like these are tough to prove, even without extenuating circumstances. You, Dr. Warner, are going to have to choose what's more important to you. Your research or... your private life."

The idea stopped Kale cold. He didn't know what to say, how to get off the damned phone.

Anthony concluded the conversation for him. "You think it over, Kale. I'll be in Fayetteville the day after tomorrow. We'll get together for lunch. You can let me know then if you want to go ahead with the court case."

Reluctantly Kale agreed and thanked Anthony for his time before he hung up the phone. Then he poured himself a cup of coffee and sat at the table, his hands cupped around the hot mug, his thoughts bouncing wildly between Jessie and Jennifer. What's more important? Which one did he choose?

Why did he have to choose at all? This was probably just a way of getting him out of the picture so Anthony would have a clear field with Jessie. It was a ploy. Stay away from Jessie. Ha! Kale thought. He'd show that stuffy lawyer what he thought of that advice.

But the question returned. What's more important? Anthony's advice aside, Kale knew he did have to make a choice. The research was vitally important to him. He'd poured his life's blood into it for two years now. He couldn't take any chances on Tom Jensen or anyone else walking away with his work and profiting from his efforts. And although he might doubt the validity of Anthony's advice when it pertained to Jessie, he had to agree that gaining more substantial evidence and publishing the results was imperative.

He wanted to present the world with a chicken that was genetically endowed to produce a healthier food product. He had no intention of profiting personally from the research, but he'd be damned if he'd let someone like Tom Jensen do so. It was one thing to conduct research for the betterment of mankind and quite another to research for the financial books of a corporation.

So to answer the question . . . his work was more important than his private life. At least for now. Jessie would understand. Wouldn't she?

"Kale!" The front door bounced open. A chill wind drafted into the living room and around the corner to the kitchen. "Kale!" It was Jessie's voice, coming closer, brimming with excitement. "We found her, Kale. Pancho kept singing and the birds just kind of milled around out in the yard and then—'' Jessie came to the kitchen doorway, all smiles, all flushed and lovely. A private life seemed suddenly very important. ''—I wish you'd been out there, Kale. It was so great! Pancho sang 'Sweet Lolita' in Spanish and he began to do this little dance and Jennifer hopped up to him and tried to dance, too. It was the silliest thing I've ever seen, but she did try to dance!''

''Chickens can't dance,'' he said lamely, trying to protest the rush of emotion, the quick stir of desire Jessie's enthusiasm evoked in him.

''I didn't think so, either.'' She pulled out the chair opposite him and reached for his coffee cup. ''I am so cold. Where's Grandad Joe?''

''He went to the cellar to get...something.'' Kale couldn't take his eyes off her. He had the feeling that somehow she had become forbidden fruit, the one thing he wanted, the one thing he couldn't have. Dumb. He was overreacting to the whole thing. He'd just tell her. Jessie, he'd say, would you mind not being in my life while I work on my research? I'm going to have to concentrate and I can't do it with you around.

''Pancho will be inside in a minute. He's bringing her.'' Jessie sipped the coffee and frowned. ''You let this get cold. Here, I'll get another cup.'' She scurried around the little kitchen, chatting, laughing, oblivious to his internal discomfort. ''Really, Kale, you should have stayed out there with us. When Jennifer came up to Pancho, I couldn't believe it. You would have loved it.''

He loved her. What would she say if he told her? What would he do if she said she loved him, too? This was bad timing all the way around. He didn't have time for a relationship. Not now. Not with so much at stake in his work. No, he couldn't tell her. She deserved his complete attention, not a moment now and a moment later.

"Señor! I have found the chicken!" Pancho came into the house and carried a cage into the kitchen. Proudly he placed it in the center of Grandad Joe's table and spread his arms in a munificent gesture. "I told you, Dr. Warner. Theese chicken is one smart cookee!"

Kale looked at the hen and felt a stir of excitement in his chest. How could he be excited about a chicken when Jessie was in the room? How could he not be excited when his research was once again within his grasp? His work. Jessie. He couldn't get the two to balance. "Good job, Pancho," he said. "I didn't think you could do it."

"It was Mees Day's encouragement." Pancho smiled and nodded at Jessie. "She kept telling me to keep singing, keep singing. And she was right. Because here is Jennifer. I have rescued her twice."

"And caused me a great deal of trouble in the process," Kale said.

"He saved you a lot more trouble than he caused." Jessie jumped easily to Pancho's defense. "If he hadn't taken Jennifer out of the lab that night, you might have lost her for good."

"You're right." He turned a smile to her, but it faded with the certain knowledge that he was about to leave her. She'd been with him every moment of the past couple of weeks. She'd been with him last night and this morning. He didn't know when she would be with him again. And the thought of saying goodbye suffocated him. "Pancho," he said abruptly. "We'd better head back for the university. You won't be offended if I perform a few tests just to make sure this really is CTA #43, will you?"

Jessie looked startled, but she didn't say anything. She didn't ask to go with him. She didn't ask him to stay.

"These tests will not hurt her?" Pancho leaned over the cage, putting his arms around it protectively. "I must protect Jennifer. Gretchen would be unhappy with me if I didn't."

"Believe me, Pancho, nothing is going to hurt this hen. She's much too valuable." Kale caught Jessie's gaze and tried to tell her with a look that she was valuable to him. She smiled and a pang of regret smacked him square in the heart. Okay. He'd just tell her he loved her. He'd say it once, so she'd know. Before he left.

"Come on," Jessie said. "I'll walk you two out to the car. I know you're both anxious to get back." She walked through the back door and Kale heard her yelling into the cellar. "Grandad Joe! Kale and Pancho are leaving. Come up and say goodbye."

In a few minutes, they all stood beside Kale's station wagon, exchanging the polite amenities of leave-taking. When Jessie moved close to him, Kale's heart pounded in his chest like native drumbeats. *I love you.* The words pushed at his mouth, but somehow wouldn't come out.

"Goodbye, Kale." She lifted her chin, her lips tipped in a rueful expression, her eyes bright and unreadable. "You were the best vacation I've ever had. Thanks."

Thanks. He was ready to say, I love you, and she said, thanks?

He took her hand and wished he could think of a way to change what he had to do into what he wanted to do. The problem was he wanted both his work and Jessie. "I'll see you again." It sounded almost desperate and he cleared his throat. "I'll call you...sometime."

The slant of her lips became a wistful smile. "Of course you will, Kale. Sometime."

He felt like a fool, unable to say the right words, unable to just say goodbye. "Jessie? I want you to know...I—"

"Mees Day! Dr. Warner!" Pancho called from inside the car. "Look, the chicken, she is dancing again!"

Jessie pulled away from Kale and peered into the station wagon. "Oh, look, she is. Jennifer's dancing. She's glad to be going home. She probably didn't like being one in a harem of hens here on the farm. Grandad Joe's rooster is a real Casanova."

"Yes, well, we'd better get going. We will have to stop by the sheriff's office to give him a receipt for the chicken." The moment was gone and Kale wanted to get this uncomfortable farewell behind him. He'd figure out what to do about Jessie when he'd finished the research. He'd call her when the trial was over. For now, all he could do was get the hell off the farm. "Goodbye, Joe. Goodbye, Jess. See you in court."

Those were not the words he'd intended to end with, but hell, there wasn't a good way to leave someone you loved. There just wasn't an easy way to say goodbye.

He was a quarter mile down the road before he realized that he could have kissed her, should have kissed her...and hadn't.

The regret settled over him like the dust of Grandad Joe's chicken house and it wouldn't go away. No matter how much Pancho sang and Jennifer danced.

JESSIE WATCHED the station wagon disappear into a cloud of Arkansas dust. She tried to tell herself it was silly to be upset at Kale's abrupt goodbye. He was a man with a one-track mind. She'd known that since the beginning. Why should she be surprised that he was running true to form? He had his research back. He had his chicken. What did he need her for?

The answer was obvious. He didn't need her. Not at all.

Jennifer was his girl, now. Just as she'd been before. Jessie had known this would happen. A thank-you and a quick goodbye. She had no right to expect more.

But oh, she wanted more. It wasn't supposed to hurt. Not when she'd known all along it would turn out this way. Her credit card bill would come and she'd pay for the experience with a wry smile and a wounded heart.

And Kale? He'd finish his research on lowering cholesterol in eggs and move on to another study, another way of making the world a healthier place to live. That was Kale. She wouldn't have loved him if he'd been any other way.

But it was going to be a while before she could be philosophical about the whole thing. It would be a while before she could point with pride to the sacrifice she'd made for the cause of lower cholesterol.

She pressed her hands against her cheeks, felt the pressure of tears behind her eyes.

It was going to be a long while before she felt anything but awful.

Chapter Seventeen

"How soon can you start?" Jessie smiled at the young woman seated across from her at the desk. In the past month she'd hired two additional salesclerks for the Day Dreams store and an administrative assistant for the design operations. Business was good. Better than good. And life should have been rosy.

"I'll be out of the office next week," she told her new employee. "But Brenda Murray, my associate, will show you the ropes. Whatever questions you have, she'll be able to answer." Jessie stood and walked the young woman to the door of the office. "I'm sure you'll be settled into the job by the time I return."

With a word of thanks, the young woman left and Jessie closed the office door. One more task accomplished. One more detail out of the way. One more day down the drain.

She pulled herself out of the slump and began sifting through the paperwork on her desk. Her enthusiasm for her work had dropped to an all-time low and she was desperately trying to manufacture a new excitement. She'd thought that if she could just catch up on the business end and spend a few days working on new designs that that would solve her problem. But then, she'd spent three days staring out the window and accomplishing little more than a few half-formed sketches.

And they'd all looked like chicken feathers.

The door opened after a small tap and Brenda entered the office. Brenda Murray was a tall brunette who'd been with Jessie since the beginning of Day Dreams. She was a trusted employee and dear friend. "I knew you'd hire her," Brenda said. "I think she'll be a lot of help to us. We've been so busy lately."

"Don't I know it," Jessie said as she shifted a stack of orders to the out basket. "Do you remember when we used to pray for the phone to ring. Those were the days."

"How well I remember those starving-artist days. I'll take success anytime, thank-you."

"You're right, of course," Jessie said with a smile. "Now we're starving because we don't have time to eat. Life just gets more complicated, doesn't it?"

"Well, chicken-nappings and lawsuits do tend to fowl up things." Brenda paused. "That's *f-o-w-l*?"

"You don't have to spell it out. I get the idea. In fact, the next time I hear a chicken joke, I may scream at the top of my lungs."

"What's happened to your sense of humor?" Brenda said as she plopped into one of the chairs. "Last week you were cackling about your adventure in poultry like an old biddy." There was a pregnant pause and then Brenda grinned. "A biddy is another word for hen, if you'll recall."

Jessie sank into her chair. "I think you've punned me to death, Brenda. I concede that you can come up with more chicken jokes than I so, as your reward, I'm going to get you a baby chick all your own for Christmas."

"I'd rather meet your Jennifer."

"She's not mine. She belongs to the University of Arkansas."

"Then you should have visitation rights."

That was just what she needed...to show up on Kale's doorstep, saying she wanted to visit Jennifer. As if Kale would even remember that his Cholesterol Test Animal Number Forty-Three had ever gone by the name of Jennifer. "No thanks. I have to testify in court next week on behalf of Jennifer, Grandad, and the University of Arkansas. Maybe I'll see her then."

"More importantly, you will see Dr. Warner." Brenda leaned back in the chair. "I can't wait to hear how that works out."

"I can tell you right now how that will work out. I'll say my piece. He'll wonder where he's seen me before. And that will be that. I told you he's the epitome of the absentminded professor."

"You also fell for him hook, line and sinker, Jessie, so he must be a heck of a nice guy. So what if you have to keep reminding him of who you are and how you met? There are worse problems in a relationship."

Jessie had reached much the same conclusion over the past month. She missed Kale, ached to be with him, battled the need to phone and tell him so. Anthony had warned her against interrupting the scientific process, had cautioned her that Kale needed to devote his full attention to his work. It would be the best way to win the suit against Tom Jensen, Anthony had said. The best way for Kale to prove his case. But Anthony, of course, didn't know that she couldn't have interrupted Kale if she'd tried. His attention was firmly glued to that research. He could have called her. He could have sent a letter. A postcard, even. Or a singing telegram. But she hadn't heard from him at all.

"Kale isn't interested in a long-term relationship, Brenda," Jessie said, more for her own benefit than for her friend's. "Even if he remembers me."

"Oh, you're being too pessimistic. The man has had a lot on his mind lately. He'll probably sweep you into his arms and into a happily-ever-after the minute he sets eyes on you again."

"A romantic scenario, Brenda, but hardly likely. Besides, I'm not a believer in 'happily-ever-afters.' I'm in charge of making my own happiness and I'm not going to depend on a man to make it for me."

Brenda applauded. "Good for you. So if Kale Warner doesn't sweep you into his arms the minute he sees you, I expect you to sweep him into your arms. A new twist, see?"

"I see." Jessie pushed her hands against the desktop and rose to her feet. "I see that you're a hopeless romantic and we're not going to get any more work done today. How about an Irish Coffee before we head for home?"

"Sounds great. I'll be glad when this freezing weather gives way to spring." Brenda stood and waited as Jessie got her coat. "Are you driving to your sister's tonight?"

"Sunday afternoon. I thought I might get some design work done tomorrow if I stayed home. Besides, staying with Gretchen is never something I want to stretch out too long and since I don't know what day I'll be called on to testify..." She also didn't want to be in the same town with Kale, but without him, any longer than necessary. "My Grandad will be staying at Gretchen's house, too, so it promises to be quite a jolly week."

Brenda patted her on the shoulder. "I think you may need a couple of Irish Coffees, Jess. And I'll buy."

Jessie smiled and wished all of her relationships could be as pleasant and as uncomplicated as her friendship with Brenda.

THE COURTROOM buzzed with conversations. Jessie scanned the room for a friendly face and saw Anthony deep in discussion with Kale.

Kale.

He looked great. Or better.

His hair was disheveled, despite evidence of a thorough combing. He wore a suit that looked stylish and new and when he turned toward her, she saw that the knot of his impeccable tie was slightly askew. Probably no one else would notice such a small imperfection, but she wished she could straighten it for him. He needed just that tiny touch of a woman's hand. Her hand. Jessie smiled and at that moment he caught sight of her.

Her heart stopped, raced, skipped, stopped again. She was aware of the impulse to run forward, to wrap herself in his arms, to kiss the slow, sensual slant of his mouth. But she couldn't move. She could only stand and stare as an expression of warmth and welcome stole across his face. He was glad to see her. He'd missed her, too. Jessie took a step forward, but Anthony touched Kale's arm, reclaiming his attention and stripping away her opportunity. There was nothing to do except find a seat and wait.

Two hours later, she was still watching. The preliminaries stretched, one technicality after another, into the afternoon. No witnesses were called. No progress seemed to be made. Jessie didn't get to talk to Kale that afternoon. He passed within three feet of her, but they exchanged only a glance before Anthony hustled Kale past and out of the courtroom.

She told herself it didn't matter. Kale was busy at the moment. His thoughts had to be focused on the case. His time had to be taken up in discussions with Anthony. She understood.

But after an evening of playing chess with Grandad Joe and of helping Gretchen rearrange her closet, she decided that understanding the situation was no consolation. Maybe Kale really didn't want to see her. Maybe she'd misinterpreted the welcome in his expression, the emotion in his eyes. After all, he surely hadn't had to spend the entire evening with Anthony. He could have found a minute to pick up the phone.

Maybe he really had forgotten her name...

KALE was miserable.

He was tired of the legal mumbo jumbo. He was bone-weary from burning the candle at both ends, trying to hurry through a process that should not be hurried. And he was tired of not being able to see Jessie.

Never mind what Anthony said. Never mind the logic of avoiding any hint of consorting with a key witness. It made sense, he'd admit that. Why else would he have practically killed himself trying to complete research that deserved more time, more attention, if it hadn't been the knowledge that the sooner he concluded, the sooner he could see Jessie.

But he still hadn't found conclusive evidence. It had taken two of the past four weeks simply to determine, without a reasonable doubt, that the chicken he'd brought back with him from Crow Mountain was actually CTA #43. That information *had* given him a new respect for Pancho and the haunting lyrics of "Sweet Lolita," but it had also eaten up valuable time. Time he could have spent with Jessie.

The judge called for a ten-minute break and Kale rose with the intention of seeking out Jessie and at least saying hello. Anthony couldn't object to that, could he?

But Anthony had other plans, another legal angle to discuss, and the break passed without opportunity. Kale wondered, not for the first time, if Anthony had devised this stay-away-from-Jessie plan in order to give himself a clear field with her. The thought only intensified Kale's misery. Anthony was a good attorney. He could be incredibly persuasive. Kale only hoped Jessie wouldn't be fooled. Anthony might be a nice guy, but he was not the man for Jessie. Why, if she married Anthony, the two of them would be running into each other trying to be helpful, spilling chicken soup all over the place. Not to mention, the natty robes they'd probably wear. Anthony would undoubtedly give her one to match his. No, Anthony was wrong for her. He didn't need her enough. Not like he, Kale, needed her.

And he was going to convince her of that . . . just as soon as this lawsuit was over. He had to convince her, he thought. Otherwise he might never be any good as a scientist again. Usually he had trouble getting his mind *off* his work, but not lately. Lately he'd had to force himself to concentrate, had had to stop himself from sitting in the lab and day-dreaming. And it was all Jessie's fault.

Or maybe it was Anthony's fault.

He didn't know and didn't care at the moment. He just wanted to get things settled, one way or another. He'd never told a woman he loved her before, but now the words were burning a hole in his heart. If he didn't get to talk to Jessie soon, he was in danger of forfeiting years of dedicated research, weeks of agonizing study, and his tenure as a Professor of Genetic Studies by declaring his love for her right here in the courtroom.

Anthony would have to be a crackerjack lawyer to talk his client's way out of that kind of "consorting with a key witness."

JESSIE TESTIFIED on Wednesday afternoon, finishing her account of events in a half hour. It seemed odd to be able to sum up in thirty minutes the days that had altered her life. Of course, she didn't mention the personal effects of those events. And she'd been careful to focus her attention on the room at large rather than on one individual. The one who sat staring at her from his seat beside his lawyer.

His eyes were so incredibly blue. She'd almost forgotten. And there, on the stand, while Anthony directed questions at her, she began to see a new design. Sheets of blue linen, patterned with circles of gold. Wedding rings entwined with dark blue ribbons. She'd call it Promise. Or maybe Forever.

"That's all, Miss Day."

Jessie snapped to attention and realized she'd answered the last couple of questions without consciously being aware of having done so. She hoped she'd said the right thing. She hoped she hadn't blurted out something embarrassing . . . like how incredibly blue Kale's eyes really were.

But no one tittered or acted anything other than bored as she stepped down from the stand and made her way to the back where Grandad Joe and Gretchen sat. There was really no need to stay longer. Her part was over. Grandad Joe had long since given his testimony about the stolen chickens. All that kept her here now was Kale. And it was becoming perfectly clear that he had no time for her. He'd made no effort to speak to her, had made no attempt to phone her or come to see her in the evenings when the trial was on hold.

So what was she waiting for? Christmas?

"JESSIE, would you hand me that highlighter pen?" Gretchen stretched out her hand, palm up, but didn't glance away from the textbook she was reading.

With a sigh, Jessie began to search in the small amount of uncluttered space on the table. The highlighter pen eventually was found under a stack of last semester's notes and Jessie dutifully handed it over.

"You're a gloomy puss," Gretchen said, still reading. "I thought you'd be excited about testifying today."

"My life isn't all that dull, you know," Jessie said as she stirred her instant coffee absently. "Why would you think I'd be excited about a lawsuit?"

"Just a hunch. Pancho certainly thought it was a thrill. I'm not sure he was a tremendous help for the cause, but he did romantically embellish the details a bit, didn't he?"

"Do all your students fall in love with you, Gretchen? Or just the . . . very young ones?"

Gretchen laughed softly. "Jealous?"

"Just curious. Do you suppose our brother would tell us the male perspective of love?"

"Eric? Do you honestly think he's gotten the ink off his hands long enough to fall in love?" Gretchen tossed back her long, silky hair and let it fall forward again as she bent to highlight a passage in the book. "You'll be the first to go, Jessie. You're always the first to experience the good stuff. You'll be the one to tell me and Eric all about it."

"Me?" Jessie said in surprise. "I'm so busy taking care of you guys, I'll never have a chance to find someone to take care of me."

"I'd like to see the man who could 'take care of you,' Jess. Even if he exists, which I seriously doubt, he'd drive you crazy in a couple of weeks. Take that guy in the courtroom today, your neighbor, that prissy attorney. I'll bet you tomorrow morning's breakfast that he irons his underwear."

"Irons—? Oh, that's ridicul—" But it was just the kind of thing she could imagine Anthony doing, and she began to laugh. It was not something, however, that Kale would ever do. Oh, no. When he was in the midst of a project, he might need to be reminded of where his underwear was kept, but he wouldn't be ironing it. And she wouldn't really mind if he forgot which dresser drawers were his. She had a good memory for things like that.

"What's more . . ." Gretchen began to giggle, a signal of sisterly hilarity about to commence. " . . . I bet he wears pajamas to bed. You know, those fancy ones with silk piping and a matching handkerchief in the pocket?"

Jessie began to laugh, too. "He has this robe, Gretchen. I've seen it. He brought it over one night when the power was off and it was cold and it's made out of this, this woolly stuff and this striped velvet material and—" She began to laugh harder. "It's so—so—awful. . . ." Giggles overtook them both and from there, it took only a look at each other to set them off again. They ended up on the floor, laughing so hard at nothing that it was embarrassing.

It had been a long time since Jessie had gotten so silly with her sister, but it felt good. Like a much-needed release of tension. There were times when no one could help like a sister.

Someone tapped at the door and Gretchen sat up on the floor and wiped the tears of laughter from her eyes. ''Get that, would you, Jessie? I'll find the tissues.''

Jessie pushed herself to her feet. ''I hope it isn't Grandad Joe. He should have arrived at the farm by now.''

She pulled open the door...and froze. It was Kale. Kale, in dark slacks and a pullover sweater, with a coat and a wool scarf draped over his arm. Kale, who looked worried and concerned and tired. ''Kale,'' she said. ''Come in. Is everything all right? Can I get you some coffee? Tea? Soda?''

''You've been crying.'' He reached out and brushed her cheek with a fingertip. ''You're not supposed to do that.''

''No, no. I've been laughing.'' She stepped back so he could enter. She gripped the doorknob hard to try to stop herself from trembling. ''Gretchen and I were...laughing.''

''I heard you from outside. It sounded . . . painful.''

''It wasn't. We were laughing.'' Jessie realized she was repeating herself. ''Because of Anthony.''

''Is he here?''

''No. I don't know where he is. Were you looking for him?'' Her spirits sank faster than a lead balloon. ''Isn't he staying at one of the motels?''

''I thought he might have left for Tulsa by now. We settled the case this evening. Jensen-Homestead said enough was enough and offered a generous settlement. Anthony wanted to continue the trial, but I was ready to compromise. Jensen-Homestead Farms has been hurt by all the media attention of the trial and I guess Tom Jensen realized he might as well admit what he'd done. Anyway, they came to us with an offer and, after consulting with university officials, I told Anthony to accept. But then, after everything was settled, Anthony disappeared. I was afraid you might have gone with him."

"To Tulsa?" Jessie's heart was beating so fast she could barely think. "Why would I go with Anthony? I have my own car."

"And your own credit cards. I know, but that's not what's important, Jessie. You have to understand—"

"I found them." Gretchen stopped in the doorway, a box of tissue in her hand. "Oh, hi. I was just looking for the tissues."

"Kale was looking for Anthony," Jessie explained. "He thought he might be here."

"No." Kale reached for and took possession of her hand. "I've been looking for you. All my life, I guess. And now that you're here, I'm not going to let you make the mistake of marrying Anthony. He's not right for you, Jessie. Genetically he would be the worst choice you could make. Any children you had with him would have terrible taste in robes."

Gretchen buried her nose, and her snort of laughter, in a tissue. Jessie tried to ignore her. Sometimes there was nothing more irritating than a sister. "I'm not going to marry Anthony, Kale. It never crossed my mind. Never. He's just a . . . a neighbor."

"But he takes care of things and he's been dropping little hints about wedding plans and he told me to stay away from you until after the trial. He said I could put the university in a legal bind if I saw you or talked to you before the trial."

"He told me the same thing," Jessie said breathlessly. "About the trial. Not about wedding plans. If he's planning to get married, I didn't know anything about it. He's not someone who could ever be more than a friend to me. No matter what he said."

Kale dropped the coat and scarf on the floor and took both of Jessie's hands in his. "He's just the kind of guy you said you wanted, but I'm a better match for you, Jessie. I know I am. I love you."

It took a full thirty seconds for the words to sink in, for the wild hammering rhythm of her pulse to slow down enough for her brain to absorb the message. "You love me?" she asked.

"Yes. I think I loved you that first night, when you glared at me through the windshield of your car. I don't usually try to arm-wrestle automobiles, but something about you has me doing the craziest things."

Behind her Jessie heard movement and she glanced over her shoulder to see Gretchen trying to ease her way into a front row seat. "Do you mind?" Jessie asked her sister. "This is kind of private."

"Oh, Jessie, let me stay. I'll be quiet. How else am I going to learn how to be romantic?" A few scathing seconds later, Gretchen blew her nose and edged out of the room. "I'll make coffee, okay?"

"You need fresh coffee," Jessie said. "Go to the store and get it."

"Will you tell me everything when I get back?"

Jessie gave Kale a pained look. "My sister," she said, as if that explained anything. "She'll leave in a minute."

"I don't care if she stays. I almost stood up in that courtroom today and told everyone there that I was in love with you. But I couldn't bring myself to jeopardize the case that way. My research is valuable to the university. I had to weigh my desires against other considerations."

At one time, Jessie would have considered that as putting her in second place, squarely behind his work. But now, she accepted it as a fine and honorable quality in the man she loved. Kale wouldn't be Kale if he didn't care so very much for the work he had to do, the vision he had to follow. "It's all right," she said. "I wouldn't have wanted you to declare your feelings in public like that. I'm sort of a private person."

"You're a wonderful person, Jessie. You remember little things I seem to forget. Like luggage and credit cards and umbrellas. I have been so miserable without you the past weeks, I could hardly work. If we don't get married soon, I may never be able to finish my research. The world may never reap the benefits of a lower-cholesterol egg and it all depends on you, Jessie."

"An awesome responsibility," she agreed, beginning to relax with this new and wondrous experience of requited love. "But I'm not sure that's a valid reason to marry you."

"We'll have beautiful, talented children. They'll carry our luggage and umbrellas for us. As I said before, genetically, we're a perfect match."

"Have you done a scientific study on that?"

"No. Heaven help me, Jessie, I'm so crazy in love with you I haven't been able to think straight, much less concentrate on genetic studies. Isn't that a good enough reason to marry me? I love you, Jessie, and I've missed you so much the past few weeks, I thought I might catch a cold."

"Oh, you want my Nas-O capsules." She reached up to stroke his face because she couldn't stand there and not touch him any longer. "It's a package deal, Kale. Nas-O capsules, vegetable soup and me."

"Yes?" His lips slanted into a slow, happy smile. "Does that mean yes?"

"Yes," she said. "Yes."

He gathered her into his arms like a drowning man hugging a life jacket. He looked into her eyes as if he couldn't believe this was actually happening. "I'll make you happy, Jessie. I promise."

"I know," she whispered in the split second before he captured her lips in a devastatingly sweet kiss.

When he lifted his head and smiled, she thought she might simply melt with the heat of desire that flooded her. Why, she wondered, hadn't she suggested that Gretchen take an all-night drive?

Kale's hand cupped her chin. "I can hardly believe how good I feel at this moment. After spending so much time cooped up with chickens—no pun intended—I was beginning to think I'd forgotten how to enjoy life. You showed me, Jessie. I know our relationship is based on a relatively short acquaintance, but I'll be happy to court you as long and as carefully as you like. I'll commute from Tulsa every day, just as long as I can spend every night with you."

"You'd be a very long way from Jennifer."

"She can commute, too."

Jessie laughed. "She'd be happier on Grandad's farm."

"Maybe so, but she'll have to settle for your apartment. We could always get a rooster."

"I have a better idea. I've been wanting to devote more time to designing, instead of spending so much of my day on administrative duties. I have an associate who can handle the office and, at the moment, there are plenty of employees to handle the sales. Why don't I move in with you and commute to Tulsa on an as-needed basis? That way, you—and Jennifer—can stay at the university until the research is completed."

"I love you, Jessica Day. Are you sure you want to do that? You're not just saying that about designing for my benefit?"

"No. I have an idea for a new line of sheets and towels in blue and gold. I'm calling it Feather Duster."

He pulled her closer and sighed happily. "I'll try not to be too demanding. Your work is every bit as important as mine."

"I'm glad you understand that, Kale. But you don't have to worry about being demanding. I seem to thrive on being needed. I'm more comfortable in taking care of the details for someone else than I am in having someone take care of me." She smiled up at him. "Although you did a wonderful job when I was sick. I need to be needed, Kale, and I knew, right from the first, that you needed me."

"I'll always need you, Jessie." He bent to kiss her again.

Sometime later—Jessie had no real idea of how much time had passed—someone cleared her throat. "Uh," Gretchen said. "I couldn't find my car keys. Does anyone still want coffee?"

"Gretchen," Jessie said with a sigh.

"He said I could stay. I heard him." Gretchen hastily offered as an explanation as to why she was still in the house and not at the store. "And I tried not to eavesdrop, but this house is not well insulated and I couldn't help but hear . . ." She grinned at Kale. "Does this mean I can start calling you brother?"

"Sure." Kale reached for his coat and slipped it over Jessie's shoulders. "See you later, sis." He pulled open the door and urged Jessie outside.

"But, wait—"

Kale closed the door on Gretchen's protest and led Jessie down the steps to his car. "We'll take my car," he said as he helped her in.

"Where are we going? To the lab?"

He shot her a frown as he turned the key in the ignition. "Trust me, Jessie. I know just the place. A refined atmosphere. It's private. No sisters. No research. Good food. Great wine."

"A feather bed?" Jessie asked.

"No feather bed, but you'll never know the difference."

And he was right. She didn't.

Feathers, after all, belonged on chickens.

HARLEQUIN
American Romance®
RELIVE THE MEMORIES....

From New York's immigrant experience to San Francisco's Great Quake of '06. From the western front of World War I to the Roaring Twenties. From the indomitable spirit of the thirties to the home front of the Fabulous Forties to the baby-boom fifties...A CENTURY OF AMERICAN ROMANCE takes you on a nostalgic journey.

From the turn of the century to the dawn of the year 2000, you'll revel in the romance of a time gone by and sneak a peek at romance in an exciting future.

Watch for all the CENTURY OF AMERICAN ROMANCE titles coming to you one per month over the next four months in Harlequin American Romance.

Don't miss a day of A CENTURY OF AMERICAN ROMANCE.

A CENTURY OF
AMERICAN ROMANCE
1960s

The women...the men...the passions...the memories...

If you missed #345 AMERICAN PIE, #349 SATURDAY'S CHILD, #353 THE GOLDEN RAINTREE, #357 THE SENSATION, #361 ANGELS WINGS, #365 SENTIMENTAL JOURNEY or #369 STRANGER IN PARADISE and would like to order them, send your name, address, and zip or postal code along with a check or money order for $2.95 plus 75¢ for postage and handling ($1.00 in Canada) *for each book ordered*, Canadian residents add applicable federal and provincial taxes, payable to Harlequin Reader Service, to:

In the U.S.
3010 Walden Ave.
P.O. Box 1325
Buffalo, NY 14269-1325

In Canada
P.O. Box 609
Fort Erie, Ontario
L2A 5X3

Please specify book title with your order.

CA-60-R

**Don't miss one exciting moment of you next vacation
with Harlequin's**

FREE
FIRST CLASS TRAVEL ALARM CLOCK

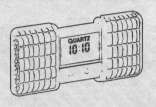

Actual Size
3 ¼ " × 1 ¼ "h

By reading FIRST CLASS—Harlequin Romance's
armchair travel plan for the incurably romantic—
you'll not only visit a different dreamy destination
every month, but you'll also receive a FREE
TRAVEL ALARM CLOCK!

All you have to do is collect 2 proofs-of-purchase
from FIRST CLASS Harlequin Romance books.
FIRST CLASS is a one title per month series,
available from January to December 1991.

For further details, see FIRST CLASS premium ads
in FIRST CLASS Harlequin Romance books.
Look for these books with the special FIRST
CLASS cover flash!

JTLOOK

Take 4 bestselling love stories FREE

Plus get a FREE surprise gift!

Special Limited-time Offer

Harlequin Reader Service®

Mail to

In the U.S.
3010 Walden Avenue
P.O. Box 1867
Buffalo, N.Y. 14269-1867

In Canada
P.O. Box 609
Fort Erie, Ontario
L2A 5X3

YES! Please send me 4 free Harlequin American Romance® novels and my free surprise gift. Then send me 4 brand-new novels every month, which I will receive months before they appear in bookstores. Bill me at the low price of $2.74* each—a savings of 21¢ apiece off cover prices. There are no shipping, handling or other hidden costs. I understand that accepting the books and gift places me under no obligation ever to buy any books. I can always return a shipment and cancel at any time. Even if I never buy another book from Harlequin, the 4 free books and the surprise gift are mine to keep forever.

*Offer slightly different in Canada—$2.74 per book plus 49¢ per shipment for delivery. Sales tax applicable in N.Y. Canadian residents add applicable federal and provincial sales tax.

154 BPA NBJG (US)   354 BPA 2AM9 (CAN)

Name _____ (PLEASE PRINT)

Address _____ Apt. No. _____

City _____ State/Prov. _____ Zip/Postal Code _____

This offer is limited to one order per household and not valid to present Harlequin American Romance® subscribers. Terms and prices are subject to change.

AMER-BPADR   © 1990 Harlequin Enterprises Limited

REBECCA YORK

Labeled a "true master of intrigue" by *Rave Reviews*, best-selling author Rebecca York makes her Harlequin Intrigue debut with an exciting suspenseful new series.

It looks like a charming old building near the renovated Baltimore waterfront, but inside 43 Light Street lurks danger...and romance.

Let Rebecca York introduce you to:

> *Abby Franklin*—a psychologist who risks everything to save a tough adventurer determined to find the truth about his sister's death....
>
> *Jo O'Malley*—a private detective who finds herself matching wits with a serial killer who makes her his next target....
>
> *Laura Roswell*—a lawyer whose inherited share in a development deal lands her in the middle of a murder. And she's the chief suspect....

These are just a few of the occupants of 43 Light Street you'll meet in Harlequin Intrigue's new ongoing series. Don't miss any of the 43 LIGHT STREET books, beginning with #143 LIFE LINE.

And watch for future LIGHT STREET titles, including #155 SHATTERED VOWS (February 1991) and #167 WHISPERS IN THE NIGHT (August 1991).

HI-143-1

Harlequin romances are now available in stores at these convenient times each month.

Harlequin Presents
Harlequin American Romance
Harlequin Historical
Harlequin Intrigue

These series will be in stores on the 4th of every month.

Harlequin Romance
Harlequin Temptation
Harlequin Superromance
Harlequin Regency Romance

New titles for these series will be in stores on the 16th of every month.

We hope this new schedule is convenient for you. With only two trips each month to your local bookseller, you will always be sure not to miss any of your favorite authors!

Happy reading!

Please note there may be slight variations in on-sale dates in your area due to differences in shipping and handling.

HDATES